THE ONLY WAY OUT

The Bishop Smoky Mountain Thrillers
Book 12

LAUREN STREET

STERLING & STONE

THE ONLY WAY OUT

Prologue

A WOMAN HURRYING UP THE STAIRS REFUSED TO STEP OUT of Reuben's way as he slowly descended them and bumped his shoulder, mumbling curses as she veered around him. She hadn't noticed him. Not surprising. Most people didn't. Or if they did, the fleeting image washed immediately out of their minds. He didn't know why that was, but he considered it a gift and had learned early in life to cultivate his own "forgettable-ness." Or "forget-ability," because it was definitely an ability. He leaned into it, never made eye contact, arranged his face in an expression of benign indifference, neither smiled nor frowned, adopted non-threatening body language, his elbows tucked. No witness would ever pick Reuben out of a police lineup, not that he'd ever left any witnesses alive to try.

His ordinary face, devoid of a single remarkable characteristic, and his calculatedly unobtrusive demeanor were the foundation upon which he had built his entire career, one of many reasons he had risen through the ranks to become the most feared assassin in the world. Reuben Lablonski was "El Viento," Spanish for "The Wind." He came and went silently and left no trace of his passage. No one remembered what he looked like. There were no pictures of him anywhere. No mark had ever survived to tell the tale. And if police had ever actually found a witness after El Viento had blown through a crime scene, the image a sketch artist could have produced from his description would have been so nondescript as to be useless.

El Viento got to the bottom step in the subway station, lifted his head to glance around, couldn't even remember walking here from the doctor's office. He did remember rising to his feet in the middle of the doctor's explanation and interrupting the spiel of medicalese with a simple question: How long?

"Well, that's hard to say. It depends on—"

"Give me a straight answer, damn it!" The doctor was taken aback by such an outburst from the meek and mild-mannered man.

The doctor's look of surprise softened into one of pity and Reuben considered that the doctor had no idea how close he had just brushed up against his own death. Under other circumstances, Reuben might very well have decided to come back later and kill the man just for that look the doctor had given him. He'd killed people for much less. But now he merely stood looking down at the doctor, waiting.

"Think weeks, Mr. Lablonski, not months."

The words had hit Reuben in the chest like a wrecking ball. He felt his soul hammered backwards and was surprised that he was standing upright instead of lying flat on his back on the floor. Surprised that he had survived the blow.

"And during that time, your condition will steadily ... worsen."

Condition.

2

The symptoms that had sent Reuben to a doctor, who'd sent him to another doctor, who'd conferred with two other doctors before sending him to a third, had not been so much severe as strange. He would find himself staring into space. He'd be seated in a restaurant or on an airplane or on a park bench and he would come back to himself and realize that he'd just been staring. That had been before the blinding headaches that came and went without warning, the on-again, off-again blurred vision, and the sudden weakness in his right knee, but none of them had concerned him and confused him as much as the blank stare. The doctor had described the condition as a petit mal seizure.

"Those seizure things, are they going to get worse?"

"They will increase in frequency, duration and severity, yes."

Then Reuben had turned on his heel and walked out of the office. The doctor was still talking. He hadn't closed the door behind him, just walked out, walked down the hall, bumped into a nurse and knocked her sideways and never looked back. He thought perhaps the doctor had called out after him. He didn't know or care. He just kept walking.

Now he found himself in the subway station, staring, not knowing how long he'd been standing there staring. He moved toward the turnstiles. They all were empty except for one, and in that one, a fat man had managed to get stuck. He was grunting, trying to push the turnstile forward, trying to wedge his huge bulk into the small space to get through, cursing and squirming.

Reuben could have used any of the other turnstiles, but he didn't. He reached into his coat pocket and pulled out a switchblade, walked up behind the fat man who was struggling, grabbed a hunk of the man's stinky, greasy, gray hair, and yanked his head back so his neck lay bare. Then El Viento sliced the sharp blade of the knife across the man's neck in one swift stroke, using such force that the blade cut all the way through the carotid artery and lodged against the man's spine. The creature made disgusting, gurgling, choking sounds as Reuben pulled the knife free, wiped the blood off on the man's coat, went to the next turnstile, through it and down the hallway to the station, seeking a train going in any direction. As the train pulled up to disgorge its few passengers, he heard a scream from the turnstile area and knew someone had come upon the body. Reuben actually smiled a little, picturing the scene, before he stepped onto the train and the doors closed behind him. He sat down in a plastic seat and considered the enormity of the reality he was facing. The most feared assassin in the world was dying.

The train lurched forward and he glanced around in the car. At the teenager juking and jiving to the beat of music only he could hear in those ear buds. At the fat woman talking in some foreign language too loudly on a cell phone. At the businessman and the young mother with two snot-nosed kids. At the humanity that the whole lot of them represented. He felt a wave of such nameless fury that it almost took his breath away. How *dare* these people, these ants, these cockroaches, be allowed to continue breathing after he was gone. How did the universe dare allow the dregs of humanity to continue to live in a world without Reuben Lablonski, El Viento? He felt such outrage at that obscenity that for a time, a few seconds, a minute, half an hour, he didn't know, his world completely grayed out and was not there at all. Eventually, the protoplasm of nothingness resolved itself into a subway car again, filled with different passengers from the ones that had been there before.

Reuben shook his head, looking around like a mole that'd just crawled out of a hole. Looked at the *vermin* — and made a solemn vow, swore by everything within him, that if he had to die, he would take with him as many despicable, parasitic human worms as he could.

The only life that mattered — his own — would soon end. There was no longer a future out there of days and nights, weeks and months and years stacked one on top of the other to accomplish the things he longed to accomplish. The reality of having to give that up was staggering. He had fantasized his whole life about one day finding the others who plied the same trade he did — mercenaries, hired guns, assassin wannabes — killers who possessed nowhere near the skill and tenacity and sense of excellence he'd brought to his profession all these years. He'd fantasized that someday he would track them down, one by one. He would be predator, and they would be prey. And he would kill them all.

And now there was no time for that. They were scattered all over the country, and he didn't have time to track them down. *Think weeks, not months.* The thought that he would leave those killers upright and walking when he had drawn his last breath was not to be borne.

But there was one thing of primary importance that he *would* do — if it required the last breath in his body. He would leave behind a record without blemish. He would be remembered as the most accomplished and feared assassin who had ever lived — a killer who had *never* failed to fulfill a contract, who had killed every person he had been paid to eliminate. Every one, without fail. He would set that record straight. The one kill that had gotten away — he would take that shot, fulfill the lone outstanding obligation.

And then El Viento was in his hotel room. He was in the subway car and then in his hotel room and he had no memory of the time in between those two events. It was dark outside now. He stared at the screen of his computer, willing his mind to concentrate. He had gotten his start in his line of work as a hacker, was a man who knew his way around the Internet, particularly the dark web. That is where he had found his home. That was his community, not the world, that place where nameless people swam in and out of the dark waters around him.

He went to the dark web now, eased into the back door, and floated in the murky waters, looking around, wondering, planning, thinking.

When Reuben Lablonski next came back to himself, the ashtray was completely full of butts. The dryness of his mouth, the throbbing of his head, the fullness of his bladder, they all told him he'd been sitting there for hours. He didn't remember any of it, but that didn't matter any more than it mattered what had caused the brain tumor that was growing in his head. It didn't matter how he had gotten there, but somehow through those hours, he'd come up with a plan. It was a brilliant plan. And he smiled, feeling how uncomfortable that felt on his face, a smile.

Reuben leaned over his computer and with a few quick strokes entered the "assassins" chatroom — Beyond Here Be Dragons. Then he began to type:

"Catch me … if you *can!*"

He laughed out loud at his own words. And then in just a few sentences, issued a challenge to all comers, violent men and women, sharks cruising the cold waters of the dark web looking for prey.

"I'm dying," he typed. "I have only weeks to live. My life's being taken from me, so I've decided to extend to anybody who cares to play an invitation to an equally deadly game. I have tattooed on my body the number of a Swiss bank account where I have on deposit more than fifty million dollars. Find that number and the money is yours. Just know that while you are hunting me, I will be hunting you. This game is winner take all; loser dies.

"If you can kill me before I kill you, you grab the gold ring. If I kill you first … game over.

"All you have to do is catch me … if you can."

Then he posted a screenshot of a newspaper clipping. As his finger hit return, he heard a sound so insignificant that no one but El Viento would have attended to it. But his were the keen senses of a predator, senses that had made him successful when others had failed and kept him alive when others died.

The sound came from the hallway. There was a window in the bathroom of the hotel room. El Viento had never in his life stayed in a room that didn't have an escape.

And when the man outside in the hallway finally rushed into the room with his weapon drawn, a breeze was blowing through the room — from the open window in the bathroom and out through the door into the hallway. The wind, *el viento*, lifted a piece of newsprint on the floor and scuttled it across the room like a dry leaf. The man picked up the newspaper clipping and read it. It was the announcement of a wedding.

Chapter One

LUCILLE CRENSHAW LET OUT A CRY THAT WAS A MIXTURE of joy and relief, underscored by such agonizing sorrow as to break your heart. Rileigh Bishop turned from where she stood beside the crumpled pieces of tin and metal and wood and drywall and shingles — but mostly mud — that had once been the Crenshaw family's home.

"What is it, Lucy?" Rileigh asked. The old woman had been digging in the pile of mud and debris looking for something, *anything* that had been hers before the mud and rocks had come sliding down the mountainside and bull-dozed everything in their path, leaving nothing but devastation behind.

Lucy turned toward Rileigh, and Rileigh could see the tears running down her cheeks. They were easy to see because they were twin tracks of clean in a filthy, wrinkled face. She was hugging something to her breast and rocking back and forth, her face raised to the sky, crying maybe, though Rileigh suspected the old woman was about cried out.

"Look what I found," Lucy said. Then she took the

9

object that she'd been clutching, hugging to her chest, and turned it around for Rileigh to see. It was a photograph. The glass across the front was cracked. The edge of the frame broken off, but the picture still remained. Rileigh recognized the image. There was one similar to it on the wall in Mama's house. The standard dress-uniform picture every soldier had taken after basic training.

Picking her way across the broken pieces of timber and rocks to where the old woman stood, Rileigh took the picture from her and studied it.

"That there's Billy Ray," the old woman said and sniffed. "He was killed three years ago in Afghanistan."

Rileigh's heart sank. She put out her hand to the old woman's shoulder. "I'm sorry for your loss."

"This picture's all I got of Billy Ray."

"No, Lucy, you have much, much more than this picture of your son. You have images of him in your mind, memories of him in your heart, things no stupid hurricane can take away from you."

The woman cocked her head to the side. "You didn't strike me as somebody that was full of it-ain't-as-bad-as-you-think platitudes," Lucille said. "In case you was wonderin' — yeah, it is every bit as bad as I think. Times ten."

Rileigh was momentarily at a loss for words. Now, it was the old woman's turn to comfort Rileigh. She patted Rileigh's shoulder with her arthritis-gnarled hand.

"Don't take that wrong, sugar. Ain't nobody else doin' any better'n you. What can you say to somebody who's lost every single damn thing they ever owned except the clothes on their back and the shoes on their feet?"

Lucille was right, of course. What *do* you say to someone who has lost everything?

When Hurricane Helene savaged Florida and came

roaring up into the southeast, Black Bear Forge, Tennessee, deep in the Smoky Mountains, had been spared the hammer blows that had fallen on places farther to the east. Rileigh had awakened on Saturday morning, September 28, to see news reports of devastation that was absolutely staggering. The mountains had been drenched by rain — Busick, in North Carolina, received nearly thirty-one inches, Spruce Pine recorded twenty-six. The rainfall swelled creeks, and flooded the French Broad, Nolichucky, and Pigeon rivers flowing from North Carolina into East Tennessee, causing mudslides and landslides that washed away houses and barns, cars, roads, bridges … everything.

The little towns of Greenville and Newport were washed away, just gone. They were so far inland, how could they be devastated by a hurricane? They were up in the mountains, for crying out loud. Of course, that's why Asheville, North Carolina, was devastated. It was in a catch basin for rain that rushed down mountainsides four thousand feet in elevation. And it was the intersection of two rivers, the French Broad and the Swannanoa. The French Broad, typically about seventy yards across and shallow, had spread out to more than fifteen hundred feet wide.

Rileigh'd sat stunned with Mama and Jillian in front of the television that morning — and by afternoon she and Jillian had joined the ranks of volunteers making their way into the ravaged communities to do whatever they could do to help.

Beaver Dam Hollow, in the mountains of East Tennessee, had been erased from the map by a mudslide that came roaring down the mountain along the meandering path of Little Creek — a waterway you could wade across in the summertime.

Rileigh had heard dozens of stories of loss and devastation and harrowing escapes in the eight days she'd been working in the relief effort. The death toll in East Tennessee had passed a dozen and was still rising. This morning, she'd been trying to keep Lucille Crenshaw busy, keep her mind focused on digging through the rubble to distract her from the terror that gripped her soul. No one had seen her 79-year-old husband since the night of the storm.

The couple had been in their mobile home, one of those that clung to the mountainside, the kind that Mitch said were held in place by satellite-dish stick pins. They'd had no warning that their lives were in danger. Of course they'd never seen a storm with rain like what was coming down.

"We heard this rumbling sound," Lucille had told her. "It sounded like somebody put gravel in a blender and turned it on puree. This rattling sound like nothing I ever heard, then I looked at Albert."

Lucille had paused in the telling of the story then. Rileigh watched her relive it in her mind. The image of her husband's face. "I ain't never seen Albert scared, but he was scared then. We was both scared."

They felt the trailer begin to slide sideways. Albert had fallen to the floor and cried out in pain. And Lucille had reached down to try to help him up, trying to keep her own footing as the floors she was standing on was moving. The walls were moving. She heard crackling and crumbling sounds as her home split apart. The candles they had lit when their electricity went out fell over and were extinguished, and then it was just dark. She could hear Albert crying her name, but she couldn't get to him. Then she was in water and mud and swirling around knowing she was going to die, crying, "Jesus, I'm coming home." Then she had slammed up against something solid. It was hours before she realized that the mudslide had deposited her in the top branches of the oak tree, a quarter of a mile down the mountain in the yard of the Henderson family, whose house was not there anymore. Neither were the Hendersons.

Lucille didn't know what had happened to the Hendersons or to Albert or to her daughter and two teenage sons who lived in the next hollow. She didn't know that night and had heard nothing since. Yet she clung to the hope that somehow they were all just fine. They had all survived, her daughter and her grandsons and all of her neighbors. She clung to the belief that she'd see them come walking up that muddy stretch of dirt that once had been a road and they'd call out to her, "Hey, Lucy, we was worried to death about you."

Rileigh knew that's what the old woman was thinking as she held the picture of her long-dead son to her chest, rocking it back and forth as if it were a newborn in her arms.

"They'll be coming along any time now," Lucille said, looking down the mountainside that was unrecognizable now, bore no resemblance to the mountainside she's looked at every day for seven decades. "You'll see ... they'll be coming along directly."

"Sure they will, Lucy. So we need to do the best we can to recover some of your stuff."

Rileigh gestured toward a flat place where they had been putting the items they had been able to dig out of the mud. A lamp but no shade. Albert's tackle box. They'd place the smaller items, figurines, a saltshaker from the salt-and- pepper shaker set they'd gotten in San Diego on vacation in the kitty litter box that they had found. They'd found the box but not the cat.

Jillian had been helping the Barnaby family down the road — Joe and Gladys. They'd been having breakfast that morning. There was a light rain falling but nothing concerning. But when they heard the rumbling up the mountainside, George grabbed his wife and their dog and said, "We've got to get out of here." They didn't make it out in time before the mud and the water hit the house. They clung to an old mattress for a while and onto a piece of wall that eventually broke apart, separating them in the fast-moving water. That was the last time Joe saw his wife.

Major relief efforts were underway for the places with larger populations, but not up in the little hollows like this one where individual families, not even small towns, just individuals, were stranded by downed trees and mud. Their vehicles were gone. They had nothing to drink or eat.

And today, as Rileigh helped Lucille dig through the debris of her house, she didn't comment, of course, on the smell that she had grown accustomed to in Iraq and Afghanistan. The smell of death. It was all around them.

Rileigh's phone dinged with an incoming text. Ah, so there was coverage here. She glanced at the screen and saw three hearts, nothing more. It was from Mitch. They didn't talk. Her cell phone didn't have the juice for prolonged conversations, and she judiciously guarded her usage. Gratefully, she'd had the presence of mind to gather up the four charging battery packs in the house. Mama and Jillian both had one and Rileigh had two. Each contained the power to charge her phone from dead to full charge three times. The battery packs had been a lifesaver, giving her the ability to power her phone so isolated families could call and reassure out-of-state family who were worried sick about them.

Lucille saw the message and the look on Rileigh's face.

"That from your honey back home? A pretty girl like you must have a line of beaus out in front of your house."

"My fiancé."

"When you gettin' married?"

"The twelfth."

"Why, that's next Saturday. In a week! You got a wedding to plan in a week — what're you doing here?"

"I'm digging around in the mud. What does it look like I'm doing?" Rileigh said with a grin. "This is better than planning a wedding."

In truth, she almost believed those words. Digging around in the mud trying to find even a tiny sliver of a life that had been totally shattered was certainly more rewarding, and a whole lot less stressful, than planning a wedding.

"Oh, don't worry," Rileigh said. "My best friend Georgia is taking care of all the details for me while I'm here."

Rileigh thought again how grateful she was to Georgia for being willing to step in and handle it all when she and Jillian went dashing off to east Tennessee. She had swung by Georgia's house and dropped off everything she had accumulated in the planning stages of the wedding. It wasn't much, but the wedding was going to be small and intimate, so she didn't need much.

She told Georgia her budget, how much money she had to spend, and described the small, intimate ceremony she had in mind. She also gave her a tentative guest list with a dozen or so names on it, and she thought even that crowd was too big.

"I'll handle everything," Georgia'd said. "Don't you worry about nothing. You just go help those people in the mountains. God knows they need it. I'd go myself if..." She gestured toward the chaos of children around her and shrugged. Rileigh would rather go dig people out of a mudslide than have to corral Georgia's five children.

"You sure she's going to do it like you'd want her to?" Lucille asked.

Rileigh laughed. "Georgia and I have been friends since kindergarten, when she put a piece of gum in my hair the first day of school."

"Oh, my goodness. And you're *friends?*"

"Oh, at the time I did what any normal five-year-old would do. I hauled off and slugged her."

Lucille chuckled a little.

"And the teacher was so horrified that she took the two of us into the coat room, put me with my nose in one corner and Georgia with her nose in another, and told us to stand there until she came back. And, of course, during the time we were in there, we became fast friends and have been as close as sisters ever since."

"Well, I guess you know what you're doing," Lucille said. "But if you ain't careful, a wedding can get away from you." The old woman clucked her teeth. "Them things has a way of getting bigger and bigger and bigger."

Rileigh smiled. Thank goodness she didn't have to worry about that with Georgia.

Chapter Two

REUBEN LABLONSKI, EL VIENTO, STEPPED OUT OF THE building and closed the door behind him, the little bell on it tinkling merrily. What was that about? The tinkling bell sound was something you'd expect in a children's toy store or a mom-and-pop grocery. This was a tattoo parlor. The artist here was reputed to be among the best in the world. Not that it mattered to El Viento now. It didn't take a whole lot of skill to tattoo a fifteen-digit number. Still, he was used to getting the best of everything, so he'd set out to find the best of the best to ink this all-important tattoo on his body.

But it had hurt, like *really* hurt. Getting a tattoo wasn't supposed to hurt. He'd heard men complain about their tattoos — that the ink faded, or that the girlfriend whose name was inscribed inside a heart on their bicep had turned out to be a slut. But he had never heard anybody complain about getting a tattoo that hurt. But *this* tattoo — it had burned, felt like his skin was on fire. He'd had to grit his teeth to keep from crying out.

El Viento shook his head violently as if to fling the

memory of the flaming pain away. Then he squinted. The sunlight on this October day was so bright the whole world looked over-exposed, made his eyes water, sending twin streams of tears down his cheeks as if he was crying.

Was that ... the pain and the bright light ... were they because of Ole Arch?

He stopped at the corner. The little emblem of the walk/don't walk stick figure was green, indicating he could cross the street. The people near him at the intersection began stepping around him and off the curb into the street. But El Viento merely stood there, staring.

"Hey buddy," said a man who'd almost bumped into him from behind, "you can walk now. That's what the green sign means."

El Viento heard the man's words as if he were underwater. He understood them, but they seemed to be coming from a great distance, words shouted from the top of a cliff down onto the rocks hundreds of feet below. He shook his head again, offered the man a lopsided thank-you half smile and stepped off the curb into the crosswalk. He'd stood staring for so long that the little green man on the sign turned red when he was halfway across, and he had to hurry to escape oncoming traffic.

Archibald's fault.

Archibald was the name Reuben had given to the thing growing in his head that the doctor had said reminded him of the roots of a tree. The brain tumor that was killing him was Archibald, because El Viento believed that something as significant in your life as the thing that was going to kill you was significant enough to have a name. But there was no sense wasting a good name on it. Still, he didn't like referring to it as "that thing" or the "tumor" or "the growth" or "the cancer" — definitely not "the cancer," because the dreaded C-word had always horrified him.

The thing in his head that was killing him was Ole Arch. But giving it a name didn't grant him automatic permission to attribute to it every subtle change in his life.

Or did it?

A simple little tattoo that set his skin on fire? The sun was so bright — in autumn — that he couldn't see through his tears?

Maybe Ole Arch was causing the physical changes and maybe he wasn't. And maybe El Viento was simply imagining the changes in some kind of hypochondrial response to the knowledge that a deadly thing was *growing* inside his skull.

Still, being as unbiased an observer as he was able to be, it did appear to him that all his senses were now *heightened*. He was more aware of everything in his environment. As he walked down the street, the aroma of car exhaust and hot rubber, as if somebody had peeled out, hung in the air. And street-vendor hot dogs with onions and grilled peppers for sale out the window of a parked truck. Perfume. He thought it was Shalimar on the woman who had just passed him. Popcorn. And urine. And…

Stop it!

He had to stop obsessing over what was clearly a symptom of Archibald's relentless advance through his skull. The bottom line was that Reuben needed to get his head out of his own ass and stop wallowing in the quagmire of emotions and physical responses to his deadly brain tumor. He needed to put his game face on and get about the business of settling the final score.

Months ago, Reuben had been hired by a man who was the ex-sheriff of some little county in Tennessee to kill a woman named Rileigh Bishop. He'd been paid for the job up front, the whole amount. He only required a twenty-five percent deposit, but this guy had the cash and wanted to settle the deal. Reuben'd had to sit through the client's in-depth description of the mark, way more information than he needed. The man named Mum had told him the mark's whole damn life history, as if he needed to know that her sister had disappeared on the night before her wedding and that the mark had spent two tours in Iraq and Afghanistan. All he needed was the make and model of her car and what she looked like and her address so that he could follow her around for a while, see what places she frequented, what roads she took to get there and to get home. That was all the information he needed to set up an ambush. He didn't need all the rest of that shit. Once he'd stalked her for a few days, he had done as he had done on every other job, he had set up an ambush, he had sighted in, had the crosshairs on her temple, and squeezed the trigger. But she'd hit a bump in the road or a pothole or something, the car jogged and the shot went wide.

He'd been seriously pissed about that. Had considered going down the hillside, crossing the road, and following the smashed vegetation where her car had run off into a river and finishing the job. But that was dangerous, and he hadn't gotten to be the single most successful assassin of his generation by taking unnecessary chances like that. He would pick another time and another spot and complete his contract. He'd said as much to the man who'd hired him. And the man who'd hired him had retorted that he didn't need his services anymore, he would handle it "personally."

Paid assassins didn't give refunds. They completed their jobs, took out the marks they had been hired to take out. He'd never failed to complete an assignment, and he'd certainly never given a refund. But the client was adamant that *he* would make the hit. Mum would kill Rileigh Bishop.

That had left El Viento hanging until the next day when the whole town was abuzz with stories about how the ex-sheriff named Mum had eaten his gun. Had gone down into his basement and blown his own brains out. Nobody knew why. Neither did El Viento, nor did he care. But it had left him with a conundrum. He'd been paid to kill this woman, and she was still alive. In all his years as an assassin, he'd never left a victim alive. So he decided on the spot that he'd finish the contract, whether the man who'd hired him was still alive or not. But he didn't have the time at that point to work on it. He was an assassin who had more than one contract to fulfill. So he had merely decided that when he got around to it, after he had fulfilled the other contracts he'd signed up for, he'd come back and finish the job.

But since the ex-sheriff had told him Rileigh Bishop's whole life history, El Viento had decided to have some fun with her. He'd been personally *offended* that she had survived. When El Viento put the crosshairs on your temple, you didn't walk away from it. But this bitch had. So he decided to make her pay. And he'd sent her a postcard, because postcards had been tangled up in her family's history. And decided that every time he made a kill, he'd send her a piece.

El Viento was walking down the street away from the tattoo parlor, remembering that and chuckling, when suddenly someone was talking to him. He could hear the voice and see the man standing in front of him, but he couldn't make sense of the words.

"Dropped this." The words clanged into his brain too loud. "Hello. Knock knock. Are you in there? You dropped this."

El Viento focused his attention on the man standing in front of him, holding out the newspaper he'd bought out

21

of a rack that morning. He looked down at it, realized he must have dropped it, pasted what felt like a smile on the inside but might not have looked like one on the outside on his face, and said, "Thank you, sir."

He took the newspaper — though he could no longer remember why he'd purchased it — and continued back to his hotel. Once inside his hotel, he took a long, hot bath before he opened his computer and went through the technical gymnastics required to slide into the deep, cold waters of the dark web, where he had posted yesterday his Catch Me If You Can challenge. He smiled then, looking at the responses that had been posted by those who'd seen it. People who were chatting, cross-chatting with each other about the challenge. He recognized some of the screen names, and his smile grew wider when he saw who he had attracted. Oh, they weren't all of the assassins he daydreamed about one day killing. But there were some.

And there were other people as well.

Nighthawk.

El Viento knew who Nighthawk was, that was for damn sure. The man had been tracking him down to get payback for El Viento snuffing his brother. He was such a klutz that El Viento had been aware of him ever since he started the chase. Was just dangling carrots to keep it interesting. El Viento had taken the contract on the brother from the Russian Mafia, had offed him and dumped his body in Lake Michigan. But not before cutting off his little finger. He had sent the little finger along with a frowny face postcard to Rileigh Bishop.

He considered the other marks he'd hit in the months since his bullet blew out the side window of Rileigh Bishop's car and sent it careening into a river … instead of blowing her brains out through a two-inch hole in her temple as he'd intended. He had become more and more entertained by the game as time went on. The hardest, and he believed the most interesting, gift he'd sent to Bishop was the piece of skin from the back of one of his victims. Not just any piece of skin. It was a piece of skin with a tattoo on it. Removing the skin from the man's back, then drying the skin, a little like drying a deer hide, had proved to be way more difficult than he'd anticipated. But he'd been proud of the final product, and was certain the sight of it had raised the hairs on the back of Rileigh Bishop's neck.

His goal in the game was to freak out the Bishop woman more and more with every little gift. He was sure he'd accomplished his goal when he'd snipped off a piece of her own hair to include with his final gift. He laughed out loud whenever he imagined her shocked expression when she saw it, wondering how on earth someone had managed to snip off a piece of her hair without her knowledge ... coupled, of course, with her realization that the killer who'd been sending "little surprise packages" for months had been so close to her he could touch her ... and she hadn't noticed.

It really hadn't been that hard. He'd followed the woman and a friend — and a carload of noisy little kids — to see *Toy Story 3*. The adults had been too busy corralling the rowdy youngsters to notice the totally nondescript man seated in the row behind them. When the cartoon toys were on the conveyor belt about to be dumped into the fiery furnace — all the rambunctious children were sitting frozen in dread ... El Viento had reached up and carefully snipped off a lock of the woman's hair. She'd been as engrossed in the scene as the kids. He could have run clippers across her head and removed every hair on her scalp and she wouldn't have noticed.

El Viento read the responses to his Catch Me If You

Can post, noted who had responded. Besides Nighthawk, there were several other screen names he recognized. Born2BEvil was a hulking mercenary who took what El Viento considered the crumbs from his own table of hired killing. The big man wasn't skilled, had no repertoire of weapons to select from — he either choked his victims and dumped the bodies where they could easily be found, or slashed them, making such a mess that he left covered in blood. Amateur. Born2BEvil indicated he was in on the chase. Excellent.

IronJackal.

IronJackal had tossed his hat in the ring as had Bang-URDead. El Viento knew those screen names, knew both the assassins were skilled enough to blend into a scene and not be noticed.

And there was another name he recognized, and it made him laugh out loud. BloodHarpy. That fat clown had bungled half the jobs he took. He had been busted so many times he finally had his fingerprints removed. And he thought he could catch and kill the mighty El Viento? What a monumental joke. El Viento would take him out *first*, use him as a calling card. He smiled even broader. This was going to be more than just interesting. Oh my, yes indeed. This was going to be *fun.*

Chapter Three

GEORGIA STUMP WAS IN THE BACK THE DOUBLE-WIDE trailer, sitting in the middle of the queen-sized bed jammed into the tiny bedroom. She was surrounded by pieces of paper and brochures, pages out of a legal pad, and pictures of wedding parties that she'd gotten Chigger to print out on the printer in the library in town.

Mayella was screaming, her high-pitched wail so grating and loud that though Georgia understood that the principle of opera singers being able to crack a wine glass with a high note didn't apply to her daughter's shriek, Georgia still sometimes wondered if one day a crack would appear in one of the windows in the trailer.

"Chigger, give her a banana."

"Where are the bananas?"

"You know where the bananas are. They're where they've always been."

"On the countertop by the bread box?"

Georgia let out a sigh and hopped up off the bed. It would be easier and faster to go into the kitchen and find the bananas for Chigger than it would be to holler out to him where to look.

Why was it that men didn't know how to look for things? It had to be something on the Y chromosome because it certainly wasn't the fault of any woman she knew. She knew lots of men, though — her brother, her father, and most certainly her husband — who simply did not know how to search for a thing. Chigger would open a cabinet in the kitchen, stand in front of it, and holler to Georgia in the next room, "Where's the potato soup?"

She would come into the kitchen and find it for him — on a shelf right in front of his nose. Why couldn't he see it? All those thoughts blew through her mind as she hurried down the hallway, opened up the potato box where the bananas were stored, were always stored, had always been stored since the day they moved into the trailer, pulled out a bunch of them, and handed them to Chigger.

"How long are you going to be in there figuring?" he said. "I need to get some work done."

Translate that: Chigger needed to go out and sell some weed. That was what he did, his line of work. He sold weed. But right now Georgia had things she had to get done, too. After all, she had only a few days to set everything in place, start the snowballs rolling downhill before the wedding on Saturday.

"I've got calls to make, honey — I've got to check on the bridesmaid dresses, make sure Ian picked up the cherry lumber for the grape arbor, and confirm the Foote Notes for the whoop-de-do—"

Chigger held up his hand. "You don't have to explain it to me. I don't care, just get it done as fast as you can, okay? I got stuff to do."

Georgia stepped over the stack of Legos, assembled in a shape that was either the Eiffel Tower or an oil derrick, moved nine-year-old Liam and six-year-old Conner out of the way.

"Mommy, Eli hit me," four-year-old Mason cried.

"I did not," Eli shot back.

"Did, too."

"Did *not*."

"Did—"

Georgia closed the door on the accusations, went back to the bed, and sat back down in the middle of it amid her mountain of wedding "notes."

She had been both thrilled and honored … and intimidated when Rileigh'd asked her to take over the plans for the double wedding of Rileigh Bishop to Mitchell Webster and Jillian Bishop to David Hicks on October 12, 2024.

Ever since Mitch had proposed to Rileigh — as the two of them stood together in the pouring rain — and they'd decided to make it a double wedding with Jillian and David, Rileigh and Georgia had talked often about how Rileigh envisioned the ceremony, what she wanted in the service.

Georgia had smiled and nodded her head like a good little bobblehead — no, like the best friend that she was — at Rileigh's plans. But in her heart of hearts, Georgia had been deeply saddened by Rileigh's lack of imagination. Georgia had gotten pregnant with Liam right after she graduated from high school, soon after Rileigh had gone off to the military, and Georgia's "wedding" had been performed by a justice of the peace when she and Chigger had eloped.

Since that time, Georgia had secretly pined away for the traditional wedding she'd been denied, had daydreams about it and could see it in her mind's eye.

She'd be walking slowly down the aisle on the arm of

her father, the train of her huge white dress trailing out behind her.

The church would be jammed with well-wishers.

A line of beautiful, identically-clad bridesmaids would be standing on one side and an equal number of tuxedo-clad groomsmen would be standing on the other. A little girl and boy would be walking out front, tossing rose petals into her path.

She dreamed of a wedding reception like the well-loved tradition of a mountain whoop-de-do — a full sit-down meal with men manning the barbecue grills, grilling hot dogs and hamburgers and ladies filling the tables with pastries and side dishes — every woman competing with every other woman to provide the tastiest dish

Georgia dreamed of a dance floor lit by soft lights where she would dance slowly in her princess gown, careful to hold up the train so she didn't step on it, moving to soft music, staring up into Chigger's face as he stared down into hers. Then she would dance with her father and Chigger would dance with his mother, and afterwards the entire crowd of hundreds of people would dance the night away, drinking and laughing and enjoying a memory that would be a shining city on a hill in her mind for her to return to time and time again when life was gray, a wedding so memorable that everyone in the community would talk about it for years afterwards.

What she hadn't dreamed of was the reality of literally climbing out her bedroom window, sneaking through the woods to the other side of the creek where Chigger waited in his pickup truck so that they could drive across the county line to Beaufort County and be married by a justice of the peace.

When Rileigh had first told Georgia that she'd accepted Mitch's wedding proposal, all of those daydreams came crashing back down on her and she hoped to be able to live them vicariously through Rileigh — until she found out that Rileigh wasn't the slightest bit interested in having a big wedding.

In fact, Rileigh would much have preferred to elope, and she might very well have done that had it not been for Rileigh's mama.

For Mama, an upcoming wedding had been the occasion for the greatest traumas of her life. Her oldest daughter Jillian had disappeared on the night before her wedding and was not seen again for almost 30 years. And Mama's husband, J.R. had committed suicide over it — or so Mama thought, and everybody in her life wanted to protect her from the truth of what had really happened.

Jillian had announced earlier in the summer that she and David Hicks were going to be married, that she was going to walk down the aisle to the groom she'd walked out on — not of her own free will, of course — almost three decades before. And Rileigh'd decided she would accompany her sister to the altar and the two would be married at the same time.

The two had set about planning a ceremony, and then suddenly, a couple of weeks ago, Rileigh had called Georgia to say she and Jillian were going to eastern Tennessee and to help in the recovery efforts for the poor people whose lives had been devastated by Hurricane Helene. She'd asked Georgia to take over the wedding planning while they were gone, and Georgia had been intimidated at first ... and then exhilarated.

She really hadn't started out to change everything Rileigh wanted. Though now, looking back, she was pretty sure she had unconsciously transformed Rileigh's wedding into the fantasy she'd had of her own wedding for her whole life. And Georgia had had a willing accomplice, of course, in Mama, who couldn't imagine why Rileigh didn't want to invite every man, woman, and child in Yarmouth and all the surrounding counties to celebrate the most wonderful day of her life.

In truth, Rileigh hadn't given Georgia much to work with, and when Georgia called Mama to ask what she thought about making a few little changes here and there, Mama had supported her wholeheartedly.

And after that, it had just … grown.

Georgia thought it was like looking out into the yard after a rain and suddenly there were all kinds of tiny little mushrooms that hadn't been there the night before. She would swear they hadn't. They had just popped up overnight. Well, the preparations for Rileigh's wedding had done something similar.

Georgia sat back and looked at the list of to-do items that had started out at five or six and now she was marking off numbers 39, 40, and 41.

Number 39 — check with Bestowing Sewing and make sure Cynthia Waters had delivered the fabric to the ladies who were making the bridesmaids dresses. Bestowing Sewing was Mama's sewing group at the church that numbered from a half a dozen to three dozen ladies who got together to make quilts for orphanages and knit booties for pregnancy centers, and who had been pressed into service by Mama to make the bridesmaids dresses for Rileigh and Jillian's wedding.

Georgia was to be Rileigh's maid of honor, and when she had asked Rileigh what she wanted her to wear, Rileigh had blown her off with a simple, "Green's my favorite color, come up with something green."

When Georgia had mentioned to Mama what Rileigh had said about "something green," Mama'd offered to make a green dress for Georgia to wear. Three days later, she'd called to say she had "a whole bunch of fabric" she could use to make the dress out of — thanks to Cynthia Waters.

After Cynthia's mean-as-a-snake husband, Claude, died a few years ago, Cynthia had moved back to the Forge and "blossomed." She'd joined every woman's group in the county, taught Sunday school, made quilts and baby blankets to give to the Red Cross, crocheted scarves and doilies to sell at the church bazaar before Christmas, and was always the first to volunteer help if someone was in need. Georgia hadn't seen Cynthia since Cynthia had painted faces at the school festival months ago, and since then, according to Mama, Cynthia had somehow come by the contents of a bankrupt craft store. Mama was vague on the details, just said Cynthia had dozens of bolts of fabric — all different colors and kinds.

Then Mama and Cynthia had calculated it out. A simple sheath silhouette and train would take at least four yards of fabric. An A-line gown, five to seven, depending on the train length. A tea-length dress, around three, a mini dress at least two, and a ballroom gown would take eight to ten.

"She said I could have a bolt of green satin and an equal amount of green chiffon," Mama'd said. "A bolt's a hundred yards, so if we went with ballroom gowns, we'd have enough for at least ten of 'em — chiffon over satin. So let's go with ten bridesmaids. If we're real careful how we lay the patterns out on the material, we can get another two tea-length gowns for the maids of honor."

The sewing circle ladies would also use Cynthia's fabrics to make tablecloths for the tables at the whoop-de-do, and cloth coverings for the benches that'd be set up for guests in the amphitheater.

Georgia quickly thought of ten girls in town who

would love to be bridesmaids in Rileigh and Jillian's wedding, particularly if they didn't have to pay for their own dresses. And with ten bridesmaids, there would, of course have to be ten groomsmen. Georgia'd called Beau Mullins at the Sheriff's Department, who'd come up with more than a dozen possible groomsmen off the top of his head. Gus Hazelton, the county coroner and Mitch's best friend, was to be his best man and he had already let it be known that "I'm coming in a tuxedo. Deal with it."

Georgia had been present when he made that announcement one Sunday at church and had seen the look on Mitch's face.

"A tuxedo?"

"Hell, yeah, I'm coming in a tuxedo. I bought the damn thing to escort a girl I was dating to some hoity-toity dinner party years ago and it's been hanging in a plastic bag in my closet ever since. This is a chance to wear it, and I'm not going to pass it up."

Mitch said that he would be in uniform, thank you very much — his Yarmouth County Sheriff's uniform.

The groomsmen who were deputy sheriffs — there would be four of them — could come in uniform, too. The rest could wear black suits and white shirts. Bestowing Sewing would make each of them matching green satin ties.

The size of the wedding Georgia was planning was fast outgrowing any of the church buildings in town ... but what if they held the wedding outside? Then nature would be their cathedral. Everyone knew how much Rileigh loved fall in the Smokies, when the mountains were decked out in their bright red/gold/yellow fall finery. Georgia asked Mama to find some outdoor venue where the service could be held, and Mama had called back in half an hour saying she had reserved the Breezy Creek Recreation Area in the Great Smoky Mountains National Park.

Breezy Creek was huge! No way did the budget have money to pay for a venue that size. But Mama'd shushed her when she pointed that out.

"Ain't gonna have to pay for it," she'd said.

Lily Bishop had gone to work at the Cades Cove Visitor Center at the Great Smoky Mountains National Park right after she got out of high school, and over the years she'd worked at each of the other three visitors' centers — Oconaluftee, Clingmans Dome, and finally at the biggest one, Sugarlands. Eventually, she ran the Back-country Information Center there, which issued permits for all manner of activities. If you wanted to scatter Uncle Herbert's ashes in the park, go fishing or spelunking, stage a war protest, or *get married* in the park, Lily Bishop had to issue a permit for it.

"I got me lots of friends in high places," Mama'd said, and she'd handled it.

But in a facility that big, with a wedding party that large, they'd need tons of decorations. How on earth could Georgia afford to pay for the kind of flower arrangements they would need? Bouquets for the bridesmaids alone would cost a fortune. Not even mentioning the flowers that would be necessary to set as centerpieces on the tables at the reception and use to decorate around the amphitheater.

Liam had solved that problem for her. When she'd told Chigger she couldn't afford to pay for the number and array of flowers she would need, her nine-year-old-son had piped up, "Why do you need flowers, Mama? It's autumn. Can't you just use colorful leaves?"

"Leaves?"

"You know, put wax on them like you showed me for that science fair project."

For that project, Georgia'd shown Liam what her Mama had shown her — how to put a piece of wax paper on an ironing board, a leaf on top of it, another piece of wax paper on top of the leaf, and a dish towel on top of it all. A warm iron applied on the dish towel transferred the wax to the leaf, and would preserve it, keep it supple without drying out for at least a week, maybe longer.

Georgia got on the phone to the bridesmaids, and they were all in. Each said they would go out and gather up leaves. The trick was to pick them off the trees before they fell to the ground and began to dry out and curl up. Each of the girls would bring a bushel basket of waxed leaves to Breezy Creek the day of the ceremony. They could gather then to make the leaves into garlands and centerpieces and bouquets.

Mason was to be the ring bearer, and Chloe Morgan would be the flower girl. The sewing circle ladies would make whatever they needed to wear.

But after that…

Georgia had reached her limit in terms of people, volunteers, and supplies. Paying for fancy photography and videography, and an enormous wedding cake, was way beyond her means.

Until she got a call from Forever Memories.

The young man from Forever Memories said he had heard she'd been calling around getting prices on photographers and videographers and such. He said he was a wedding planner and he was prepared to offer her a special deal. He'd been trying to work his way into the market in Gatlinburg and Black Bear Forge and the communities around them, so he was willing to provide a wedding planner, a photographer, a photographer's assistant, a videographer, and a three-tiered wedding cake for the bride and groom to cut at the ceremony … in addition to sheet cakes to cut up and serve the guests — all at a ridiculously low price. In return, Georgia had to agree to display the work of his photographers and videographers to her friends and neighbors in Yarmouth County and recommend his services to the community.

Georgia had leapt on the idea.

And now she sat in the middle of her bed, checking items off of her to-do list, both looking forward to and dreading Rileigh's return home tomorrow. In truth, Georgia wasn't completely certain how Rileigh was going to react to the changes she had made in the plan that Rileigh had for her wedding.

Georgia let out a sigh — who in their right mind would turn down the opportunity for a fairy-tale wedding?

And why Georgia was giving her best friend the gift of a lifetime?

Chapter Four

It was almost midnight on Monday when the exhausted Bishop sisters, Rileigh and Jillian, got back to Mama's house from east Tennessee. Mama took one look at her two daughters and ordered them both to take a bath.

"You stink, smell worse'n that picnic basket I left the tuna salad in for a month."

They hadn't had a chance to clean up for more than a week, working non-stop from first light until after dark helping devastated families dig out of the mud.

Mitch was away in Nashville for a Tennessee Sheriffs' Association convention and wouldn't return until tomorrow — or Rileigh would have gone there first … well, after she'd had a bath. She'd tried to call him as they drove back, but one of the consequences of Hurricane Helene was damage to cell phone repeater towers all over the mountains. Sometimes all the carriers had service. Sometimes none of them did. It was a crapshoot, and she couldn't get through. It was too late now to call him. He'd be sound asleep. David Hicks had been out of town on business since the day they'd left for east Tennessee.

While Rileigh and Jillian bathed, Mama made corn-bread and popped it into the oven to go with the pinto beans, favored with ham hock and bacon, that had been simmering on the stove all afternoon. The sisters came into the kitchen dressed in pajamas and bathrobes, their hair still wet, and wolfed down the hot food, a treat after days of sandwiches and cold coffee.

Jillian glanced at the clock on the wall and said, "You gotta love a family that has a full sit-down meal at one o'clock in the morning."

Mama did what Mama always did. She waited on the two of them, making sure they had full glasses of lemonade or tea with lots of ice, piping bowls of beans, and big plates of cornbread slathered in butter. Finally, she sat down in her traditional chair at the head of the table and said, "Okay, I want to hear it. Tell me all about it."

Rileigh and Jillian exchanged a look. How could you tell anybody about what they had seen in the past ten days? How could you tack words onto a catastrophe of that scope and magnitude?

"It was … awful," Jillian said, picking up another piece of cornbread and put it in her mouth.

"Yeah, awful," Rileigh echoed.

"Oh, come on, girls. I want to know more than that. I could figure that out by watching the television. Come on, tell me what you've done. What were the people like?"

"The people were us, Mama. Mountain folks," Rileigh said.

"Just ordinary garden variety people who woke up in the middle of the night with the mountain sliding down on top of them," Jillian said.

37

"The whole town of Oak Pass where we went on the fourth day … it was just gone."

"I've driven through Oak Pass a time or two," Mama said "Pretty little place, what, maybe three or four hundred people? I 'member because I stopped there at a place called Higginbotham Grocery to get me some headache powders because I've been driving for hours and my eyes was tired and my head was starting to hurt. You see that store?"

"It's not there anymore, Mama."

"Not there anymore?"

Rileigh shook her head sadly. "Like I said, the whole town's gone, Mama."

"How can a town be gone?"

"It was at the bottom of the mountain with a creek running through it, but after eighteen inches of rain, that little creek you could wade across was fifteen feet deep and had washed away all the roads, bridges and half the buildings."

"And what the water in the creek didn't wash away, the mudslide that came after it buried," Jillian said. "When hurricanes hit Florida and blow people's houses away, they come back and find nothing but the foundation. So they build back a new house where the previous house had been. But what do you do when the spot where your house had been is now covered in mud fifteen feet deep mud?"

"How'd they cope with a loss like that?" Mama asked.

"Most of them had bigger fish to fry than digging their house of the mud," Rileigh said. "We didn't meet a single family who hadn't lost somebody."

"And a lot of them didn't even know," Jillian continued. "They had relatives living up in some hollow or in a house stuck down at the end of some little road with trees knocked down over the road and they couldn't get to them to help."

"There was one woman named Daisy McKinley," Rileigh said. "She was trapped on the roof of her chicken house all night and all day, and right before sunset, a helicopter flew over and spotted her and plucked her off the roof. She was the only member of her family who had made it out of the house before it washed away. We met people who hadn't had water or food in two or three days, drinking out of puddles in the road.

"It's hard to imagine everything you own, every picture, every chair, every bed, every towel, every spoon, fork, everything completely gone. And it was so unexpected," Jillian said. "They say that they issued warnings, flash flood warnings, and mudslide warnings, but not one of the people I spoke to heard any of them. They could tell by the quantity of the rain and watching their own creeks rise that it was going to be ugly. But there was no evacuation order. Those people were on a mountainside. Who worries about drowning when you live on a mountainside?"

"And of course none of them had flood insurance," Mama said.

Jillian shook her head. "These weren't the kind of people who could afford insurance anyway."

"How'd you folks get to them people to help?"

"We went as far as we could in a Range Rover, then got out and walked, leading pack mules for four miles up the mountain to a little washed-out place in a hollow that once had been a town. But there wasn't a single building standing."

"Except the church on the hill," Rileigh said.

"God takes care of his own," Mama said.

Rileigh felt like pointing out that all of the people who lived in that little hollow had been God's own too. But she didn't. There was no understanding why bad things happened to good innocent people.

"That church became the Rescue Center," she said. "We set up there and they helicoptered in supplies and drinking water. There was one woman had a baby, and she hadn't had any diapers in four days — or formula. She'd been giving the child soft drinks because she had snatched a six-pack out of a pile of mud and at least it was something to drink."

"That baby looked terrible," Jillian said. "They were medevacked out of there because the baby was getting dehydrated. Dr. Pepper didn't agree with his stomach, and he kept throwing it up and then having diarrhea. It was bad. But it made you believe in the natural goodness of humanity when you saw all the people who turned out to help."

"Including the two of you."

"Including neighbors from farther up the hollow who didn't have a whole lot more left than the people they were helping. One fella came along and spent four hours with us digging through the debris of a house, only to discover that he was sleeping on the floor in the church because his own house, a little trailer house, went floating down the river. He said it looked like a gum wrapper. There were people who wrote their names on pieces of canvas and stretched them out, hoping the news crews that came along would pan over them and their family members would see the telecast and know they had survived.

"It's not going to take years to clean up all that mess," Rileigh said. "it's going to take *decades*. The mountainsides are *gone*. They're down in the hollows now clogging up the creeks. All those beautiful old trees. They're blocking the roads. There are no bridges. Highways are washed out." She shook her head. "Decades."

They went silent then, finishing their beans and cornbread.

"You girls need to go to bed and just sleep as late as you can in the morning," Mama said. "I know it's hard to shift gears, but you girls is gettin' married on Saturday. And you got a right to be happy 'bout that. To be joyful and glad that you found the men you want to spend the rest of your lives with. It's a wonderful time for a family and you need to relax and enjoy it."

Rileigh and Jillian's eyes met again, conveying one to the other the understanding that they would never look at life the same way after what they had seen. That their joy would be tempered by an understanding of what others only a few miles away were suffering. But in at least one way, their joy would be multiplied by an understanding, a real gut-level understanding of how precious life was. How important it was to love the people in your life. Every day. All day. And tell them so. And how quickly everything that you knew and cared about could be snatched away.

Rileigh went to the bathroom and brushed her teeth and washed her face, looking at the woman in the mirror who stared back at her. Her cheeks were hollowed, dark circles lay under her eyes. She was going to make a beautiful bride.

Bride.

Mitch.

Suddenly Rileigh felt that butterflies-in-the-belly feeling she always did when she thought about Mitch. And the realization that they were going to be married in less than a week brought joy to her heart and a smile to her face that even the horror she'd seen could not erase.

When Rileigh fell into bed, glorying in the smell of sheets that had been hung out in the sunshine to dry, she felt an ache in every joint and muscle in her body, a symphony of discomfort that slowly slid away as she lay on the feather mattress, knowing she wouldn't be able to sleep. But she closed her eyes, and when she opened them again, it was morning. She looked at her cell phone for the time and saw the voice mail icon blinking. She must have been so sound asleep she didn't hear it ring.

At the sound of Mitch's voice, the butterflies-in-the-belly feeling returned with a vengeance. Though all he said was that he loved her, that he'd be busy all morning but would see her for lunch, and that he loved her. Again.

She played the message all the way through three times before she finally dragged herself out of bed.

Chapter Five

EL VIENTO STEPPED OUT INTO THE BRIGHT FALL SUNSHINE
and stood there, staring. The mountainsides were covered
in their fall grandeur of red, gold, yellow, different shades
of green — a patchwork of autumn leaves at their peak.

How long had he stood there staring into space? He
didn't know. He looked around and could tell that no one
seemed to have picked up on it, but he did, after all, look
like he belonged. He had stolen some orderly scrubs from
the employee locker room on the first floor of the
Carrington House and had even picked up a name tag to
stick to the front of his shirt. He made sure that the flap of
his collar covered up most of it.

El Viento walked with purpose out into the open area
of sidewalks and trails and trees and benches behind the
facility, surrounded by a tall chain-length fence that was
intricately hidden by bushes and trees so that you didn't
know it was there … until you tried to get out.

The renowned assassin knew all the tricks. When you
were trying not to be noticed, you walked with purpose,

not as if you were in a hurry but not ambling either, walking as if you had somewhere you needed to be and something you needed to be doing. He'd gotten one of the other patients to point out the person he'd come to see, and gratefully she was sitting on a bench under a tree by herself, off away from the other patients.

"May I sit down?" he asked her, pointing to the empty space on the bench.

"No," the old lady said. "Go away. I don't want company."

He'd been expecting that, and it didn't deter him. He simply sat down anyway.

"You're Daisy Gillespie, aren't you?"

"Well, I guess that makes you better than me in every way because you know who I am, but I don't know who you are." Then she reached over before he could stop her and lifted his collar up off the name tag so that she could read it.

"Tom Arnold." she looked from the name tag to his face. He was wearing a face mask, so little was revealed. Ahh, face masks — the greatest gift to the criminal element in the society the world had ever known. And she was a bonkers old lady, not astute enough to catalog other features she could use to identify him. "You ain't Tom Arnold."

El Viento had not been expecting that, had not been expecting the woman to be sharp and quick. He had expected her to be vicious and vindictive and a willing accomplice in the mayhem he wanted to deliver to her family. But he had misjudged her mental acuity and hoped he didn't have to pay for it. All she'd have to do was start screaming, and he would have to find a way to climb over the fence and make his escape.

She didn't call out, though. She just looked at him, lifted one eyebrow.

"So you're pretending that you're Tom Arnold, got his shirt and pants on and his name tag, but you ain't Tom Arnold. So who the hell are you and what are you doing here? It ain't real often that somebody breaks *into* a mental hospital."

"My name doesn't matter, but what I came here for is to see you."

"Me? What for? I got a face so ugly it'd make a train take a dirt road. What do you want to see me for?"

"It's about Jillian Bishop and Rileigh Bishop," he said, dropping the names individually like stones into a pond. "Ring any bells?"

"Oh, yes, they ring bells. They're my nieces. What about 'em?"

"As I understand it, you arranged to have one of them sold off to a sex trafficking ring, and the other of them — you tried to cut off her head with a chainsaw. Is that true?"

She pulled back from him then and lifted the other eyebrow. "Everybody knows I went after Rileigh with a chainsaw. That's what I'm doing here," she said, looking around. "It was when I was off my meds," she said sarcastically. "But don't nobody but a handful of people know that it was me that got Jillie kidnapped away for almost 30 years. And you ain't in that handful of people. How the hell do you know?"

"I was hired by a man who's no longer with us. His name was Jedediah T. Mumford."

"Mum hired you? To do what?"

"To kill Rileigh." That was a bit of a conversation stopper, but she didn't show great shock or emotion of any kind.

45

"Well, apparently you botched the job, 'cause she's still breathing."

"That's why I'm here. I'm here to remedy that."

"That explains here in Yarmouth County. It don't explain here on this bench beside me. What do you want to talk to me about?"

"I'm here to fulfill the contract I got paid for. It's a matter of professional pride." The old woman made a sound in her throat of derision, but he went on. "And the here as in sitting on this bench talking to you is to make you an offer."

"What kind of offer?"

"An opportunity to join in the fun. I know how you feel about Rileigh and Jillian Bishop, and I thought you might like to participate in their demise." She lifted the lone eyebrow again. "I'm going to kill them both. Do you want to help?" She sat for a moment, absolutely motionless, no look of any kind on her face.

"I do."

"Can you get your sister to get you out of here so you can be at the wedding?"

"I can."

"Good."

"What do you need me for?"

"I need a distraction."

"Distraction?"

"They're going to figure out that I'm here pretty quick, and they're going to be looking for me among all the different strangers who are going to be at the wedding."

"And?"

"And as far as I can determine, they're pretty good detectives. I need you to keep them off balance. I need you to do whatever you can do to distract Rileigh, keep her mind occupied, make it hard for her to concentrate on looking for me. As I understand it, you are a very clever woman, and you'll know just what to do to take her eye off the ball."

"And what do I get out of it?"

"Well, you get out of this jail for a few days, and you get to watch Rileigh and Jillian Bishop die."

For the first time since El Viento had sat down, Daisy Gillespie smiled.

"I've got some props you can use," he added.

"Props?"

He leaned over then and whispered in her ear, not because he feared anyone would hear, but because he wanted it to be a "conspiratorial conversation."

"You got one of those?" she asked when he was finished, her eyes wide. He nodded his head.

"I do, indeed."

"How am I going to get it?"

"You need to tell me somewhere that I can leave it, someplace at your house or in your yard. Or…"

The old woman was quick, her mind sharp.

"The bird feeder. That's where you ought to put it."

"A bird feeder?"

"Yeah, there's one out in the front yard hanging from a limb of the sycamore tree. I never put no seed in it, but Lily did sometimes. It's a box you can get into the back of. You can it there."

"I'll do that." He paused. "I don't suppose I have to tell you that I'm going to be at the wedding pretending to be someone I'm not, so I need you to keep my secret."

He'd come to this meeting assuming that if he wore a mask, the old lady would not be able to recognize him later. Now, he wasn't so sure.

She smiled. "I'm good at secrets. I kept the secret about where Jillian was for 28 years. I figure I can pretend I don't know you for a day or two."

"So we have a deal."

"Indeed, we do." She smiled again, but it was a cold smile. One that never reached her pale, gray shark eyes.

Chapter Six

RILEIGH SHOULD HAVE PICKED UP ON THE FACT THAT something was amiss by several things Mama said that morning as she flitted around them like a butterfly serving them breakfast.

Something about the girls in Rileigh's graduating class getting together. It was an odd time for a class reunion.

And Mama mentioned the Breezy Creek Recreation Area. But Rileigh didn't catch specifically what she said about it. She was anticipating Georgia's arrival so they could talk about the wedding on Saturday that Rileigh had left to Georgia to plan. She was anxious to see what Georgia had put together for her and Jillian, Mitch, and David. More than anything else, Rileigh was anxious to see Mitch. He would come by as soon as he got home from Nashville and she could hardly wait to feel his strong arms around her.

When Georgia showed up, she had a big file folder full of papers. Her hair looked like she hadn't gotten around to combing it yet this morning, but Rileigh knew she probably had. It had just gone askew again in her frantic efforts to get her five children parked somewhere so she could talk to Rileigh and Jillian about the wedding. She blew in the front door like a whirlwind, grabbed Rileigh, and hugged her, literally picking her up off the ground and spinning her around.

"Five days. It's only *five days*. I'm so excited!"

It was impossible not to catch her enthusiasm.

"Oh, I've just got so many things to tell you. So many things!" Georgia picked up the file folder stuffed with papers, looked at Rileigh, burped out a little nervous giggle, and then just dumped the papers out on the table.

"This is what I've been doing since you've been gone," she said, "and I have been one busy little bee."

Rileigh felt a niggling itch of discomfort at that. Certainly it was a lot to orchestrate any wedding. There were so many things you had to organize and put together, but certainly not so much as to achieve "busy little bee" status.

"Okay let me, where should I start?" Georgia said. "Where should I start?

"Just tell us about it … where's the ceremony going to be?" Jillian asked.

"The Breezy Creek Recreation Area."

Rileigh and Jillian exchanged a look.

"That enormous facility would dwarf a tiny little wedding ceremony. Why on earth?"

"Mama helped me with all of it," Georgia said. "If it hadn't been for Mama, I wouldn't have been able to land Breezy Creek. But she knows people who pulled strings for her at the Great Smoky Mountains National Park."

"I don't understand why—" Jillian began.

"I don't understand what…" Rileigh stopped. "I tell you what, Georgia, we're gonna just sit here and you're gonna tell us *everything* that you've arranged for the wedding. We won't interrupt with questions. You just lay it on us."

Georgia smiled wide and her eyes crinkled. Mama brought out her cup of coffee and set it on the table, but Georgia was too focused on her "presentation" to notice.

"Well…"

And then she told them. She told them about the bridesmaids, how there would be ten of them, all in matching green satin and chiffon dresses. Mama's sewing circle, Bestowing Sewing, is making them from bolts of fabric Cynthia Waters got from a crafts store that closed .

"Last I heard they've finished nine of them — and the flower girl's dress."

"Flower girl," Rileigh said, not as a question, just repeating the words aloud to make them real.

"Chloe Morgan. I asked her mother, and she was thrilled. You did save the little girl's life when she was kidnapped, after all."

Rileigh couldn't breathe, couldn't talk, couldn't do anything but grunt out something that sounded like "Who?" But maybe it was only a monosyllabic grunt, which was all Rileigh felt able to produce at the time.

Georgia took it as a question.

"The bridesmaids? They're girls out of our graduating class."

Georgia ticked their names off on her fingers. "All in matching dresses. Sylvia was the challenge, of course, since she's pregnant. Mama's making it special … and the dresses for the maids of honor, me and Aaliyah Al-Masri." Jillian had asked her therapist to be her maid of honor. "Millie wouldn't let Mama make her own dress, so she's doing that one." Mama was doing double duty as matron of honor to both her daughters. Mildred Hanover was Mama's best friend.

"The groomsmen — the deputies will be in uniform and the others in black suits, white shirts and matching green satin ties — like the bridesmaid dresses. Bestowing Sewing is making the ties, too."

"But … but … flowers, and—"

"I've got that covered."

Then Georgia explained about the waxed leaves. And even in her present state of shock and disbelief, Rileigh did give her credit for that. It was a wonderful idea. Not just because it didn't cost anything, but because there would be nothing more beautiful than using the autumn leaves that decorated the mountainside to decorate the amphitheater.

Georgia described how their classmates were going to show up on the day of the wedding, each with a bushel basket full of leaves that they had waxed. Then they would join forces to make the bouquets and decorations for the tables at the reception.

"Reception?" Jillian croaked.

"Well, not a traditional reception. We're going to have a whoop-de-do."

"Whoop-de-do." Rileigh repeated the phrase, realized she sounded like a parrot.

"That way, we don't have to send out wedding invitations, which saves us a lot of time, energy, and money," Georgia said. Rileigh thought to point out that she hadn't been all that concerned about time, energy, and money with the plans she'd made for her own wedding because the plans didn't require a great expenditure of any of them. But she didn't have the air to say that right now, as the enormity — both figuratively and literally — of the whole thing began to settle in.

The whole county was coming to her wedding.

The breath was so totally knocked out of Rileigh at that point that it took her a little while to digest the rest of

Georgia's rambling description of the three-ring circus that Georgia had planned for Rileigh's and Jillian's wedding day.

"So you're wondering about the photographer and the videographer, the cake and, of course, the wedding planner."

"Wedding planner," was all Rileigh could say.

"Why sure, you need a wedding planner to get it all down right. You know, figure out who's supposed to sit beside who at the bachelor party, the bachelorette party, the rehearsal dinner."

"…parties…" Rileigh repeated.

"Rehearsal dinner." Jillian was the parrot this time.

"You know, Friday night, the rehearsal dinner. That's supposed to be the groom's family's responsibility. So I called Ellie Hicks, and she said she'd take care of everything. I'm sure she's got something wonderful planned."

Jillian's face blanched even paler than it already was.

"All the rest of it, I turned over to Forever Memories."

"And Forever Memories is…?" Rileigh was surprised she had managed a whole sentence.

"It's this new business that's just started. They called me and offered a special deal. See, they're trying to work their way into the Gatlinburg/Black Bear Forge market. A big wedding like yours is a wonderful opportunity for them to show off what they can do. And because it's free advertising for them, they're giving us all kinds of services. It's a package deal for two hundred fifty dollars. Hell, a photographer alone costs five thousand."

"And you said yes?"

"Well, duh. Of course, I said yes."

Two hundred fifty dollars was roughly half of the budget that Jillian and Rileigh had given Georgia to work with to make plans for the wedding.

"Look right here." Georgia pulled one of the pieces of paper out of the pile she'd dumped on the table. "That right there, that's the bottom line. That's all I spent. See, I came in sixty bucks under budget." Georgia smiled, sat back beaming, waiting for Rileigh's response, obviously expecting Rileigh to jump up and grasp her in a bear hug of appreciation.

That's not what Rileigh did. What she did was look at her best friend and say coldly, "Cancel it."

"Excuse me, cancel it?" Georgia looked genuinely confused.

"I told you I wanted a small ceremony, a little intimate family gathering. You made this whole thing into a Macy's Thanksgiving Day Parade." Rileigh jumped to her feet. "No, absolutely no. Cancel all of this."

Georgia had gone pale. "Rileigh, today is Tuesday. It's too late to cancel a Wednesday bachelor's dinner, a Thursday bachelorette's dinner, a Friday rehearsal dinner, and a Saturday wedding. I can't cancel all that now."

"Oh yes, you can. And you will."

Rileigh was so angry at Georgia that she knew if she kept talking, she would say something she would regret for the rest of her life. She ground her teeth together to keep the words behind her lips and merely growled,

"I should have left you duct-taped to the damn chair."

She threw the budget piece of paper down onto the table, turned around, and marched into the house, slamming the squawking screen door and then the front door behind her. Georgia, Mama, and Jillian sat in stunned silence.

"I don't understand," Georgia stammered. "This is the most gorgeous, perfect wedding, every fantasy I ever had."

"See, that's the problem," Jillian said quietly. "It's your fantasy. It's not Rileigh's fantasy, and it's not mine. We didn't want a huge affair with bridesmaids and groomsmen and wedding cakes and … we wanted something small and private. That's what Rileigh told you to organize."

Color began to return to Georgia's cheeks. "What she told me was to take five hundred dollars and see how far I could stretch it to cover the expenses of a…" She paused, omitted the words small and intimate, and simply finished with "wedding. And I did just that. In fact, I came in sixty dollars under budget. I'd think a little gratitude might be in order right now, but I'm not seeing a lot of love."

Georgia rose to her feet, snatched up the papers on the table, stormed down the porch steps out to her car, and roared away. Mama and Jillian sat silently on the porch.

"I suppose I should have reined her in," Mama said in a small voice.

"Ya think?" Jillian replied caustically, then relented immediately. "Yeah, you should have reined her in."

"But it all sounded so lovely, and she was making it all happen without it costing any money, and she was so excited about it, and she really believed…" Mama paused then, looked at the front door that Rileigh had slammed behind her, and looked back at Jillian. "She honestly thought that Rileigh was going to think this was the most wonderful thing Georgia had ever done for her. She saw this as the absolutely perfect wedding gift." Mama sat back in the rocker. "Well, wrong-o, Moosebreath."

"What?"

"Rocky the Flying Squirrel and…" Mama began and then let it go. "Never mind."

RILEIGH WAS LYING on her bed, looking up at the ceiling,

her hands knotted into fists at her sides. When Jillian came into the room, she sat up instantly.

"Can you believe that? Can you believe what she did? How are we going to cancel it all?"

Jillian came to the bed and sat down on it. She reached out and took Rileigh's hand in hers and patted it.

"We're not."

"What do you mean we're not? We're—"

"We can't."

"Of course we can. We can just tell everybody—"

"Everybody in the whole county?"

That stopped Rileigh.

"And if I know Georgia, she has stirred up enthusiasm all over Yarmouth County, has made this mountain whoop-de-do something everybody is looking forward to. There's no way to cancel it all now."

Jillian let go of Rileigh's hand.

"Remember *Raiders of the Lost Ark*?"

Rileigh nodded dumbly.

"You remember when he was running away from that big rock rolling down the tunnel behind him?" Rileigh nodded again. "Well, that's you and me. And that big rock isn't something we can turn around, hold out our hands to stop. It will mow us down if we try."

"But I don't want—"

"Neither do I," Jillian said. "It's the last thing I want." She let out a breath. "But it's what we've got."

She paused before starting over quietly.

"All those people in the mountains who'd lost every-thing ... they made me realize how everything you own can be snatched away in an instant. Those people didn't have anything left ... except their memories. And the rela-tionships in a community just like Black Bear Forge — folks as close knit as steel wool, where everybody lives in everybody else's pocket. A place full of people who will show up at all the important events — both good and bad — in your life, and look for your face at the important events in theirs. Like it or not, our wedding has become a community event here, and after the devastated lives I saw in east Tennessee, it feels very important to me to honor that."

Rileigh remained silent.

"Look. On Saturday, I'm marrying David Hicks. Finally. You're marrying Mitch. That's what matters. Not the how and the where and all the trimmings. I figure we can either throw up our hands and say fine, and join in the revelry, or we can be angry and pout, try to cancel it, hurt everybody's feelings — including Mama's, who, as I'm sure you noticed, thought Georgia's ideas were glorious — and wind up getting married in a wedding remembered as a disappointment to half the population of Yarmouth County."

"I could strangle Georgia."

"She thought she was doing something wonderful for you."

"Wonderful? I told her—"

Jillian held up her hand. "You know what you *said*, but you don't know what she *heard*."

Rileigh stopped. "I'm guessing Georgia didn't have a big wedding."

"No, and she always wanted one. She used to tell me how she dreamed of…"

"That's it, isn't it?"

Jillian nodded her head. "Georgia is giving to you, to us, the wonderful fairy-tale wedding that she didn't have. And she's doing it out of love."

Rileigh sat holding her sister's hand, her head spinning, knowing that Jillian was right, trying to shed her anger and disbelief and disappointment, too. She'd been looking forward to the quiet little ceremony she had envisioned instead of the three-ring circus/mountain whoop-de-do that Georgia had orchestrated for Saturday.

"I think we have to go all in," Jillian said. "We can't mope and whine and make everybody around us miserable. We have to accept and enjoy what we're getting instead of what we wanted."

Rileigh said nothing.

"You know I'm right."

"Hell yes, I know you're right. That doesn't mean I like it."

Rileigh let out a sigh, then it occurred to her — Mitch knew what was going on. Maybe David didn't — he'd been out of town the whole time — but Mitch had to know what Georgia was planning if she was asking his deputies to be groomsmen.

"Mitch knew. Why didn't he tell me?"

"How many times did you talk to Mitch while we were gone?"

"Oh, just a couple of times — conserving the cell charge," Rileigh admitted. "And every time I talked to him, I cried."

"What did he say?"

"He didn't say much of anything. I did all the talking — and crying. I told him about the damage, the people's lives destroyed, how devastated…"

"And I suspect Mitch decided that was not the time to tell you that your plans for our wedding had gone totally off the rails."

Jillian was right, of course. Mitch had known what was going on, but Rileigh was sure that by the time he'd found out, it was too late to stop Georgia. So he'd spared Rileigh, hadn't piled on any more emotional load.

"I need to talk to Mitch. He won't be home until this afternoon, but maybe I can catch him while he's driving."

"David's supposed to call me from the airport. I'll wait until then to share the 'good news' with him."

As Rileigh rose, Jillian reached for her hand again. "First, you need to call Georgia."

"And say what?"

"Tell her thank you for all her hard work and for giving you a fairy-tale wedding."

Rileigh ground her teeth. Damn, she hated when Jillian was right.

Chapter Seven

Rileigh looked at the huge pile of accumulated mail and sighed. She was going to have to go through it piece by piece. While she'd been gone, Mama had made no effort to throw out any of it. So there were circulars for grocery stores, coupons, and junk mail of every other sort mixed in with credit card bills and the electric bill and mail Mama really needed. And it was a way bigger pile than there would ordinarily be, because mixed in were congratulatory cards to Rileigh and Jillian, wedding cards, and a small stack of wedding gifts. Mama had simply dumped it all in a big bushel basket, which was now overflowing, sitting on the floor beside the couch in the living room.

Rileigh went into the kitchen and got the garbage can and took it outside and set it beside the porch swing on the front porch. She hauled the bushel basket of mail out to the front porch, turned it upside down, and poured the contents on the porch floor. She had to go back into the house with the bushel basket and pick up all the overflow of mail that had accumulated around it after it was full.

Then she sat down on the porch swing and looked at the pile and started to go through it.

Circulars, ads, grocery store sales. Wouldn't you love to have a credit card interest-free for the first six months — and then in print so small a gnat walking across it with muddy feet would have obliterated it. Oh, by the way, the interest rate is 24% after the free period.

She found wedding gifts that she set aside so she and Mitch could open them together.

Mitch.

Rileigh felt that butterfly feeling in the pit of her stomach just thinking his name. He would be here soon. She'd called and left him a message that she was sure he got as soon as he started to drive home. But all she had said was that she couldn't wait to see him this afternoon. She didn't bother to tell him about the wedding catastrophe. She didn't want to do that on the phone anyway.

She looked at her watch and smiled. He'd be here soon.

Mixed in with all the mail was a stack of cards of congratulations. The word had gone out through town, of course, on Mama's phone tree. So there probably wasn't a man, woman, or child above the age of five in all of Yarmouth County or the surrounding counties who didn't know there was going to be a double wedding and a mountain whoop-de-do on Saturday. Rileigh let out a sigh. A double wedding and a gigantic community-wide whoop-de-do at the Breezy Creek Amphitheater in the Great Smoky Mountains National Park. She sighed again. It was what it was.

"Get over yourself," she told herself aloud. Shook her head and smiled. "You and Mitch were getting married. Married ... as in *married*. So how about you tell your face that that's what's about to happen because clearly it didn't get the memo. Your face looks like your best friend left you and your dog died."

She picked up a big grocery store circular out of the pile and beneath it was a small box. It was wrapped in brown paper, mailing paper, and she turned it over in her hand and saw that there was no return address. It was simply addressed to Rileigh Bishop, 629 Bent Twigg Road, Black Bear Forge, Tennessee.

Rileigh felt a cold stone settle into the bottom of her belly. She didn't move, just sat staring at the box in her hand. She felt as if the day outside had grown dim. As if there had been a sudden and unannounced full solar eclipse and the sun were fading out behind the moon. It felt not only dark but cold on this beautiful warm October afternoon. She was proud that her fingers weren't shaking when she put her fingernail under the edge of the tape on the box and ripped off the paper. It was a plain box, probably three inches deep, four inches wide, and a foot long. She opened the box and inside was a doll.

A doll in a white dress.

A *broken* doll in a white dress.

A broken doll in a white dress *with a bullet hole in the chest.*

Her eyes flitted from one characteristic of the thing in her hand to another. The doll looked like it had been run over by a truck. But on closer examination, it was clear that someone had systematically broken the doll's arms and legs and neck and body. The white dress it was wearing was wrinkled and soiled and splattered with some red substance that she would like to think was maybe tomato juice, ketchup, perhaps wine, but she knew better. She knew that the red splotches had turned sort of a rusty brown in on the fabric of the dress was blood.

The doll had no face. It had been scraped away, and in

its place, someone had crudely drawn a frowny face that she recognized.

And in magic marker on the very front of the dirty doll's white wedding dress — just below what could only have been a bullet hole — was a number one.

As if all that weren't horrifying enough, the monster who had been torturing her all these months left a final signature cruelty. The doll's hair had been cut off. In its place was human hair just stuck down to the head with a piece of scotch tape. It was a single lock of hair chestnut brown with gold streaks.

A lock of Rileigh's hair.

Somehow Rileigh managed not to scream, not to make any sound at all. She sat holding the box, watching it wiggle in her hands because her fingers had started to tremble so violently that she finally had to set the box down on the table. She fumbled in her pocket for her phone, punched favorites, and called Mitch.

"Hi" was all she said when he answered the phone, and he instantly recognized the alarm in her voice.

"What's wrong?"

"You need to see…" And then her words trailed off because she couldn't summon an explanation.

"I'm only about ten minutes away," he said.

"Then just come as fast as you can. You can see what's wrong when you get here."

It seemed that at least an hour passed between her frantic phone call and the sight of Mitch's cruiser bumping up over the lump at the top of Mama's driveway and pulling to a halt in front of the fence.

Mitch leapt out of the cruiser, ran through the gate and up the sidewalk, and folded Rileigh into his arms. She clung to him, trembling, listening to him whisper words that weren't words into her ear, soothing words, kind words, loving words.

When she could finally manage to let go of him, she pulled back and said, "I've missed you."

"I've missed you too, sweetheart," he said. "Tell me what's wrong."

She pointed to the box that was sitting on the table with the rest of the as yet unopened mail. The doll was laying on the seat of the porch swing.

"Oh no," Mitch said, and she could hear something like despair in his voice. "Not again."

He reached out and picked up the broken doll and turned it over in his hands, looking at the spotted dress, the broken limbs, the number, the bullet hole and the lock of Rileigh's hair stuck on top of the doll's head.

"He knows I'm getting married," she said. "That's not just a random white dress, that's a *wedding* dress. That's my hair. How did he get it?"

She realized that her voice was quaking, so she clamped her jaws shut and said nothing more. Mitch had let go of her and was pacing back and forth on the porch, holding the doll in his hands.

Rileigh had seen Mitch in the throes of just about every possible emotion working cases with him in the past year. Shoot, they'd almost been burned at the stake once. But she didn't believe she'd ever seen him as angry as he was right now. She watched the jaw muscles in his face tense as he ground his teeth, keeping himself from spewing out the obscenities she was sure were rolling around in the back of his head. Then he turned to her and sat down abruptly on the swing, took her hands in his and pulled her down beside him

"So here's what we're going to do. I'm thinking we need to blow this popsicle stand."

Rileigh looked at him as if she didn't understand … because she didn't understand.

"We get out of here. You and me. We elope. To hell with this wedding. I don't know if you know yet, but Georgia—"

"I know what Georgia did."

"Then you know it isn't the quiet intimate little service that you wanted. So let's just skip it all together."

"So we run off because this guy knows we're getting married."

"Because he knows *you're* getting married," Mitch began. Then he gestured at the doll he had tossed onto the table beside the empty box when he sat down. "And he's been close enough to…"

Mitch stopped then, probably realizing that he'd stepped in it. He probably shouldn't have mentioned what was obvious to Rileigh, but she hadn't mentioned to him. And that was the fact that whoever this monster was, he had somehow, at some time, been right beside Rileigh. So close she could have reached out and touched him. Close enough to clip off a lock of her hair.

"I can't imagine how he got that close and I didn't see him. How?" Her words trailed off.

"It doesn't matter," he said. "He's been that close, so he knows not just that you're getting married but when and where and to whom."

"And the number one," Rileigh began. "In a count-down, after the last number, something happens. So what's the something?"

"You and I both know what it is. He's planning on being here. Remember 'bang, you are dead' *this time*. He intends to shoot you on your wedding day. So that's why we're not going to be here. We're not going to be sitting ducks for this guy."

65

"We're not going to run off and then be looking over our shoulders for the rest of our lives wondering who he is and where he is, when he's going to strike."

She heard the edge of incipient hysteria in her voice and dialed it back.

"Look, for the very first time since the first one of these boxes arrived," she said, "we know something about him."

"And that is?"

"And that is where he's going to be this Saturday. He's going to be here. Right here."

Mitch said nothing.

"Don't you see?" Rileigh said. "This is our chance. This is the only chance we have. The only chance to catch him and stop him is to catch him on Saturday when he shows up here."

"To kill you," Mitch whispered.

"Well, we just won't let him do that part," Rileigh said, trying to sound more forceful and confident than she felt. Mitch rolled his eyes.

"I should have called you and told you what Georgia was planning," Mitch said in something of a non sequitur. "You could have called her and clamped down on her enthusiasm and she wouldn't have turned this wedding into a public event."

Then Rileigh understood what he was getting at. It was obvious. If they'd had a private wedding in a small venue with only close friends and family present, they could have locked it down so nobody could get anywhere near them.

But that's not the wedding that was planned for this Saturday. It was going to be in a damned amphitheater, for crying out loud, with hundreds and hundreds of people, and not just neighbors and friends either. There would be people they didn't know. Photographers and videographers and wedding planners, a herd of strangers. It was an absolutely perfect place for the killer to hide among all those people they didn't know until he was ready to strike.

"So fine, we know he's going to be here somewhere on Saturday. How do we catch him?" Mitch said plaintively.

Rileigh sat back and thought for a moment. "We don't," she said. "Not just you and me anyway. But if we're talking 'we' as in the communal 'we,' we can find him."

"I'm sorry, you lost me."

"We, meaning *all of us*, all the people we know and care about. We have to tell them what's going on. It won't be just you and me looking for somebody behaving strangely. It will be 20 people, 50 people, 75, who knows how many, looking at every person they don't know, watching their actions, keeping their eyes on them." Rileigh paused before continuing. "That's a pretty good-sized posse."

Mitch said nothing. Just stared off into the distance.

"So if you see something, say something," she said, parroting the Homeland Security slogan about terrorists. And this guy certainly qualified as a terrorist. He'd been terrorizing Rileigh for months, and it had to stop. She had to catch the son of a bitch and lock him up. Or kill him.

Mitch looked at her and sighed. "Okay, we have everyone we know on the lookout. Whoever this guy is, he won't be expecting that every third person is watching out for him to make a move."

Rileigh could hear the false conviction in Mitch's voice. He was trying to sound positive about the simple admonition to their friends. That it would be enough to stop a cold-blooded killer, a stalker who wanted to kill Rileigh.

"Oh, that won't be our only defense. We will come up with a surprise or two he's not expecting." She had no idea what those surprises might be, but they'd think of something.

"If you see something, say something," Mitch said. "I'll

start tomorrow at the bachelor party." Mitch struggled to smile but couldn't pull it off. "Can you believe it? A bachelor party."

"Poor you."

"Poor both of us. You have a bachelorette party on Thursday night."

"It's a damn three-ring circus," Rileigh said, shaking her head. Mitch reached out and took her hand.

"And smack dab in the middle of it, we're going to get married."

Chapter Eight

RILEIGH WAS GLAD SHE AND JILLIAN HAD HAD THE foresight to select their wedding dresses before the hurricane struck, though you really couldn't call it foresight given that they didn't know the disaster was coming. You only got credit for foresight if you knew something was about to happen and you prepared very well for it. So, not foresight — just plain dumb luck. Rileigh would take that.

Both she and Jillian had already selected, purchased, and brought home their wedding dresses, their veils, and their matching shoes. Jillian's dress was a pale blue satin gown, Rileigh's was a deep green satin gown. They weren't matching, had been purchased separately, though both of the women had similar tastes, so the dresses were somewhat alike. Neither one of the dresses was floor length, neither one of them wanted a gown, but Rileigh's had a full billowing skirt of satin with a layer of light green tulle on top of the satin, and simple poof sleeves of lace. Her veil fit around a crown of daisies with green leaves and hung just below her shoulders. Jillian's dress was longer, came to mid-calf, but it wasn't as full as Rileigh's, more form-fitted. The bodice of the dress was pale blue satin covered in lace, and it was sleeveless. Jillian's veil was similar to Rileigh's. It fit around a crown of flowers too, but hers were bluebells instead of daisies, and her veil came all the way down to her waist.

Rileigh still couldn't get her head around the brides-maids. *Ten* — a whole herd of them. She wondered absently if there was a correct collective noun for brides-maids — flock? Covey? Swarm? Troupe? School? Herd would do. The fact that there would be a herd of brides-maids marching in before she and Jillian came down the aisle made Rileigh uncomfortable. It seemed to her that the two brides in the weddings were a bit of an afterthought after ten bridesmaids, an also-ran in the race, but she didn't say any of that, of course, to Georgia. They had made a truce on the phone when Rileigh had called to apologize, an apology she did not really feel, and to thank Georgia for making a beautiful fairy-tale wedding. Rileigh had claimed that Georgia had given her the wedding she had secretly wanted, and Georgia was so relieved that Rileigh was no longer angry at her and was on board with what was about to happen that she was willing to pretend she believed Rileigh's claim.

On Wednesday morning, Rileigh and Jillian hauled out their wedding dresses and the accompanying matching shoes and veils and they tried them on to see how they looked together. Jillian was a couple of inches taller than Rileigh, tall and stately with long arms and legs. That's how Rileigh had always thought of her big sister. And the two of them standing side by side in their wedding dresses were a beautiful combination of different looks that somehow managed to complement each other, each making the whole impression bigger than the sum of the parts. Two beautiful women, one with pale blonde hair hanging long around her shoulders and one with short chestnut-colored hair and bright hazel eyes that Mitch had determined were jade green. Sometimes, when Rileigh looked in the mirror, that's what she saw too. She hadn't told him that her wedding dress would be green. That would be a surprise.

Rileigh spun slowly around in a circle and when she did the full skirt of the dress swished out around her.

"You look absolutely gorgeous," Jillian said, studying her.

"It fit when I bought it. Before I lost—" She stopped. "I didn't get on the scales. I didn't really want to know how much weight I lost while we were in Tennessee, but I can certainly tell it in this dress."

"It's not loose. It looks great."

"But neither is it form-fitting anymore," Rileigh observed, which was kind of the point.

Jillian stood beside Rileigh, not spinning to make the skirt of her dress poof out because there wasn't that much fabric. It flew through Rileigh's mind that Jillian could have been a model. Shoot, Jillian could have been a movie star. She could have been in anything if—

And that's where Rileigh slammed the door in the face of those thoughts and moved resolutely on, but she did love looking at her beautiful sister in her beautiful wedding dress.

Mama came into the room, hauling a huge box.

"Here, let me help you with that, Mama," Rileigh said, and tried to take the weight out of her mother's arms.

Mama turned away from her. "I got this. I got it. Leave me alone." She walked to Jillian's bed and plopped the box down on top of it.

"What's in there, Mama?" Jillian said.

Mama smiled, an enigmatic smile, and said nothing.

Just looked at her two beautiful daughters. "Them's beautiful wedding dresses."

"What's in the box, Mama?" Jillian pressed her. Mama turned to the box and lifted the lid off of it and pulled out a white wedding gown.

"Oh, Mama, that's gorgeous," Jillian said.

"Your daddy thought so, too," she said, smiling. Rileigh tried not to wince at the mention of her slime-bag father.

"That's your wedding dress, Mama?" Jillian said. "Why have I never seen it before?"

"Because I never showed it to you before. That's why," Mama snapped. "You think if I'd shown you girls this wedding dress when you was growing up, you could have resisted pleading with me to play dress-up in it and asking me if you could try it on? Please! Could you play with it? I kept it hid up in the attic for that very reason."

"So why did you pull it out today?"

Mama stopped and looked from one to the other. "Because I was thinking, well, maybe hoping that one of the two of you would want, you know, would want to wear my wedding dress."

Jillian and Rileigh exchanged a look.

"Well, you might have mentioned it before we both went out and got our own," Rileigh said.

"It's better that you already got your own dresses. Then you got a choice. You ain't got to wear my dress because it's all there is. Now you can choose."

"And it won't hurt your feelings if we don't choose yours?" Rileigh asked.

"Of course it won't."

Translate that: "of course it will."

Jillian reached down and picked up the beautiful dress out of the box. It was no mere dress. It was a wedding *gown*. Floor length, pure white satin and lace. It had little

72

pearl beads all over the bodice beneath the lace. No plunging neckline here, a roller was fitted up around the neck like a priest's collar. It was solid lace. The arms of the dress were lace too. Rileigh saw that there was still fabric lying in the box as Jillian was admiring the dress, and she picked it up and shook it out.

"Oh my, look at this train," Rileigh said.

The train attached to the dress at the shoulders and at the waist and then stretched out ten feet beyond it, satin covered in lace. The veil hung down from a crown of white pearls all the way to the floor in the back and to the waist in the front.

"This is a staggeringly beautiful wedding gown, Mama," Rileigh said admiringly. "How on earth did you afford a dress this spectacular? It must have cost hundreds, thousands…"

"Don't know what it cost, 'cause Papa didn't pay for it."

"Where did he get it?"

"I ain't got no idea. But…" She looked away, "I'm pretty sure he didn't come by it legal. When my sisters got married, they all wore the same dress, handed down one to the other. I was the last one, the baby … I'll admit I was Papa's favorite, and one day he come wagging this dress home, wouldn't say where it come from. It was too big for me — Mama had to take it up to fit."

"It's like what a princess would wear to marry a king," Rileigh said. "But it's just *too much* for me."

"And as for me … it would probably look a little silly if one of us were dressed in that and the other in these." Jillian gestured down to the beautiful but simple wedding dress she was wearing.

"So don't neither one of you want to wear it," Mama said, trying to keep the hurt out of her voice.

"Mama, you can't spring it on us at the last minute."

She held up her hand. "I know, I know, I should have shown it to you sooner, but it never occurred to me that you were going to be gone for two weeks right before the wedding, and time just got away from me."

"Yeah, time got away from all of us," Jillian said.

Rileigh went to Mama and put her arms around her and drew her into a deep strong hug. "It's a beautiful dress, Mama. I'd love to get married in it." Rileigh was opening her mouth to say that if Mama wanted her to, she'd switch. Prudent and thrifty person that she was, she had kept the receipt on the wedding dress she had purchased. She could take it back if she had to, but she'd fallen in love with it as it hung on the mannequin in the store, and it had looked just like she'd hoped it would look when she put it on. But she'd be willing to swap if it mattered to Mama.

"Look, Mama, I'd—"

Mama held up her hand. "Now I know what you're about to do. You're about to tell me that you'll wear my dress if I want you to and then you're going to make me be the one to decide. So I'm deciding. *Both* you girls are going to wear the wedding dresses you picked out for yourselves." She glanced down at the ivory gown. Rileigh couldn't decide if it had been white to begin with and had yellowed slightly with age, but if it had, the yellowing had only made it more glamorous. "Maybe someday one of you girls will have a daughter, and…"

She stopped abruptly. "A daughter." Her brow crinkled.

Rileigh leapt to the rescue.

"Mama," she said, "let me hold this dress up against you so I can imagine how you looked in it."

There was no wedding picture of Rileigh's parents. They'd been too poor to pay for a photographer. Rileigh looked at Jillian, who took the hand-off. "Yeah, Mama, let's hold it up and see in the mirror what you looked like."

Both of Rileigh and Jillian were hurrying to distract Mama from the memories they were afraid she was about to recover. Memories of Jillian's daughter Michaela, who had come to find her mother — except it wasn't Michaela at all. Mama had been so thrilled to finally have a grandchild that she'd been devastated when she discovered that not only was the girl who'd shown up saying she was Michaela a fraud, but that there had been a real Michaela and she had been murdered. She had grieved the loss for several days and then woke up one morning her usual cheerful self, and her two daughters breathed a sigh of relief that Mama's dementia had erased the memory and the pain. They certainly didn't want to revive it now with talks about a grandchild someday wearing the wedding dress.

Mama looked from Jillian to Rileigh, then back to Jillian. "You girls know how happy I am. My heart just almost bursts out of my chest at the thought of what's 'bout to happen. You girls is gonna have the most beautifulest wedding anybody in Yarmouth County's ever seen. Why, I bet this is a wedding won't nobody who's there will ever forget."

Rileigh felt a cold chill at the words. Mama was probably right.

Chapter Nine

"EXACTLY WHO IS IT THAT YOU THINK YOU'RE FOOLING?" said the voice of Cole Chandler's brother.

Cole looked around the small coffee shop in Carlisle, in Weatherford County, to see if anyone had heard. Taking the phone off speaker, he picked it up, put it to his ear, and caught the end of his Jake's response. "...not me or anybody else in the family or anybody who knows you."

"I'm not trying to fool anybody."

"Except yourself."

"How do you figure that?"

"Oh, come on, Cole. You're in love with Natalie. A blind cave fish could see that you are. You want to marry her. I know it. Mama knows it. Dad knows it. Every friend you have knows it. So who is all the 'I'm going to take time to think about it' crap for?"

Cole grinned a little and pushed back.

"When have you ever known me to make a major decision without—"

Before he could finish, his brother interrupted. "Without thinking about it ad nauseam, without *overthinking* it ad nauseam. When you decided to become a park ranger, you took — what? A month in the woods to be alone to consider it?"

"It was a *week*. And you don't think this is as important as deciding to become a park ranger?"

Ben let out an audible, theatrically whiny sigh.

"Okay, bro, I get it. You're using this as an excuse to spend a week in the woods camping before you ask Natalie to marry you."

"To decide if I *should* ask her."

"So if you haven't decided already, what were you doing looking at rings?"

Cole froze. How in the world could Ben know that he'd already looked at rings?

He stammered and stumbled. "I, well, I, what do—?"

Ben burst out laughing, roaring. "Gotcha," he said. His younger brother hadn't seen him looking at rings, just made a calculated guess and hit it on the nose.

"You just don't want me to be gone for a week because you'll have to get up *every morning* at four while I'm gone."

Cole's father owned a dairy farm. Cole helped out milking the cows three days a week.

Ben shifted gears. "So when are you going?"

"Today. Nobody will see or hear from me for a week."

"Have fun."

Ben clicked off. Cole stood, stuffed his phone in his pocket, and headed out of the coffee shop to what he liked to think of as his "cruiser" outside — his official Great Smoky Mountains National Park patrol car.

As he was walking to it, a large woman in a floral dress that looked like it was made out of upholstery fabric stopped him on the street.

"Are you one of those park rangers?"

His gray uniform, green jacket, and park ranger badge had given him away.

"Yes ma'am," he said, tipping his hat.

"Well, I just want to know — actually Gertie and I want to know." She turned and called to an equally large woman in an equally ugly flowered dress. Cole had the image of a couch and matching love seat, but he pushed it out of his head. "We want to know if there really are bears in those woods."

"Yes ma'am, there are. Black bears. If you see one, you need to give it a wide berth."

"Do they hunt humans?" asked the other woman.

Cole managed not to roll his eyes. "No ma'am, they don't hunt humans."

"Well, that's not what I heard. I heard that just the other day a bear went into a campsite and stole a little baby girl, took off into the woods with her, and ate her right there in front of her mother."

"I'm not sure where you heard that, ma'am, but it's not true."

It took Cole ten minutes to finally extricate himself from the tourists, who were also convinced that raccoons broke into locked cars at night and chewed on cell phone charger cords.

Already packed to go wilderness camping, he just had to change out of his uniform. Then he could spend a week in the woods thinking about Natalie and making the decision.

He stopped. A grin slowly took over his face, and he shook his head. Ben was right. He already knew what he was going to do. This camping trip was perhaps a last hurrah before he settled down. There'd never been any doubt in his mind that he loved Natalie. The fact that she had rheumatoid arthritis complicated things, though. It was a progressive disease that would disable her in ways that couldn't be predicted, and when she found out she had it, she stopped dating, told Cole that she'd made up her mind not to get married, since she didn't want anyone else to suffer through what she was facing. Putting off proposing wasn't really about deciding whether or not he wanted to marry her. It was about the resistance she'd put up that he would have to fight through when he did. He was dreading that part.

It was late evening, and the shadow of Blinker Mountain was stretching out to claim the hollow when he pulled into his small frame house nestled beside Cricket Song Creek and got out. Cole Chandler was a big man, tall, six-six, broad shoulders. And he wasn't possessed of what others called a "big man's grace," like with athletes who moved with such fluid movements that their size didn't matter. He was always bumping into something, clocking his head on something, knocking something over, breaking something fragile. And he spent his teenage years cringing inside himself while a rabid case of adolescent acne chewed up his face. He'd been shy before, but during that time, he had been unable to produce anything more than monosyllabic grunts as his contribution to a conversation. He'd kept to himself, went camping alone, enjoyed the solitude and the beauty of the mountains that stretched all across east Tennessee and into North Carolina. But it was during that time that he first noticed Natalie. And what he noticed about her was that she didn't seem to notice that his face looked like ground meat. She was a beautiful, popular girl, and it was before the RA diagnosis when she had still believed, like every other girl, that the life out in front of them was fairy tale-bright. Even then, she was always kind and sweet to Cole. In fact, she told him later that she'd begun falling for him then — not later, when his skin cleared up, not after laser treatments removed the scarring. And not after she discovered that she had a debilitating illness and wasn't destined for the fairy-tale life. It was before all that, she said, that she'd fallen in love with Cole.

Cole went inside and gathered up his gear, loaded it into the back seat of his old Ford Taurus, went back into the house to get the final bag, and was putting it into the trunk when he sensed something off, some kind of change in the world around him. It was a sense he'd picked up from prey animals in the woods who survived by knowing when a predator was near. He started to turn toward the presence when he felt a garrote slip around his neck.

The thin nylon rope was pulled tight so quickly that he couldn't even call out, couldn't do anything but struggle ineffectively. He tried to use his elbows to bash the person behind him who was pulling the rope tight, but he had no leverage, no way to strike a blow that mattered. He clawed at his neck where the rope was buried deep in his skin, but it was useless. He gasped in a lone breath, but after that, his throat was sealed. He couldn't breathe at all. He felt dizziness swirling around him. His head was leaned back and he was facing the mountains at dusk, looking at little wisps of mist above the trees, the tattered mist that made work in the fire towers so difficult because the mist looked like smoke. He felt his knees going weak, and as he watched the world graying, he tried to think of Natalie's face, tried to pull it up into his mind, but there was not enough light in his mind anymore. All he could see was a ghostly image, and then darkness.

ANTONIO ROSSI, who was called Tony by his family and friends back when he'd had a family and friends, held tight to the two wooden handles he had wrapped the nylon rope around, continued to put pressure on the man's neck as he folded up and dropped to the ground. Rossi dropped with him, put his knee into the man's back, and continued to pull tight. He maintained that position long after the man was dead. He always did. Garroting someone was just about the only thing left in Rossi's life that made him feel alive, that gave him strength and power. It was a pleasure way more immersive than sex — the euphoria he felt bubbling in his chest as his victims squirmed and struggled and then went limp. He was always reluctant to loosen the rope, always reluctant for the experience to be over.

Rossi, known on the dark web by the screen name "Born2BEvil," had become an assassin because that was the only way that he could continue to get high on killing people. He'd been in the military. After that, he'd become a mercenary. But even then, when he was sent to do a job, it was not necessarily to kill somebody, and that's what he wanted. That's what he *needed*. He needed to be able to choke the life out of victims, to feel a spark of life in his own chest, if only momentarily. He lived for that.

And right now the euphoria was heightened by the thought of collecting the multi-million-dollar bank account that El Viento had offered in his "catch me if you can" game.

Rossi had gone to the little town, had cased the place, had gone out to the site where this wedding was to be held, and had settled on taking the role of a park ranger as his disguise. That wasn't as simple a task as it might seem, because Antonio was a big man, over six-five, and finding a park ranger whose uniform he could use had taken a little doing. He'd followed a couple of candidates from the

visitor center at Clingman's Dome, and when this big boy
had shown up there this morning, Antonio had actually
smiled, and that was not an occurrence that happened
often. He had followed the young man home and killed
him, was grateful that his particular method of murder was
clean and neat and tidy, not a speck of blood on the gray
uniform with a stupid green jacket and badge and the even
dumber hat. He'd stick the body in the car trunk, put the
car in the garage where the body wouldn't be found for a
few days, and by then he would have unmasked the elusive
El Viento, would have found the magical number on his
dead body, and would be sunning on some beach in
Monaco.

Chapter Ten

GEORGIA HAD SECURED THE USE OF THE AMERICAN LEGION Hall for Mitch and David's bachelor party. It was a big open facility that had tables and chairs and a bar. All the alcohol and food had been bankrolled by Mitch's best man, Dr. Gus Hazelton, the county coroner and lottery winner who had worked with Mitch and Rileigh on several cases in the past year. The American Legion Hall had big grills set up outside and a no-kidding, for-real jukebox, though you didn't have to put real money in it. There was a jar full of tokens on the top of the machine.

The food Gus had ordered catered to the affair came from a Gatlinburg deli: potato salad, macaroni salad, pasta salad, Cobb salad, Waldorf salad, along with yummy desserts — pecan pie, chocolate cake, key lime pie, cheesecake with fruit toppings, blackberry and blueberry cobbler, crème brûlée, and pumpkin rolls. But the big-ticket item was steak. Gus had ordered ribeyes, sirloins, t-bones, prime rib, any kind of meat you could imagine, and had hired cooks to man the grills and keep the red meat flowing, cooking each steak to order.

Mitch had been told to show up at seven o'clock, but obviously a large number of people had shown up at 6:30 because the tables had all been unfolded. Chairs were set around them and there was music blaring in the air, country music of course, and a general air of celebration and exuberance.

Mitch was going to put a damper on all that, and oh how very much he didn't want to have to make the announcement he had to make, but he didn't have any choice. As soon as he walked in, a roar of approval and applause echoed in the big open space. Cheers of "for he's a jolly good fellow" and jibes flew at him, like "You're finally going to get hogtied, huh?"

There were banners and humorous signs hanging on the walls. On the back wall was a banner that featured the face of each one of the 10 groomsmen along with the faces of the ten bridesmaids. There was a sign on the wall by the bar that stated the party rules. The first was "don't do anything you don't want tagged on Facebook," and the rules went downhill from there.

The men who'd shown up seemed to be in the mood to have a party. David Hicks was already there. He came to Mitch and stuck out his hand, then put his arm around Mitch's shoulders and said quietly, "Jillian told me all about it. I'm with you. Let's catch the bastard."

Mitch looked up into the big man's eyes and decided he was going to enjoy having David Hicks as a brother-in-law.

Then Gus approached Mitch, shaking his head. "I got bad news, bro." Mitch tensed.

"Sundeep just called. He can't make it."

"Oh no," Mitch said. Sundeep was a very good friend and would be performing the task of escorting each of the brides down the aisle, since their father was not alive to do it. "Why not?"

"Kidney stones."

Mitch grimaced in sympathy. He'd had them once.

"He's home all doped up and miserable but he told me to tell you he was sorry he'd had to bail tonight, but he definitely would be there on Saturday." Mitch smiled. Gus returned his smile and then said quietly, "What the hell's going on?"

"Huh?"

"You look like you've shown up for a wake instead of a bachelor party. Something bad's going down. What is it?"

"I can tell you now, or you can listen to the whole story when I tell everybody later."

Gus stepped back. "Everybody. It must be really bad."

Mitch nodded.

The men were a rowdy lot, singing along with the music and drinking beer, but the huge sit-down meal made it possible for Mitch to say what he had to say to a group of men who were not already three sheets to the wind. If they chose to get drunk afterwards, they could get drunk after he told them what was going on. As soon as everyone was seated, chowing down on steaks with Dolly Parton wailing "Jolene, Jolene, Jolene, Joleeeeeen," in the background, Gus got to his feet and picked up his spoon and clacked it against his glass.

"Okay everybody, settle down," he said, quelling the conversation and the laughter around him.

"It can't be time for speeches," someone called out.

"We don't have to make speeches until the rehearsal dinner, do we?" someone else yelled.

"True that," Gus said. "So you better get your notes together between now and then, because speeches are a requirement at the rehearsal dinner."

There was banter back and forth about the requirement before Gus turned toward Mitch and said, "I'm going to turn it over to one of the grooms, our sheriff and soon-to-be man locked up in leg irons by Rileigh Bishop, Mitch Webster."

The men pounded their fists on the table and cheered. Mitch got up and smiled.

"Do you guys know this whole big wedding thing wasn't my idea or Rileigh's or Jillian's or David's?" he said.

Some of the men laughed and nodded, others shook their heads in surprise. Mitch continued. "Rileigh and Jillian were out of town in Tennessee helping with the hurricane relief for more than a week."

The mere mention of the hurricane put a damper on the exuberance of the crowd. They all knew what had happened, and you probably couldn't find a man in the room who didn't know personally someone who'd been affected by it.

"And while they were away, Rileigh entrusted the planning of her wedding to her best friend, Georgia Stump. What Rileigh had envisioned was a small, quiet, intimate ceremony. A few close friends, a minister, and family members turned into…" He gestured by throwing his arms wide. "This," he finished.

All the men roared and applauded. "So this wasn't your idea?" someone yelled.

Mitch covered for Georgia, of course, to make sure nobody believed she'd done something amiss.

"When Rileigh and Jillian found out what their wedding had become — a mountain whoop-de-do — they were thrilled and glad to participate."

More cheers, more applause.

Mitch took a deep breath. "I hope the revelation that

this whole affair wasn't our idea didn't put a damper on the festivities."

"It didn't!" men cried out, but Mitch wasn't finished.

"But what I'm about to say probably will."

There was a little ripple of laughter, mostly confusion, and the room grew quiet. "I hate to have to dump all this on you," Mitch said, "but I don't see that I have any choice." He took another breath. "There's a man out there who plans to try to murder Rileigh at her wedding."

If ever there was a conversation stopper, that was it. There were gasps.

"What?"

"Huh?"

"What are you talking about?"

"*Murder?*"

"A few of you know this. Most of you don't. It's a long, story and we don't know why it started. But last summer, Rileigh started receiving packages from some unknown individual. The contents are … ugly."

Mitch went on to explain to the gathering of men about the boxes, the finger and thumb bones, the dried skin, the frowny faces, and the countdown. When he stopped to draw a breath after he described what had been going on, there was a rumble of anger in the group. Mitch held up his hand.

"There's more. Yesterday, Rileigh opened what she thought was a wedding present, but it wasn't. In a box, she found a doll that looked like it had been run over by an 18-wheeler. Its arms and legs were broken. It was crushed. Torn up. And it was wearing a wedding dress."

There were gasps and then silence.

"And there were drips of blood on the fabric."

The silence stretched out. "The doll's face had been scraped away, and in its place, somebody had drawn a frowny face. On the front of the doll, they'd printed the number one."

Mitch let out a breath and drew in another, squaring his shoulders.

"The doll's hair had been cut off, and in its place was a lock of Rileigh's hair.

That set off a rumble through the crowd, and Mitch waited for it to die away before he continued. "The message this guy's trying to send is pretty obvious. He plans to make an attempt on Rileigh's life at her wedding."

Mitch shook his head, then a rueful smile spread across his face. "Of course, I tried to talk Rileigh into canceling the whole thing and eloping, but I guess all of you know how Rileigh responded to that."

A few of the men chuckled softly.

"She's determined she won't run away, and she made a good point. There's some guy after her, and we have no idea why, by the way. No idea whatsoever, but he's been after her for months, and if he's set up to try to shoot her at her wedding and she doesn't show, he'll just come up with some other place, some other time, and we'll spend the rest of our lives looking over our shoulders, tensing for a blow."

"She pointed out — *wisely* — that at least we have a where and a when right now. We know the guy's going to show up here on Saturday, and we have to catch him and stop him then once and for all."

There was a rumble of approval and dismay mixed together.

"And that's where I need your help."

"Anything."

"Whatever you need."

"Glad to help."

Every man there was ready to stand beside Mitch to protect Rileigh.

"If Georgia hadn't turned our small private ceremony into a mountain whoop-de-do, this wouldn't be so complicated. In a small ceremony, it'd be easy to spot the 'away from here's.'"

He lifted his hand before anyone could say something.

"And I realize that I number among that giant group of people, but I intend to spend the rest of my life becoming a local."

The men laughed and clapped and cheered.

"But with this circus that Georgia has orchestrated, they're going to be strangers everywhere. Workmen coming in to set up benches and chairs and tables and to build the 'whatever' thing we're going to be standing beneath during the ceremony. There'll be florists and wedding planners and photographers and videographers, and on the day of the wedding, a good-sized chunk of the population of Yarmouth County.

"It doesn't help to be able to spot a stranger. There'll be plenty of them. So how you can help is…" Mitch stopped and took a breath. "You know what they said … remember after 9/11 — 'if you see something, say something'?"

The men murmured in understanding.

"That's what I need from you. I can't do this alone. But we've got what, 45 men in this room? That's 45 sets of eyes watching every stranger's every move. And if you see anything, anything at all out of the ordinary, you come tell me."

Mitch paused, then continued. "Watch every stranger like a hawk. Try not to look like you're watching them. We'd like to catch this guy by surprise. But with this many people on the lookout for anybody who does anything out of place, that's all I got. My only shot. You guys ready to help?"

The men cheered, stomped, and then rose to their feet, clapping their hands, hooting, and yelling. This was an army, and every one of them would be itching to find the bastard who was threatening Rileigh's life.

Joe Willis called out from the back above the rumble. He'd arrived slightly late but had heard everything Mitch had said.

"If you see something, say something, right?" he called out. "Well, I've seen something."

Everyone sat back down and looked at him. "I got here just a little while ago and was parking in the lot, and there's some guy out there I don't know. He's just wandering around. I don't know what he's doing, but he's from away from here, that's for damn sure."

The sounds of chairs scooting back and men leaping to their feet was a rumble Mitch had to shout over.

"No, wait, let me," he said. He turned to the nearest deputy, Jeb Rawlings. "Let's go see what the son of a bitch out there in the parking lot wants. Everybody else hang in here. It's probably nothing. Most everything you're going to report will turn out to be nothing, but we'll check out every lead you give us. So get back to eating. Gus brought a shit ton of booze, and the bar's open."

All the men rumbled their approval and smiled, but the exuberance was gone. The party atmosphere was gone. The celebration was muted, nobody in the mood anymore to party hardy.

Chapter Eleven

THERE WERE TIMES WHEN LILY BISHOP UNDERSTOOD THAT something was wrong with her, that she didn't see the world the way other people saw the world. Sometimes she would get up and her mind would feel as clear as the morning after a spring rain, when the dew on the spider-webs sparkled like little diamonds. She felt calm at those times, in control. Steady.

But then there were all the other times, the times when Lily woke up fine, but at some point, it was like those old English movies where fog rolls in off the sea. Lily had never lived near the sea, had never lived anywhere except in the mountains, but what happened in her mind was not like mist over mountain creeks — light and fluffy and you could see through it. Fog rolling in off the sea was thick and gray and impenetrable. There were times when Lily felt like her mind was filled with that kind of fog. Some days, everything was bright and crisp and clear, and she understood people, what people said, and it made sense, and she made plans, and she talked. But other days, it was like she was walking around in fog. And she couldn't see where she was going until she was almost there. And people would appear out of the fog and speak to her and then disappear back into the fog again, and she didn't know where they'd gone. When she was in the fog, she couldn't find her way around. And when she tried to talk to people, it was like she had cotton in her ears when they talked back.

When the world was full of fog like that, the most crisp and clear images were of unlikely people. Rhett Butler had shown up out of the fog, sitting at her kitchen table, and he was so crisp and clear, and she could talk to him, and he'd talk back. But at the same time, Rileigh and Mitch and Jillian were just mumbling out there in the fog, and sometimes she couldn't understand a word they said. The same thing had happened with Buzz Aldrin or whoever it was who'd been the first man on the moon. It wasn't Aldrin, was it? It was Neil Armstrong. Yes, that was it, Neil Armstrong. He told her all about being on the moon, and the Dalai Lama had been the clearest of them all, had spoken to her, and they had big, long conversations.

And when the fog cleared, left behind were pieces of memories, little vignettes, snatches of a scene or a conversation or maybe just the look on someone's face. They all floated around in the soup of her mind, and she couldn't connect them to anything. She had an image of Jillian standing beside David, smiling up at him, but sometimes she thought that image was from before Jillian went away for that time when she went away. Other times, she knew that it was recent, that Jillian and David had gotten together after all these years.

Lily had awakened this morning with her mind crisp and clear, but the fog had begun to roll in about ten o'clock, and she had trouble understanding what was going on around her. The thing was, she still felt the emotions of whatever was reality; she just wasn't sure what reality was. She was happy, but she wasn't sure why, and if she'd been sad, she wouldn't have known why she was sad either.

While her mind had been clear, she had wandered around the house, looking at all the preparations that reinforced the reality in her mind that her daughters were getting married. Not just one, not just Rileigh, and not just Jillian, both of them, on the same day, and it was … soon. Lily didn't know what today was — Tuesday? Wednesday? But she knew that the wedding was soon, and that was all she really needed to know.

The "soon-ness" meant there were preparations to make. And she functioned flawlessly when the girls just gave her a task to do — *Mama, would you make this bridesmaid's dress? It's the hardest one. It's for Sylvia, and she's so pregnant she might end up having that baby in the middle of the ceremony.*

So Lily had adjusted the pattern so that the billowing skirt of the beautiful, flowing green gown would fit over Sylvia's belly sticking out in front — but the length of the skirt in front was adjusted so it wouldn't be shorter than the rest of the dress because of the bulge. When she showed Jillian the dress, Jillian said it was the most beautiful thing she'd ever seen.

She had just given Jillian the dress when a brief moment of clarity illuminated her thoughts, and she knew there was a name for what she had done about the wedding. She wasn't quite sure what that name was. Had it been a crime, it would probably have been something like "accessory after the fact." That's what she had been when Georgia went off the rails and started planning a huge wedding for Rileigh and Jillian. Mama knew that wasn't what they wanted. Mama knew that's not what they hadn't planned, and it's possible that Mama could have put out Georgia's fire before it caught all the woods ablaze. But she didn't, because the big wedding that Georgia was planning was exactly what mama secretly wanted for her girls. She wanted a mountain whoop-de-do. She wanted the whole county to celebrate the wonder of her girls finding the loves of their lives and pledging their truths to the two wonderful men, Mitch and David.

So she kept her mouth shut … maybe even blew on the flames from time to time. Now she'd just about convinced herself that Rileigh and Jillian had liked the big wedding now. Were happy about it. If they weren't, they were obviously willing to pretend they were.

Lily went out to feed the chickens.

Had she fed them already today? Maybe. Hard to tell, but there was no seed left on the ground and she'd rather feed them twice than not at all. While she scattered the seed — crooning "here chick, here chick, here chick, chick, chick," her phone rang. She pulled it out from her pocket and looked at the number and couldn't place it. It was familiar, but she couldn't remember whose number that was.

"Hello," she said.

"Hello, baby sister. How are you today?" came the voice out of the phone, and for a few moments, Lily had absolutely no idea who she was talking to, who in the world would call her baby sister.

Then she knew it was Daisy, her older sister.

"Daisy, hi Daisy. I haven't talked to you in a while. What you been up to?"

Fact was, Lily had no idea when was the last time she had talked to her sister Daisy, nor what they had talked about, nor what Daisy was doing these days.

"I hear you're getting ready for a big wedding."

"Oh, I am, I am, I am!"

Then Lily was off to the races, telling Daisy wonderful

things about the dresses and the leaves instead of flowers and who was making the food for the reception and on and on. When she paused to draw breath, there was silence on the other end of the phone, and she wasn't sure that Daisy was still there.

"Daisy, you there?"

"Sure, I'm here," Daisy said.

"What's wrong, Daisy?"

"I want to come to the wedding," she said.

"Well, of course, you're coming to the wedding," Lily said.

"No, I ain't. I'm locked up here."

"You're locked up where? What are you talking about?"

"I'm here at the Carrington House, remember?"

As soon as Daisy said it, Lily did remember. She remembered that Daisy had been committed to that mental hospital, that she had to stay there whether she liked it or not, that she was indeed mentally ill, went off on these screaming tangents, had to have shock therapy and all kinds of medications to keep her on an even keel, but she'd forgotten about the part about her being "locked up."

"Do you want me to come to the wedding?" Daisy asked, and her voice sounded so sad and bereft it broke Lily's heart.

"Why, of course, I want you to come to the wedding. Why would you ask a question like that?"

"If you want me to come, you're gonna have to get me out."

"Get you out of what?"

"Of the Carrington House," Daisy said. "You can do it. It's not that hard."

"Do what?"

"You need to come out here and talk to the director. You need to ask if he will release me into your custody on compassionate leave to go to my two nieces' wedding."

"Compassionate leave?"

"Yeah, they give that all the time, and they know I'm fine now." Daisy hurried on before Lily could comment. "I know there were times I wasn't, times I behaved real crazy like, but I've been staying on my meds, and taking them regular. I been helping out in the library. I've been as nice and sweet and kind as I could be to everybody. I know they'll let me out."

"So, what is it I have to do?"

"You have to come out here and talk to the administrator. You have to tell him you're willing to be responsible for me and that he's welcome to put an ankle bracelet on me."

"An ankle bracelet? What do you mean, an ankle bracelet?"

"You know, something where they can track me and know where I am. Will you do that for me?"

"What makes you think they'll let you out just 'cause I ask them?"

"'Cause you're Lily Bishop, that's why. There ain't no more upstanding citizen in all of Yarmouth County than Lily Bishop. And hell, one of your daughters is marrying the sheriff, and all the deputies is going to be there. It ain't like I could run off somewhere with all of them people around, particularly if I've got on an ankle bracelet."

"Do I have to say all that to them, explain all that?" Lily asked.

There was a silence on the other end of the phone, and then Daisy said, "No, you don't have to do nothing, Lily."

Daisy sounded so sad. "What do you mean?"

"I can tell you don't want to come out here and say all that stuff. You don't care that I have to miss the wedding because I'm stuck here. It don't matter to you. I just want you to know I wouldn't have done a thing like that to you if it was my girls who was getting married. I'd damn sure see that their aunt Daisy — who helped to raise both them girls — was going to be at the ceremony."

"No, I'll come, I'll do it."

"That's all right, Lily. I'll just sit here, and maybe you can take some pictures and come out here after and show me the pictures of all that I missed."

"No, you're not going to miss nothing!" Lily was scrambling now, feeling terrible about the fact that she hadn't thought a thing about Daisy, hadn't even considered inviting her to the wedding. She wasn't sure exactly why that was. It was something that she was supposed to know about Daisy, and perhaps it was just that Daisy had been committed to a mental institution, and Lily had assumed she was stuck there, but maybe not. Lily felt a wave of guilt wash over her, as she considered all the ways her big sister had looked after her when she was a little girl. The time she beat the crap out of the Langford boy when he blew his nose in Lily's hair in second grade. The way she had helped out after Lily married J.R. She was always there, available, to help with the girls and whatever needed doing. She had moved into their house when Jillian was small and had damn near raised her, and here Lily was all these years later, not even bothering to invite Daisy to Jillian's wedding. Lily felt terrible.

"Now you listen to me, Daisy Gillespie. I'm going to come out there and have me a talk with that administrator and tell him he ought to let you come to your nieces' wedding, both your nieces' wedding."

"Take me with you when you talk to him," Daisy said. "It will be helpful to have me there."

"Okay, I'll come today."

Rileigh and Jillian weren't home right then. Lily was supposed to be making the finishing touches on the last of the bridesmaid's dresses. Well, she could do that tonight, and wouldn't it be great if she could have Daisy there to help her? Lily grabbed her purse and headed out the door to the Carrington House.

～

Daisy Gillespie sat with her phone in her hand, a genuine smile on her face. Poor stupid Lily had fallen for her tale of woe hook, line, and sinker. She always did.

Daisy considered sometimes why it was that she was the only one of the bouquet of flowers who had a lick of sense. The rest of her sisters, all named for flowers, had dwelt their whole lives in the black hole of incurable stupid. Lily was the dumbest of the bunch.

Daisy let out a sigh, but it was Lily who had snared the only man Daisy had ever loved — J.R. Bishop, and it was Lily who married him, took him away from Daisy, and Daisy would never forgive her for that.

It was after her last round of electric shock treatment that J.R. had come to visit her. She shivered at the thought, even now all these months later, J.R. had come to her room in the Carrington House, walked right in with the door locked, and told her how much he loved her, told her how sad he was that the two of them hadn't been able to make a life together, told her how much he hated Jillian for keeping J.R. from Daisy.

Even though Daisy had been religious about taking her meds, she would stop today and it'd take them maybe 24 hours to get out of her system, and then she would be able to think clearly, because she *needed* to think clearly after the visit from that man yesterday, outlining how he planned to kill Jillian. Daisy hadn't slept a wink. It was all she could think about. She would give her life to be able to end the life of the bitch who had stolen her one great chance at true love. All of this had come up at a very opportune time. There was no real administrator at the moment, just an "interim," Dr. Eckstein, who'd taken over after Mr. Garrison had quit, or got fired, suddenly about six weeks ago. So there was nobody with any real authority running the place, and Daisy was sure she could bamboozle that poor schmuck, if she put her mind to it.

She packed up what little she had in a small suitcase and sat on her bed to wait for Lily to come for her. Lily arrived frazzled and befuddled as Daisy had known she would. But when they talked to the interim hospital administrator, Daisy had been lucid and docile. All she wanted was to go to a wedding. They could put an ankle bracelet on her. It wasn't like she had anywhere to run, and she was, after all, 78 years old, so *running* wasn't exactly an option. And the wedding she was going to was the wedding of the Yarmouth County *sheriff,* and every one of his deputies would be there, as well as several of his friends who were sheriffs and sheriff's deputies in surrounding counties. Add to that the Black Bear Forge police officers — nothing but meter jockeys in uniform, but the interim director didn't know that — along with a handful of Tennessee State Police Troopers. Hell, that place would be broke out with law enforcement. It was certainly a safe place for a 78-year-old woman who only wanted to watch her nieces get married.

She'd thrown in the zinger at the last minute, pointing out that she'd seen various practices and procedures in the Carrington House that were not up to Tennessee state code. She'd never mentioned them to Mitch, of course, who was about to be married to her niece, and she never would mention them, of course, particularly since the administrator was going to give her a compassionate leave to attend the sheriff's wedding.

An hour after Lily pulled into the parking lot of the Carrington House, she pulled back out again with her sister Daisy sitting in the front seat, smiling happily beside her.

Chapter Twelve

MITCH AND DEPUTY RAWLINGS LEFT THE BUILDING OUT the back door. Using hand motions, Mitch pointed to the east side of the building. Rawlings nodded and headed that way. Mitch took the west side, so the two of them would approach the parking lot from opposite sides. Both had their weapons drawn, pointed at the ground. Mitch made his way through the woods near the American Legion hall toward the parking lot and instantly spotted a man beside the far end of the parking lot in the trees. The man seemed to be bent over something, then he stood up. Mitch leveled his pistol at the man and called out, "Police! Freeze!"

The man's head snapped toward Mitch, and then he simply lifted his hands slowly and clasped his fingers together over the top of his head. Then he very carefully and slowly got down on his knees. That was odd.

Mitch and Deputy Rawlings hurried to where the man knelt in the brush beside the end of the parking lot. As soon as Mitch arrived, the man asked, "Are you Sheriff Mitchell Webster?"

"I'll ask the questions. Who are you and what in the hell are you doing skulking around this building?"

The man gestured with his chin toward the inside pocket of the sports coat he was wearing, but didn't unclasp his fingers.

"My ID's in there," he said, and kept his hands where they were. "And I'm packing, shoulder holster."

Mitch nodded to Rawlings, who kept his pistol trained on the man on his knees. Mitch holstered his weapon, pulled open the man's jacket, lifted out the pistol and then searched his coat pocket. In it was a leather case that flipped open to reveal a badge on one side and a picture ID on the other. The badge was circular, with a star in the middle — looked a little like the plastic sheriff's badge that had come with the cowboy hat and boots Mitch got once for Christmas. Except on the circle surrounding the star were engraved the words: United States Marshal. The picture ID identified the man as U.S. Deputy Marshal Joseph Craig Dylan. The photo was a head-and-shoulders shot of the man kneeling in the dirt before him — except the man in the picture had a beard. Seeing that Mitch noted that, the man explained, "I was working undercover, narcotics and the gang unit." He gestured with his chin — but did *not* move his arms — to his full sleeves of tattoos. "Any woman who claims she can do a 'temporary' tattoo is a witch and should be burned at the stake."

"What's your name?" Mitch asked.

"Craig Dylan." He was looking up at Mitch and paused, as if he were expecting some kind of response. "Which makes me 'Marshal Dylan.'" He paused again. "As far as I know, there's only one federal marshal whose first name is Chester, and I have never had the pleasure of working with him."

Though what he said made no sense, the man exuded

an air of confidence and was careful to make no sudden movements or attempt to remove his fingers clasped above his head. He paused a third time and then smiled a little half smile. "My girlfriend's name isn't Kitty either," he said.

Mitch got it then, understood, his reference — the vintage television western, *Gunsmoke*, where Marshal Matt Dillon and his trusty deputy, stiff-legged Chester, kept the peace in Dodge City, Kansas, while the marshal flirted with Miss Kitty, the owner of the Long Branch Saloon.

Mitch nodded at Deputy Rawlings, and the deputy holstered his weapon. Mitch held out his hand to the man, who took it, then Mitch pulled him to his feet. Mitch handed back the gun, which the marshal returned to his shoulder holster.

"So what are you doing here, Marshal Dylan?"

Even Mitch smiled a little.

"Looking for you."

"Did you think you'd find me in the woods?"

"I went by the sheriff's office, and they told me you'd be here."

"So what are you doing out here in the weeds?"

"I pulled up and got out of my car and was about halfway across the parking lot when I saw some guy come running out of the woods, jump into a car, and peel out of the parking lot."

"Some guy?"

"White male, six feet tall, slender, no facial hair, wearing a University of Tennessee ball cap and jeans. I couldn't see the license number because of the dust that flew up behind the tires, but I could tell it was a Tennessee plate. Black Ford Taurus, at least ten years old — maybe even 2012."

"So you…?" Mitch left the sentence dangling.

"I came over here to see what the guy had been running from in the woods … and I found it." The marshal nodded toward the tree line. "He dumped a corpse, an Ichabod Crane. Have a look for yourself. I'm sorry I tromped on the weeds, but the ground's so hard I don't think you'll get any prints."

Deputy Rawlings and Mitch headed toward the trees, cutting a wide path around the straight-line entrance in case the marshal was wrong about footprints. About 25 feet inside the woods, they found the body that the marshal had told them would be there.

Mitch had thought he knew what the marshal meant by "Ichabod Crane," and as soon as he spotted the body, he was sure. The corpse of a fat man in a plaid shirt and jeans was lying on his back in the weeds. The body was missing its head.

Marshal Dylan stepped up beside Mitch as he turned to Rawlings. "Call it in, then go inside and get Gus. Make sure nobody else comes out here." Then he said to the marshal, "The county coroner's in the building."

"They told me it was a party. I didn't mean to crash it. Thought I'd just show up, let you know who I was, and set up some time we could talk tomorrow."

Mitch stood with the federal marshal looking down at the dead body and mused aloud, "So who comes out here to the American Legion Hall in broad daylight, when the lot's full of cars — three of them sheriff's department cruisers, and—"

"Dumps a dead body in the woods so close to the parking lot somebody was bound to see it," Marshal Dylan finished for him. "Appears to me the dude wanted the body to be found."

Mitch concurred. He walked slowly around the body,

staying far enough away not to mess with any evidence that Gus might be able to find.

"You say you came here looking for me? What for?"

"It's a long story. How about I wait to tell you until you're finished here?"

Gus came striding across the parking lot toward them. When he arrived, Mitch said, "This is Dr. Gus Hazelton, Yarmouth County Coroner."

Gus held out his hand to the stranger as Mitch told Gus, "This is U.S. Marshal Craig Dylan."

Gus's head snapped up, "Marshal Dylan?"

Mitch saw the marshal cringe. "Uh huh."

"The marshal saw somebody come running out of the woods and drive away. He found our headless friend here when he went to investigate."

"And a federal marshal just happened to be in the parking lot because…?"

"I haven't heard that story yet," Mitch said. "Rawlings called in a 10-46, and I'd like to get this body out of here before all the guys in that room come out and see it."

Gus squatted down close to the body, then looked up at Mitch.

"It's going to be a bitch finding out who this guy is," he said. "Hope his DNA's on file somewhere."

"Yeah, I saw," the marshal said.

But Mitch had not noticed what the two of them were talking about until Gus indicated the man's hands. Then he saw his fingers.

"Had his fingerprints removed," Gus said. "Acid, probably." He paused. "That had to hurt."

Chapter Thirteen

Mitch was certain his bachelor party would go down in the annals of Yarmouth County as the single worst bachelor party anyone had ever attended. Oh, the food was great and the booze was even better. The men had arrived ready to party, but as soon as they finished eating the glorious catered meal, Mitch had thrown a wet blanket on everyone's enjoyment of the evening. He told them about what was going on with Rileigh and asked for their help. "If you see something, say something." And if that weren't bad enough, then he found a U.S. Marshal and a dead body — a *headless* dead body — in the woods beyond the parking lot.

Hard to top this as a bachelor party disaster.

The crowd of men left early, and the ambulance took the body to Gus's office, where Gus would perform an autopsy later. Mitch and the federal marshal and Gus had stayed behind.

After the marshal had commented on how good the steak smelled, nothing would do but that Gus got one of the cooks to grill a medium-well steak for the federal marshal and then heaped his plate with all the trimmings.

Now as he ate, he explained what had sent him to the American Legion Hall that night.

"I hate to talk with my mouth full. My mama always did say that wasn't polite."

"Write that down," Gus said. "Issue a citation — illegal rudeness."

"What sent you looking for me tonight?" Mitch asked.

"I'm working a case. I've been chasing the wind for almost six months." He took a swig of his beer and continued, "My assignment is to catch a notorious assassin."

"Mob assassin?" Mitch asked.

"Not exclusively. This guy freelances. He takes contracts on anybody and everybody."

"What's his name?"

The marshal shrugged. "You got me, pal, I couldn't tell you. Nobody knows his name. He goes by 'El Viento.'"

Gus translated, "The Wind."

"Yep, The Wind. Blows through a murder scene and out the other side and doesn't leave a trace behind. Nobody knows what he looks like. Nobody's ever seen a picture of him. The man has, at least by my count, murdered nine different people in the last year and a half."

Gus whistled.

"He's wanted all over the world. Interpol would love to get their hands on him. MI6 in England has been looking for him for at least two years."

"How did he manage to land on your plate?"

The man stopped chewing, then swallowed. He picked up his beer and took a big drink before he spoke again.

"He killed my partner," he said.

"I'm sorry," Mitch said.

"Somebody took out a hit on a federal marshal?" Gus was surprised.

A quick thought about Lamar Devereaux flashed through Mitch's mind, then more thoughts about all the FBI agents and Homeland Security agents who had been systematically tortured and killed by the South American drug lord who was looking for the millions in diamonds he had stashed inside the horseshoe of a Tennessee walking horse.

"It wasn't a contract hit. Guess you could call it a freebie. Joe was working narcotics, got a tip on a fentanyl shipment, was part of the task force sent to take it down. Word on the street claimed El Viento would be there. There was a gunfight." He shook his head. "They must have made Joe, but he wasn't killed until two days *after* the gunfight. That's when his wife found him in the front seat of his car with a single bullet in his temple. El Viento *got away,* but he circled back to kill Joe … payback, I guess." Dylan's jaw tightened. "Joe had two kids, and Margie was pregnant when he was killed. He was the nicest guy you ever met. I asked for this assignment. It's personal."

He reached out and picked up his beer, took another swallow, then began cutting into his steak. "I've been trailing El Viento for months, and I got as close as I've ever gotten in Nashville last week." He paused. "Wasn't there a sportscaster who used to say when somebody missed a tackle, that they 'came up with a handful of shoestrings?'"

"Sounds like something Casey Stengel would have said, but wrong sport," Gus said.

"Well, I came up with a handful of shoestrings in Nashville, tracked him to a fancy hotel there, and I was as certain as I've ever been with anything in my life that he was there, in that room, when I broke the door down." He sighed heavily. "And I came up with a handful of shoestrings, there was an ashtray full of butts, but the last one hadn't even burned down yet! Bathroom window was open to the fire escape."

The marshal fixed Mitch with a long look before he continued. "But that's not all I found in the wake of his departure." Reaching into a coat pocket, Dylan pulled out what appeared to be a plastic evidence bag — numbered and sealed. Inside was a newspaper clipping.

"No prints on it," he told Mitch as he laid it down on the table in front of Mitch.

Mitch looked at the clipping and gasped. It was the wedding announcement from the *Black Bear Forge Gazette*, announcing the wedding of Miss Rileigh Joseph Bishop to Mitchell Andrew Webster and Miss Jillian Ann Bishop to Walter David Hicks. There was the date, and there were their pictures. Mitch was sure his face had gone white. He looked from the clipping to the face of the marshal and back down to the clipping. "You found this...?"

"I found it on the floor in that hotel room. And that's why I'm here. It would seem El Viento intends to be a guest at your wedding. I came to see what possible connection this assassin has to any one of the four people in that picture."

"I know the connection," Mitch said airlessly. "I think he plans a hit on one of the brides — my bride, Rileigh Bishop."

The man swallowed the bite of food that was in his mouth, put down his fork and knife, and said, "Tell me the story."

And so Mitch did.

He described briefly what had happened to Jillian thirty years ago and about the postcards that had begun showing up after she vanished. He described how Jillian had returned home in June and how she and Rileigh had almost been killed then.

"It's a long story, and I'll tell you the details sometime if you're interested, but what concerns you here is the fact that it was after Jillian came home — that the first frowny face showed up."

"Frowny face."

"Yep. You know how I told you the postcards that came after Jillian vanished were from exotic places with nothing but a smiley face on back. Well, Rileigh got a postcard, but the picture on the front wasn't some exotic scene from Madrid or Paris; it was a picture of a creepy cemetery, and someone had scratched out the name on one of the stones and wrote in Rileigh Bishop, and on the back was not a smiley face, but a frowny face. And there was something besides the frowny face on the back; there was a number. The first one was number six."

The federal marshal shook his head in confusion, sat back, and scooted his plate away. "Go on."

"That was the first of the frowny faces. They came pretty regularly after that. Every three or four weeks. The second one wasn't just a card with a frowny face on it; it was a box, and inside the box was a finger bone."

"Go on."

"A finger bone and the number five. There was a thumb bone along with the number four in the next box."

"So, it's a countdown."

Mitch nodded. "Along with the number three was a piece of tanned human skin — not just a piece of random skin. It was skin with a serpent tattoo on it. We got DNA matches on some of the body parts. In the box with the skin was a key, but we didn't know what it opened.

"Number two was when we found out what the key opened. It opened a jack-in-the-box. And the little figure that sprang up out of it was a clown head on a spring bouncing around. The clown was not smiling, though. Its face was a hideous, grimace. A card attached to the front of the clown had a number two on one side and 'BANG! You're DEAD this time' on the other."

"*This time*," the marshal noted.

"Rileigh opened up the last box yesterday. Inside, she found a doll in a wedding dress with a number one on the front."

"The end of the countdown," the marshal observed. Mitch nodded.

"The doll was broken, arms and legs twisted, drips of blood on the wedding dress, and a lock of Rileigh's hair affixed to the doll's head."

"This is one sick son of a bitch," the marshal said, shaking his head. "You got any idea why he's stalking her?"

"We think we know. Right before Jillian came home, Rileigh was ambushed. A sniper was hiding in the woods, took a shot at her in her car when she passed. But she hit a bump in the road, and the shot went wild, and she wound up going off the road into the river and almost died of hypothermia. A fellow in Knoxville was murdered the next day, and the bullet matched the one recovered from Rileigh's car."

"So, who wanted Rileigh dead?" the marshal asked.

"That's the long story," he said. "The condensed version is that a man who served as sheriff of this county for twenty years — his name was Jedediah T. Mumford, Mum to his friends — tried to kill Rileigh and Jillian both, and when he failed, he ate his gun."

"So, you think this Sheriff Mumford waited in the woods and took a shot at Rileigh."

"No, I don't think it was Mum."

The marshal looked like a light bulb had turned on in

his head. "You think this Mum dude took out a hit on Rileigh."

Mitch nodded. "It's possible."

"So the former sheriff hired an assassin — El Viento — to take out Rileigh, but he missed." Now it was the marshal who was nodding. "The puzzle pieces fit. El Viento had a contract, and he missed the shot. He's the kind of bastard who'd be bothered by that. So let's say he decided to come back and finish what he'd started, but he had other jobs to do first, so he—"

"Sent Rileigh pieces of those other kills," Gus put in.

"If you'll give me the files on whatever DNA matches you were able to get on the body parts sent to your fiancée, I'll do a little digging, see if they could have been hits made by El Viento."

"I'd like to back up to the fat, headless dude sans fingerprints we found lying in the weeds … that we were *meant* to find in the weeds," Gus said. The other two nodded. "The audacity … it feels like a challenge to me, an announcement: 'Game on!'"

"The last thing, the broken doll…" Mitch began. His chest was suddenly so tight it was hard to find enough air to speak. "The drips of blood on the wedding dress, the bullet hole…"

Gus spared him from having to ask the marshal the rest of it. "What's your read on what that means?"

The marshal's eyes softened, but he didn't pull any punches.

"I think he's saying he plans to shoot Rileigh in her wedding dress … on her wedding day."

Chapter Fourteen

SUNDEEP SINGH GRUDGINGLY LAID BACK ON THE PILLOWS his wife had piled up for him so that he could sit up in bed to "work." He wanted to get up and dress, but there was no arguing with Miriam when she was in taking-care-of-Sundeep mode, and he *had* been sick, sicker than he'd ever been in his life just yesterday.

He'd seemed fine, had been looking forward to Mitch Webster's bachelor party last night. He knew that Gus Hazelton was having it catered and the food would be great, and he would enjoy hanging out with all the guys. Guys who were also *voters*.

Sundeep was running for mayor of Yarmouth County against incumbent Mayor J.P. Rutherford, and the election was a little over three weeks away. Folks assured him his would be a landslide victory. Rutherford had been a terrible mayor, had only been elected because of the low turnout during COVID, and had pissed off just about every man, woman, and child in Yarmouth County during his term. Sundeep, on the other hand, had the support of churches, the Rotary Club, the Lions Club, the Knights of

Columbus, the local newspaper and the Fraternal Order of Police. He certainly didn't need to campaign at Mitch's bachelor party — those guys were voters who were already in his camp, but it never hurt to spend time with your support base.

And then out of nowhere yesterday afternoon, it had struck. He literally dropped to his knees gasping when the pain hit him. He thought perhaps he'd been shot. It hurt that bad. He gasped as Jojo, who worked with him in the convenience store, came running to his aid.

He refused to allow Jojo to call an ambulance, demanded that he simply close the store and drive Sundeep to the emergency room. Miriam was shopping in Gatlinburg, and when he called her and told her he was on the way to the emergency room, she said she'd meet him there.

The diagnosis was simple and not as grim as he had feared it would be, though it was difficult to celebrate when he was in so much pain.

"Mr. Singh, you have a kidney stone, and your body is trying to pass it."

Sundeep could barely think, could barely speak. "Why does a stone hurt so much?"

"I could show you a picture of a kidney stone, and you'd understand immediately why it is so painful. It's a jagged crystal with sharp spines all over it. An absolutely horrible little critter."

The doctor told him that after he passed the stone, he needed to come in for some tests, and they would consider the possibility of doing a lithotripsy procedure on him — using radio waves to shatter the other small stones that had shown up in the scan.

Sundeep had gone home heavily medicated, still in excruciating pain. He hated taking narcotics because he always felt terrible the day after, but he was gobbling them now, trying very hard to put a good face on it so Miriam wouldn't be so worried.

He had to bail on Mitch's party, and about midnight, his ordeal was finally over — the stone passed and the pain had subsided.

Exhausted from the pain, he had fallen into bed and had slept well. But when he awoke this morning ready to go to work, Miriam put her foot down. He wasn't going anywhere, she said. He was staying in bed. He started to argue, but she had her game face on. He understood the value of a strategic retreat so managed to negotiate a reprieve for the afternoon.

Propped up in bed on pillows with his laptop in the position its name implied, he set to work on a task he'd intended to address last night. He had been informed of a suspicious purchase on one of his credit cards early yesterday afternoon, but what with the kidney stone and all, he had done nothing to investigate the situation. Now, he went online trying to find out whether or not his credit card had been compromised. He went to the credit card site but couldn't remember his password. It was in his desk downstairs, and he would have to get past guard-dog Miriam to fetch it. Though Sundeep lacked the techie skills common to many of his countrymen from India, he knew his way around a computer, and he had several friends who were for-real, no-kidding hackers. Sundeep was convinced that one of them, Vivek Patel, could hack his way into the little black satchel that accompanied the President of the United States everywhere — the one where nuclear launch codes were stored. Vivek had once described to Sundeep how he had found a site that was not for *victims* of credit card or identity theft but was instead a chatroom for the criminals who did the stealing.

The site was deep in the bowels of "the dark web." With nothing better to do — he was stuck here until noon — Sundeep went looking for that site. If he couldn't find out from the credit card company if there'd been a fraudulent charge on his card, maybe he could find people who did things like that — stole credit card numbers and identities. Maybe there was a collaboration of thieves on that site where they talked about what they did and how they did it. Maybe they even shared "best practices" and he could figure out how a thief could have gotten access to his card.

Down one internet rabbit hole after another he went, taking his time, searching, snooping, nosing around. After two hours, he had gone down so many rabbit trails that it was a good thing they were virtual or he'd never find his way back home. He had no idea what he would find when he clicked to enter a chatroom called Beyond Here Be Dragons, and he began to run his cursor down the various conversations. It only took him a minute or two to realize that he'd somehow managed to stumble into a really ugly place, where bad people got together with other bad people to brag about crimes far worse that stealing credit cards. He needed to get out of here — hoped that his computer's IP address couldn't be traced — was hovering his cursor over the X to exit when he saw a picture that he recognized. He sat staring at it in disbelief. It was a picture of a newspaper clipping from the *Black Bear Forge Gazette* showing Mitch and Rileigh and Jillian and David and the announcement of their wedding on Saturday.

Sundeep had been pressed into service for that wedding. Since Jillian and Rileigh had no father, he had been asked to walk both brides down the aisle, one on each arm. He had already started working on the "bashing" speech he would give at the rehearsal dinner to make fun of Mitch. What was a picture of their wedding announcement doing on the dark web?

Sundeep began to read. A person whose screen name was El Viento had posted in the chat room, and several other people had made comments about his post. The post was titled "Catch Me If You Can," and Sundeep was staggered by the contents. Surely, it was a joke of some kind. The post offered the winner access to millions of dollars in a numbered Swiss bank account. It *had* to be a joke.

But the people who commented displayed no levity. Someone named Nighthawk spewed out incredibly lewd obscenities, said he was glad to see that El Viento would not be "breathing in and out on a regular basis for much longer." Other replies were even more vicious and explicit, posted by people with screen names like Born2BEvil and BangURDead and BloodHarpy.

It suddenly occurred to Sundeep that in his quest to find a site where credit card thieves talked shop, he had stumbled into a dark web chat room where mercenaries, terrorists and killers-for-hire hung out.

He burped out a bleat of nervous laughter. That was absurd, of course, it couldn't be true. This whole chatroom was probably part of some alternate reality, a role-playing game like Dungeons and Dragons. The people behind those kick-ass screen names were likely a collection of pimply-faced adolescents, fantasizing about superheroes and assassins.

But if it was some kind of game, why had the person named El Viento posted the wedding announcement?

Catch Me If You Can.

And the more responses he read, the more convinced he became that the participants in the chat weren't callow teenage boys playing a game. The jargon they used for weapons, the phrases they used that seemed paramilitary, the nature of their obscenity — these were hardened men, brutal and merciless, who knew their way around weapons too advanced for teenagers, and displayed total disdain for "civilians" or "collateral damage."

Sundeep realized his hand was trembling slightly as he took a screenshot of the chat room, complete with the Catch Me If You Can post, the comments, and the picture of his four Yarmouth County friends. He felt a sudden stab of anxiety. He didn't know if he had left footprints all across the dark web that would lead back to him from this site, but he did know he didn't want to be there anymore. With trembling fingers, he reached up to the button on the side of his computer, punched it, and the screen went blank. When he rebooted it a few minutes later, he was back in normal, garden-variety Google-Land.

Scooting the laptop off onto the bed, Sundeep got to his feet, went into the bathroom, and turned on the shower. He knew he would have to fight his way past Miriam downstairs, but Mitch needed to see this — *now*.

Chapter Fifteen

EL VIENTO STOOD AT THE TOP OF THE HILL, LOOKING down on the Breezy Creek Recreation Area in the Great Smoky Mountains National Park. It was an impressive facility, and right now, it was a beehive of activity. From where El Viento stood, he was looking down on a huge amphitheater that had been cut into the hillside, with a stage at the bottom. Three rows of wide steps marched down from the top of the hill to the stage, the widest in the center, the smaller two on the outsides. The tiers for seating that had been cut into the hillside were just flat levels of grass where people came in the summertime and spread out blankets and listened to concerts. That kind of seating didn't work for a wedding, though. The dressed-up guests — and El Viento was certain these simple people still adhered to such traditions — wouldn't find sitting on a blanket on the grass particularly appealing.

He wondered how these industrious little ants would surmount that obstacle, asked a question or two here and there, nothing anybody'd remember, and learned all manner of useful — and useless — information. It seemed that the Yarmouth County Rescue Squad had, indeed, come to the rescue. A dozen or so burly men were hauling benches from the firehouse, where they were used to seat the huge crowds at their semi-annual pancake breakfasts, up the grassy tiers. The benches were ugly, of course, but that particular flaw would soon be corrected by an organization known as Bestowing Sewing, which was a group of little old ladies who spent their retirement sewing and then giving away what they had sewn, quilts for disaster relief efforts, baby blankets for orphanages, and other more decorative items that they sold at Christmas time at a bazaar and used the money to buy food to hand out to needy families in the county at Christmas. All that information had been provided by a particularly chatty red-haired woman whose mother was a member of the sewing group. She described how the ladies had taken to their sewing machines with a vengeance for this double wedding — had made at least a dozen dresses for the wedding party — for the bridesmaids and the flower girl. And they'd made white satin covers for each of the ugly 15-foot-long benches the rescue squad had come along.

The ladies had also, or so had said the chatty, freckle-faced woman, stored away the red velvet curtains that had hung in the old high school auditorium before it closed, and had brought them out to make a red velvet skirt to go all the way around the base of the stage of the amphitheater.

Carpenters were also building something — more than one something — that El Viento couldn't find a use for. They were assembling two-by-twelves, cut in six-foot lengths ... for what? He watched until workers had completed one of the what-is-its and carried it to the bottom step in the stairs leading down from the top of the amphitheater to the stage. Then he understood — they were making caps for the steps ... to keep the high-heeled shoes of the bridesmaids and female guests from digging into the grass as they walked down them.

He smiled and shook his head. One of the carpenters making step caps ... El Viento recognized the poor bastard. Did he really think a blond mohawk would make him *less* noticeable? Seriously? He watched the man, who appeared to be a fairly decent carpenter, and decided that IronJackal could be useful to him.

El Viento turned his attention to other carpenters, who were constructing an arbor where the brides and grooms and the minister would stand during the ceremony. There were risers set up on either side, and El Viento wasn't sure exactly what those were for, but he'd overheard someone saying they were for the bridesmaids and groomsmen to stand during the ceremony, but that couldn't be right. There couldn't possibly be enough bridesmaids and groomsmen to fill up risers — could there?

Besides the amphitheater, the Breezy Creek Recreation Area had all manner of other facilities. There was a big building just above the amphitheater steps where El Viento was sure the brides, bridesmaids, and others would gather before they walked in ceremonially down the steps. He had wandered around inside it for a little while. The building had lots of large rooms with tables and chairs, and in some of them, he saw what he supposed were the gowns of some of the bridesmaids. Hell, maybe there *would* be enough bridesmaids/groomsmen to fill risers.

Along the north side of the amphitheater were several other buildings and a large gazebo where tables and chairs were being unloaded, that he supposed would be set up there for the big dinner after the wedding. He needed to know exactly what was going to happen this Saturday, the events and in what order, so he'd asked about those, too, always able to find chatty people willing to share everything they knew. A friendly lot, he'd give them that. As he understood it, there would be two events going on simultaneously that had common elements. There was to be a big mountain whoop-de-do, which was a gathering of come-one, come-all to an enormous potluck dinner where all the ladies in the county brought their favorite dishes and where men grilled steaks and turned a pig on a spit. There was to be dancing, of course, with music provided by the Foote Notes — a local band made up of musicians who regularly served as backup musicians to the stars in Nashville. After the wedding ceremony, which wouldn't take very long, the wedding guests and all the participants would swell the ranks of the revelers at the whoop-de-do for a blow-out-all-the-stops wedding reception. They were sure it would be unforgettable.

And they were right. It would most *definitely* be an event nobody would ever forget.

These people, these *insects* buzzing around, were insignificant creatures destined to electrocute themselves on the great bug light of life. But El Viento would spare them that end, some of them anyway. The rest would bear witness to a spectacle that would go down in the county's history books as the single most significant event that had ever occurred here.

It was going to be quite a show.

He chuckled, tenting his hand over his eyes to shade them from the intense glare. He was squinting — the sun seemed too bright.

Someone was speaking to El Viento. He could hear the voice and the words, but the words had no meaning, either individually or clumped together in sentences. It was as if pieces of fruit or bowling balls or lampshades or Christmas decorations — just random objects — were falling out of the person's mouth instead of words. They were meaningless.

He knew he had to come back, had to understand and comprehend. He *had* to attend to the person who was speaking to him. It took every speck of will he possessed to pull himself back into a conscious state where he shook his head and mumbled to the man standing beside him.

"Lost in thought. Sorry. What did you say?"

The man began babbling again, speaking *words* this time, though nothing of consequence, and El Viento had to stop him about three sentences in to explain that no, he was *not* the wedding planner. No, he did not know who *was* the wedding planner, he only knew who *wasn't*. The man went scurrying off in search of the illusive wedding planner, leaving El Viento to turn slowly and walk back to his car. He had parked well away from the other vehicles, and now he got in and opened his laptop, hoping his phone would work as an internet hotspot. Coverage was still spotty because of the hurricane. Today, Verizon was functioning, and he dived into the deep waters of the dark web.

When he arrived in the chatroom Beyond Here Be Dragons, he was surprised that his was the first post for today.

El Viento: *I spotted you, IronJackal. A disguise is supposed to make you blend in, not look conspicuous. You suck at this. And a shout out to BangURDead and Born2BEvil. Either you changed your minds and you're not coming, you haven't arrived yet, or you've done a better job than IronJackal at disguising your appearance. But remember, if I find you before you find me, game over.*

Chapter Sixteen

RILEIGH AND JILLIAN HAD ONLY BEEN GONE TO THE grocery store a little over an hour, but when they returned, they found an empty parking space in the back where Mama always parked her car.

Rileigh had been going to have the "Mama, I need to take your car keys" conversation with her mother for months. She'd been putting it off because she knew that Mama would feel bereft when she couldn't go where she wanted to go when she wanted to go there. Mama's grip on reality was getting more and more tenuous every day, but one of the things that kept her tethered was her sense of self and community — that she was a part of Black Bear Forge, and Black Bear Forge was a part of her. The way the people of Black Bear Forge looked after Lily Bishop, kept track of her, noticed when she looked confused, helped her find her way home when she needed it — all of those things had weighed on Rileigh's decision not to take her car keys.

It wasn't like there was any physical impairment at all. Lily could see and hear fine. It wasn't like she was some old lady who was likely to cause a wreck. It was just the niggling fear Rileigh always had when Mama left the house that she'd decide to go to Nashville or some other absurd thing and wind up getting lost there. It had never happened, but Rileigh knew that whether it happened or not was not the point; the fear of it happening was enough, the possibility was enough, and she needed to put on her big boy pants and tell her mother that she shouldn't drive anymore. All of that went through her head when she saw the empty space behind the house where Mama's car should have been parked.

Jillian agreed with Rileigh but abdicated to Rileigh the task of giving Mama the news. Why couldn't Jillian do it? They'd never talked about it and probably needed to, but Rileigh knew in her heart that it would be *her* who had to perform the difficult task. She had assumed the leadership role in the house while Jillian was gone, and Jillian's return had changed nothing in that regard. Jillian might have been the older sister, but when the rubber met the road, it was Rileigh who was in charge.

They went into the house, carried in the groceries in, and were putting things away when Rileigh heard the crunch of gravel under tires and knew Mama was home. She chastened herself for her wild fears. Wherever Mama had gone, she hadn't been there long enough to get into any trouble and had come right home.

Jillian had gone upstairs to her room, and Rileigh was still in the kitchen when she heard the back door open. She didn't look up, just said, "Where you been, Mama?"

Mama didn't answer.

"Hello, Rileigh girl, how are you?" said another voice, huskier than Mama's, rougher sounding.

Rileigh almost choked. She sucked in a breath, her head snapped up, and she stared at her aunt's ugly face in disbelief and horror. What in the hell was Aunt Daisy doing here?

She was about to ask that very question when Mama stepped in behind Aunt Daisy with a smile on her face as bright as sunrise on Easter Sunday morning.

"Look who's got out to come to your wedding," Mama said. "Ain't you thrilled?"

Rileigh was feeling a lot of emotions at that point but thrilled was not among them. She suddenly realized where Mama had been. She had gone out to the Carrington House and somehow managed to get her sister out of the psych ward there.

"Mama, what is Aunt Daisy doing here?"

"I just told you, Sugar, she's coming to the wedding on Saturday." Rileigh's head was spinning, and she was having trouble focusing on Mama's babble, about how she had gone to the director of the Carrington House, a nice young man who was just acting as the director until they could hire a new one, and she'd asked that Aunt Daisy be granted a furlough.

"...for the wedding. So they released her into my custody."

"Who released her into your custody?" Rileigh said, the rage in her building. What kind of moron released a homicidal maniac into the custody of an old woman with dementia?

"Was you listening to a thing I said? There was this young man, Dr. Einstein, and—"

"Einstein? *Dr.* Einstein? Who the hell's—?"

"*Eck*stein. I told you that, too. He's the interim director. They've done gone through two or three bosses out there in the last little while. He's the one in charge now."

Right. Some dudes from Away From Here, who didn't know jack shit about the patients or the community, had sent in some equally clueless jackass who had no idea that Daisy Gillespie needed to be locked up away from the world for the rest of her life.

Through all the exchange between Rileigh and Mama, Aunt Daisy had remained silent. She merely stood there with a placid, benign look on her face and a half-smile. When she finally spoke, her voice was even and had a hollow sound to it, like an automated attendant telling you not to leave your luggage unattended in the airport or it might be removed per NSA regulations.

"Who is it you're gettin' married to?" Aunt Daisy asked.

"You know damn well who I'm marrying. Mitch Webster, the sheriff."

What she didn't say was "the sheriff who shot you to keep you from cutting my head off with a chainsaw." She almost did but figured that Mama had forgotten all about that and there didn't seem to be any really good reason to bring it back into her mind.

Jillian! Oh dear God, Jillian. What would Jillian do when she saw Aunt Daisy? She had not set eyes on the old woman since she was an eighteen-year-old on the day before her wedding and Aunt Daisy tricked her and sold her to sex traffickers who held her captive for almost thirty years. It was Aunt Daisy who had stolen Jillian's life, Aunt Daisy who had been having an affair with their father, sleeping with her sister's husband and sold off Jillian so she couldn't go to the police and report that she had caught her father molesting Georgia. It was all so dirty and tawdry and ugly, nothing that Rileigh wanted to think about right now and certainly Jillian didn't, not right before she got married and yet Mama had brought the monster here to—

"Aunt Daisy."

The words came from the kitchen door leading into the

dining room, and they all turned to see Jillian standing there. Her face was chalky white except for two red spots on her cheeks. That blue vein in her temple that throbbed when she was upset was pulsing, her eyes were narrowed to slits, and Rileigh was sure she was grinding her teeth.

"What in the *fuck* are *you* doing here?" Jillian asked.

"Why, Jillian Ann Bishop!" Mama exclaimed, horrified. "I never heard you use language like that!"

"I asked you a question, Aunt Daisy. What in the fuck are you doing here?"

"Why, I'm going to your wedding, Sugar. Yours and Rileigh's. Lily come and got me out because she knew you'd want me to be there. It's a family event I wouldn't miss for the world."

"The last time I saw you, you lied to me, tricked me into going to a garage in Knoxville where you said the owner would help me start a brand-new life." Jillian was walking slowly toward Aunt Daisy as she spoke, her hands bawling into fists, violence in her eyes. "And I *believed* you. I believed your lies right up until that man locked me in a room for two days and raped me!"

Mama gasped. "What are you sayin', child?" Mama was absolutely horrified, her face a mask of disbelief and disgust … and fear. Tears filled her eyes and instantly streamed down her cheeks. "What are you talking about?" She was so shocked she could barely summon enough breath to speak. "What do you mean she lied to you, tricked you? What would she do a thing like that for?"

Oh, I don't know, Rileigh thought. Maybe because she was screwing her sister's husband and was trying to protect the revolting pedophile from the police.

Mama began to tremble all over, her body vibrating. She looked desperately from her sister to her daughter and back to her sister, shaking her head, "no."

"Tell her that ain't true, Daisy. Tell her that didn't happen. It didn't happen … did it? *Did* it?"

Mama's voice was high and shrill, fueled by incipient hysteria. "No, no, it can't be true. No." Then the dam broke and she burst into tears and buried her face in her hands, her whole body wracked by wrenching sobs.

Everyone else in the room stood rock still, frozen in place. The only sound was Mama's horrified, dejected sobbing. Rileigh rushed to her and put her arm around her mother's shoulders, but her mother pushed her away roughly and looked at Jillian.

"Now you tell me what you're talking about, tell me what you're saying." Mama was crying so hard she could barely speak. "You never said what happened the night you left here and I ain't never asked. Well, I'm asking now. Tell me! Did Daisy have something to do with it?"

Jillian's face, which had been a mask of rage, of suppressed fury, began to crumple as she looked at her mother, sobbing. Jillian's eyes met Rileigh's — pleading with her to do something, say something. But Rileigh had no idea what to say. Jillian had every right to hate her Aunt Daisy. She had every right to punch the old bitch in the face. She had every right to grab her by the hair and drag her out to the car and haul her ass back to the Carrington House. She had every right to …

But they had never told Mama any of it. What for? So she could be standing here like she was now, sobbing, her heart broken? They never told her the role Aunt Daisy had played in Jillian's disappearance, never told Mama that her own husband was screwing her sister and molesting her daughter's best friend — and had molested Jillian, too, for years. There'd been no reason to. At the time, the truth of what was going on had been veiled in secrets and lies, and Rileigh remembered how fragile Mama was then — after her daughter vanished and her husband committed suicide. Grief had scraped her nerves so raw that even the kindest word sounded like a scream and the gentlest touch like a blow. Mama would not have survived knowing the truth then.

Mama lifted her face out of her hands and rushed to her older daughter, grabbed her by the shoulders and shook her. "You tell me what's going on. You hear me? What are you talking about?"

Through it all, Daisy had stood in the kitchen as stiff and unmoving as a mannequin, her face a complete blank. And it occurred to Rileigh then that maybe Daisy didn't know what Jillian was talking about. She had had a complete mental collapse, two or three of them as a matter of fact. She'd had electric shock treatments, was on a cocktail of drugs treating her various mental conditions. Maybe she didn't even know. Jillian stood frozen, looking down into the anguished face of her devastated mother. And then she pulled the old woman into a hug, kissing the top of her head and patting her on the back.

"It's okay, Mama. Don't cry. It's okay. Everything's going to be just fine."

"But what you said, what—?"

"It was ... just a game Aunt Daisy and I used to play. Don't you remember? We played it all the time. One of us ... picks a movie, a scene from a movie and we ... act it out ... repeat the dialogue. The first person who breaks character loses. I was so shocked to see her, I just ... I thought it'd be fun to surprise her so I could win the game and ... I didn't think, you know, that somebody might think it was real."

The lie was so absurd and unbelievable, there was no possible way Mama would fall for it.

"It's all a big misunderstanding, Mama," Jillian continued. Jillian's eyes flicked to Daisy's face, looking for some spark of understanding or recognition there — but found only the blank stare of incomprehension. Maybe she really didn't remember.

"Everything's all right, Mama. I'm sorry I upset you. I didn't mean to. Calm down." Mama was still shaking and crying, inconsolable. "Just ... think about *the wedding.* Rileigh and I are both getting *married* on Saturday — remember." Those words penetrated, Mama looked up into Jillian's face, longing for her to be telling the truth. "We have all kinds of wedding things we need to do, Mama." Jillian gently pushed a strand of Mama's hair back behind her ear. Then Rileigh saw Jillian swallow hard as she gestured toward their Aunt Daisy. "I'm" — she almost choked on the word — "*glad* you brought Aunt Daisy home to help. We can use another set of hands."

Rileigh looked at her sister's face, at the tears streaming down. What Jillian had just done was the most sacrificial act she'd ever witnessed.

Chapter Seventeen

MITCH STOOD ON THE HILLSIDE LOOKING DOWN ON THE Breezy Creek Recreation area at all the people hurrying around below him, each with an important task they had to do. He was paying particular attention, of course, to anybody he didn't recognize, and there were lots of people he didn't recognize, but after all, he was not a true local. He was, at his core, an away-from-here who been working all day every day for months to change that draft status.

His phone rang, and he pulled it out and looked at the screen. The number identified merely as the Carrington House.

"Hello, this is Sheriff Webster."

"Sheriff Webster, this is Dr. Gunther Eckstein. I haven't had the pleasure of meeting you yet, but I'm the new interim director of the Carrington House."

Mitch had heard a lot of scuttlebutt about what was going on at the Carrington House. Some real shakeup in management. The company that had owned it had sold it out to another company who had come in to clean house and make it more efficient. They'd wound up firing a fairly substantial number of people before the new director, hell-bent on dragging the old sanitarium out of its unprofitable status, had gotten canned. Then they'd brought in someone else, and he'd only lasted a week. Mitch didn't know if this guy was interim director number two or some higher number, perhaps more than one more than perhaps there were more interim directors that Mitch hadn't heard about.

"What can I do for you Dr. Eckstein?" Mitch said.

"Actually, I'm simply calling you with an official notification."

"Notification of what?"

"I'm notifying you that one of our compulsory residents is out on compassionate leave with an ankle bracelet."

Mitch understood what he was saying, but had never heard of the Carrington House allowing "compulsive residents" — now there was a euphemism for "legally incarcerated," or "involuntarily committed" he hadn't heard — to set foot off the grounds of the sanitarium. The "compulsive residents" had been committed against their will for various reasons that ranged from fear that they would harm themselves or others to the fact that they already had harmed others. The Carrington House was the east Tennessee repository for the criminally insane. How did someone who had been judged by a court to be criminally insane walk out of the facility with an ankle bracelet?

All of that went through Mitch's head as his eyes continued to search the strangers he saw doing various tasks on the grounds below.

"How does a patient who's been legally committed to your institution get a 'compassionate leave'?" Far as Mitch knew, prison inmates didn't get furloughs.

The man took instant offense.

"Are you questioning my judgment about my patients?"

"It was just a simple question."

But Mitch had this guy's number now. It had been Mitch's life experience that anybody who took offense at nothing was someone who feared that you'd find out something they had really done that you should take offense at. Someone so insecure that they expected opposition and attacked in a preemptive strike.

"I'm sorry, Dr. Eckstein, we seemed to have a miscommunication. I'm just asking how someone who's been placed in your care by the courts can just walk away. "

"It is done on a case-by-case basis and depends on the diagnosis of the patient and the best clinical decision of the doctor caring for that patient."

"Oh," Mitch said. He saw Bill Covell, who was a lineman for the electric company, coming up out of the amphitheater toward him, walking purposefully.

"Since this particular patient was remanded to the facility by the court system, I am required to make the local law enforcement officials aware that the patient is in their jurisdiction, wearing an ankle bracelet. Which will notify us at the Carrington House if they leave the vicinity."

"All right, fine. Thank you for your—"

"The patient's name is Daisy Gillespie."

Mitch felt like someone had kicked him in the belly. "Whoa, whoa, wait a minute, Daisy Gillespie?"

"Yes, She is 79 years old, and she was committed to the Carrington House—"

Mitch interrupted. "I know why she was committed to the Carrington House. I was the officer who shot her to keep her from cutting off someone's head with a chainsaw."

"Oh," came the response from the other end. "I was unaware that you were personally involved."

"Oh, I'm personally involved all right. Daisy Gillespie is the aunt of my fiancée, and she's a *dangerous* old woman, totally batshit crazy."

"'Batshit crazy' is not a term we use to medically identify a mental disorder," Dr. Eckstein said, gleefully assuming the position of King of the Mountain on the moral high ground. "Daisy Gillespie is on various medications that control her behavior and her thought processes. She has been in therapy constantly since she was remanded into our care and has been treated with electroshock—"

"You don't have to tell me what Aunt Daisy has been treated with. I just want to know why you are letting her out and who's supervising her."

"Her sister, a Mrs. — uh, just a minute and I'll find her—"

"Her name's Lily Bishop," Mitch told him.

"Yes, yes. A Mrs. Lily Bishop requested the compassionate leave so that the patient could attend the wedding of her niece on Saturday. The furlough is of limited duration, beginning this morning and she will have to be returned by nine a.m. Sunday morning."

"You mean you've already let her go?" Mitch was stupefied.

"She was remanded into the custody of her sister, Lily Bishop."

"Who has dementia! Surely to God you picked up that when you talked to her. She believes she's dating the Dalai Lama."

His words hit the thin-skinned doctor like a drip of water in hot grease.

"Are you questioning my medical judgment? I'll have

you know I am a certified..." He continued to babble, but Mitch tuned him out as Bill drew closer, obviously with something to say.

Finally, Mitch cut the doctor off. "Look, so you're telling me that Daisy Gillespie is out, has been released from the Carrington House — is that right?"

"With an ankle bracelet."

"Released into the custody of Lily Bishop. And she's already left the Carrington House so there's no stopping it, right?"

"I was led to believe that there would be a large contingent of law enforcement officers present at the event."

"Oh, the place will be broke out with deputies."

"I have therefore discharged my duty to notify—"

"I don't have time to discuss how you have discharged your official duties right now, but we will talk later. You can take that to the bank, Dr. Eckstein. We *will* talk later."

Then Mitch disconnected.

He needed to call Rileigh and warn her that her mother had checked Aunt Daisy out of the insane asylum so she could come to the wedding.

Dear Lord, what would Jillian do when she saw her? He punched favorites on his phone and then looked up to find Will Covell standing in front of him.

"Listen, you said to say something if you saw something?" Mitch didn't punch the number. Just slipped the phone quickly back into his pocket.

"What did you see?"

"It ain't much."

"You don't have to explain or apologize. Anything. Anything out of the ordinary. That's what I told you. What did you see?"

"Well, there's this guy, one of the carpenters working on the raised part of the stage. I think that's where they're going to have a dance floor during the reception, maybe."

"And what did you see?"

"Well, he's just a carpenter but … but he's got this big bulge in his pocket, his hip pocket. And I swear, Mitch, it's the shape of a gun."

"Thanks, Bill. I'll check it out."

"Look, if you don't find anything…"

"I appreciate that you told me, either way. Please continue to keep your eyes open. If this one doesn't pan out, it means the guy's still out there."

Bill pointed to the man he was describing, a small Hispanic man. Mitch hurried down the steps to the amphitheater, crossed the stage area to the back, and hopped off onto the ground behind the man Bill had pointed out. The man glanced over his shoulder, when he saw Mitch, but continued to work.

"I'd like to talk to you," Mitch said.

The man stopped hammering and turned to look at him. He seemed nervous. "Sure, Sheriff," he said in heavily accented English.

"Down here." Mitch gestured for the man to jump off the stage to the ground beside him. The man tensed. "Keep your hands where I can see them."

"Did I do something?"

"Get down here."

The man hopped off the stage to stand on the ground beside Mitch.

"Now, turn around and put your hands on that stage and lean over."

"But I—"

"Just do it."

The man put both hands on the stage in front of him and put his weight on his hands. Mitch reached up and patted him down, and found the large bulge in his hip pocket that Bill had noticed. Reaching into the pocket, Mitch pulled out a gun-shaped object. It was an electric screwdriver.

Mitch let out a sigh.

"Okay, pal, you can straighten up."

"What's this all about? What's going on?"

"We are looking for a suspect in a crime," Mitch told him. "And you had a suspicious gun-shaped lump in your hip pocket."

"That's all?"

"That's all." The relief on the man's face was palpable. "Sorry to have troubled you, sir."

Mitch turned on his heel and walked away, certain that the carpenter was an illegal alien who thought he had just gotten busted.

Reaching into his pocket as he walked, he pulled out his phone, saw that he actually had two bars of service, and touched favorites — and almost ran into Joe Hardesty, who was suddenly standing in front of him.

"Joe, hello. Do you need—?"

"Mitch, that guy who says he's the videographer, he's a fake."

Mitch put his phone back into his pocket. "What are you talking about, Joe?"

"I'm telling you, he doesn't know what he's doing."

"And you know that … how?"

"My brother-in-law side-jobs videoing weddings and I go along sometimes to help. Ray spends every second fully focused on capturing the moment, totally concentrating. That was the first thing I noticed about the videographer here … he was looking around, watching what people were doing, not paying any attention to the things he ought to be shooting. The rule is: get the images. You don't have to use everything you shoot, but you can't use something you didn't shoot."

Mitch wasn't sure a little bit of inattention constituted dereliction of duty as a videographer, but Joe wasn't finished.

"All professional wedding videographers use a 3-axis gimbal to keep their shots smooth and stabilized. It's got a name, a DJI RS3, I think, and it's a common tool of the trade. The guy here has one … but he doesn't have a clue how to use it. I watched him fumble around, trying to balance his camera on it, and the camera was flipping and flopping around. I'm telling you, Mitch, that videographer is a fake."

"I'll check it out, Joe. Thanks."

Mitch turned around, looking for the videographer. He'd seen him earlier with his camera, but now he couldn't locate him. He began walking the grounds and saw Marshal Dylan coming down from the parking lot toward him.

"I got in some information on those DNA samples," the marshal said. "The first, the finger bone, was a Russian mafia hit, could easily have been El Viento. But nothing on the DNA from the piece of skin from Santiago Suárez — still haven't recovered his body. But he was a bagman for organized crime in Chicago, so go figure."

"I just got a tip on the videographer, that there's something hinky about him," Mitch said. "You seen him?"

"I saw some guy with a video camera up by the restrooms as I was coming down."

The marshal and Mitch turned and walked together toward the bank of restrooms at the top of the hill.

"How is the saw-something/say-something working out?"

"I've had several tips. I think people really are being

watchful. But what are the odds the killer would do something that looks suspicious? And that somebody would notice when he did? I hope this tip pans out better than the others."

"Is that why you look like somebody pissed in your Cheerios?"

Mitch cast a sidelong glance at the federal marshal.

"I'll tell you the story of Daisy Gillespie when I have the time, but I just found out that Rileigh's crazy aunt — as in committed to a psychiatric hospital nuts — has been furloughed to come to the wedding."

"Goody," the marshal said.

They got to the building containing the bathrooms, went to the door marked "Men's" and Mitch drew his weapon. With it pointed toward the ground, he shoved the door inward and called out, "Anybody in here?"

There was nothing but silence. Mitch and the marshal stepped into the room, which had three urinals along the wall facing them and four stalls along the wall to their right. Lying in the middle of the floor beside a broken video camera was a man with curly blond hair He had a thin knife, a stiletto, sticking out of his right eye.

And he was naked, his clothes scattered all over the bathroom.

Chapter Eighteen

THE MAN IN THE GRAY UNIFORM JUMPED WHEN MASON Stump asked him the question, acted like Mason had poked him in the side with a cattle prod. Then he looked down at Mason and smiled, and Mason knew right then and there that this was one of those grownups who didn't like kids.

Almost-five-year-old Mason Stump was good at figuring out things like that. He knew when grownups were just being nice and acting like they liked little kids but didn't really. There were grownups who really did like little kids. He knew lots of them. He was pretty sure Aunt Rileigh didn't like kids in general, but she really loved him.

Mason was surprised that the big man in the uniform didn't like little kids. Most everybody he'd ever met in a uniform liked kids. Sheriff Mitch did. And all of his deputies did. And the man who had come to the school to talk to the class about being careful with matches and fire because you could start a forest fire. He'd been wearing a gray uniform, green jacket, and stupid-looking flat-brimmed hat like this man, but he had liked kids.

This man didn't.

"Yes, it is, son," the uniformed man said with that smile on his face that was just hanging there. "It's a real gun."

"Can I hold it?"

Mason knew the man was going to say no. He often asked Sheriff Mitch if he could see his gun. And he always said no. But it was worth a shot. And Mason would dearly love to hold a real, no-kidding pistol in his hands. Oh, he had held rifles. His daddy took his older brothers out squirrel hunting sometimes and said that when Mason was a big boy he could go, too. But Mason wasn't a big boy yet. So he had to settle for asking men in uniform if he could see their guns even though he knew they'd say no.

"No, you can't hold it. It's loaded. Guns are dangerous."

"Are you a policeman?"

"No, I'm a park ranger."

The man was clearly annoyed by the questions, but Mason kept asking anyway.

"A ranger? Like the Lone Ranger — that guy in those old back-and-white movies Mommy watches? He wears a mask. Not a mask to keep from coughing out germs, but a mask around his eyes, makes him look like a raccoon."

"Don't you have somewhere you're supposed to be?" the ranger-man asked, obviously trying to get rid of him. "I bet your Mommy's looking for you."

The man didn't wait for Mason to answer, just turned away and returned to watching people. That's why Mason had surprised the man, because he had been just standing there, studying, looking really hard at everybody, all the workers who were running around, as Mommy said, like chickens with their heads cut off, getting ready for Aunt Rileigh's and Aunt Jillian's wedding. And he had been concentrating so hard on looking at those people that he hadn't noticed when Mason crawled out from under the table he was standing next to.

Mason was having a wonderful time crawling around under tables. Today was a good day. Mommy was so busy doing so many wedding things that she told Mason to run along and play and then didn't come looking for him five minutes later to see where he'd gone. There was nowhere to get into any really bad trouble, he didn't suppose, at the Breezy Creek Recreation Area. And everybody was so busy, nobody was interested in what Mason was doing. The ranger man sure wasn't. He wasn't busy doing something, he was busy watching everybody else doing something. Maybe he was looking for bad guys. There wouldn't be any bad guys here, though — just people getting ready for a wedding. Those weren't people who robbed other people, or maybe set fires on purpose. There couldn't be any of those people here. So Mason didn't know why the man was so intent on watching all the people who were working.

The ranger man was watching a man carrying a bag, walking down from the building at the top of the hill where the bathrooms were. He didn't even notice when Mason crawled back under the table and went on looking for gum. Workers were setting up tables here for a whoop-de-do, unfolding them and lining them up. These were old tables that'd been used for a lot of things, so it was easy to find pieces of gum that people had stuck there.

Mommy would turn him over her knee and bust his little butt if she knew he was pulling gum off the bottom of tables and chewing it. But Mommy wouldn't let him and his brothers have chewing gum. She said it wasn't good for their teeth. But he knew the real reason was that a long time ago Eli had put a big piece of it Mayella's hair and Mommy had to cut her hair off to get it out and she was real mad.

Mason crawled to the end of the table and stood up, looked back at the park ranger who was watching the man who'd come down the hill. He had stopped at one of the tables and was taking pieces of equipment out of a bag, the same kind of equipment Mason's Uncle Jody used. Mason paused in his gum search to see what was so interesting about the guy but he couldn't figure it out. Maybe if he got closer. So he got back down on his hands and knees and crawled under the next table, but he stopped halfway down the table when he found a big hunk of dried-as-a-rock chewing gum. It wasn't easy to get old chewing gum off the bottom of a table. Usually, he couldn't because it was as hard and stuck there tight like it had been put there with super glue. But if he could get the gum off... He kept tugging. Maybe he could borrow one of the hammers the carpenters were using, bang on the piece of gum and knock it off. No, he couldn't do that. Grownups would hear him banging around and look under the table to see what he was doing. It was a whole lot easier to hide under the tables after they put the tablecloths on them. But even now, nobody looked so he was pretty safe, just couldn't make a bunch of noise with a hammer.

Finally giving up on the big piece of hard gum, he remembered that he had been going to get closer to the man the ranger man was watching to see what was so interesting about him. He crawled the whole length of the table, and under the next one. When he got halfway down the length of the third table, he figured he was near where the man unloading equipment was standing. Sure enough, he could see his pants legs and his shoes.

And there was something on the top of his shoe, on the laces on the top. A big glob of red, like paint or maybe fingernail polish. The glob was as big as a quarter, and there were drips of red on the toe of his shoe, too, but nowhere else. It must be paint. No, fingernail polish. Mommy had some fingernail polish exactly that color. But if the man had spilled fingernail polish, he must have spilled the whole bottle of it on his shoe 'cause there wasn't much polish in those little bottles. Mason crawled a little closer, to get a better look. The fingernail polish was still wet. It was just on his left shoe, not his right.

Suddenly, Mason spotted a big piece of gum, stuck to the table right above his head. He reached up, tried to pull it off. It wasn't dried out, hard as a rock, and a piece of it came off in his hand.

"Maaaaaason, Mason Stump, where are you?"

Mommy was calling him. He popped the piece of gum in his mouth, chewed and chewed to get it soft.

"Mason, come here to me this minute." She was closer now, and Mason needed to get out from under the table before she caught him there because she'd know what he'd been doing. He sighed and spit the gum out onto the ground and crawled back the way he'd come to the far end of the table.

The day of the whoop-de-do, there'd be tablecloths on these tables. And it'd be easy to hide then. He could spend as long as he wanted looking, and it'd be easier to pry the gum off if he had a spoon or a fork to use.

He crawled out from under the end of the table and turned toward where he'd heard his mother's voice, casting a glance back at the man who had fingernail polish on his shoe. He could see the man clearly. Mason looked at the equipment on the table. He knew what it was for, though it made no sense to him why the man was putting it all back in his bag when he'd just taken it all out. Mason couldn't see anything interesting enough about the man that the ranger man was watching him. Then the man glanced down and must have seen the polish on his shoe. He lifted his right foot and used the sole of it to scrub the goo off the top of his left shoe. He scrubbed back and forth. Mason didn't know if that would get it all off, but it would smear it, mix it with dirt so it wasn't shiny red anymore. Now, nobody would notice it.

Chapter Nineteen

MITCH STOOD LOOKING DOWN AT THE BODY SPREAD-EAGLED on the floor in the men's bathroom in front of the urinal It appeared to him that the arms and legs were splayed out at odd angles, like somebody moved them after the guy was dead. It had been an almost bloodless death. Mitch would have to wait until Gus made a formal ruling on the cause of death, of course, but it was obvious to him that it was the wound to his left eye. That was the only mark on him, and if there had been any other wounds on him anywhere, they would have been on full display as if the body lay there on the floor. It appeared to Mitch that someone had gotten close enough to the man to stab something — a switchblade, a stiletto, an ice pick, shoot, even a pencil — into his left eye and through into his brain. He would have died instantly and would have bled very little. There was blood on the left side of his face and cheek, running down and dripping, but there wasn't much of it.

The body being stripped was what confused Mitch. Was this a sex crime?

Marshal Dylan came up beside Mitch and stood looking down at the body with him.

"So somebody kills this guy and then takes his clothes off — why?" Marshal Dylan said.

"Ya got me," Mitch said, leaning into a mountain accent.

"I think I might know a reason."

The voice came from the doorway behind them, and Mitch turned around to see Sundeep Singh standing there. "I told the deputy that I needed to talk to you, and he let me through." Sundeep's eyes went to the body on the floor, flitted across it, and then locked on Mitch's face, clearly unnerved by the nude corpse.

"Did Deputy Mullins not tell you that there was a body in here?" Mitch asked him.

"Oh, he told me, said I should wait. But I really needed to talk to you about something important." He glanced again at the body and away again. "More important now than when I got here."

Mitch noticed then the pale cast to Sundeep's olive skin and the dark circles under his eyes.

"How you doing, man? I heard you had a kidney stone."

"I did," he said. "Never had one before and this one was particularly ugly, or so the doctor said. I need to go in and have a lithotripsy before one of the smaller ones floating around in there decides to take a header."

"Lithotripsy?" asked Marshal Dylan.

"It's where they shoot radio waves or something through you into your kidneys to shatter the kidney stones before they cause a problem."

Mitch turned to the Marshal. "This is my friend, Sundeep Singh. He's running for mayor."

"Mayor? I haven't seen any of your signs," Dylan said.

With the election three weeks away, political signs were, as Mama put it, "thicker'n ticks on an old dog" in Yarmouth County. Trump/Vance. Harris/Walz. Blackburn/Johnson for senator, along with half a dozen other state races and almost as many local ones.

"I don't do signs. People know——"

"That he's a nice guy," Mitch finished for him. "Unlike the current mayor, who is a jackass."

"I wish you luck, I guess. I hear holding an elected office is only slightly less painful than passing a kidney stone."

Sundeep's eyes kept straying to the body on the floor.

"So tell me why you think you might know why somebody killed this guy and then took his clothes off," Mitch said.

"Maybe because they were looking for a tattoo."

"Somebody killed him to see his tattoos?"

Marshal Dylan's eyes fixed on Sundeep. "What kind of tattoo?"

"A tattoo of numbers."

"Are you enjoying being obscure?" Mitch prodded.

Sundeep let out a sigh. "This morning I was noodling around on my computer. I don't spend a whole lot of time doing that. Too busy with the store and the campaign. But after the kidney stone yesterday, Miriam chained me to the bed, wouldn't let me go in to work until noon. And that's why I happened to come upon a site I've never seen before." He paused. "On the dark web."

"You hang out on the dark web?" Marshal Dylan asked.

"Nope. And I certainly don't hang out in the kind of chat room I stumbled into today."

"What kind of chat room?"

"It was called 'Beyond Here Be Dragons.'"

"What does this chatroom have to do with this guy laying here buck naked?" Mitch asked.

"Maybe nothing," Sundeep replied quietly. "Maybe everything."

Then he explained what he had found in the chat room named Beyond Here Be Dragons — the "catch me if you can" post by someone whose screen name was El Viento, the offer of a reward to anyone who killed him and found on him the tattoo with the numbers to a Swiss bank account.

"That can't be real," Mitch said.

"Sounds like some kind of prank to me, probably a bunch of teenagers doing some role-playing game," said the marshal.

"Oh, I wouldn't have taken it for real if it hadn't been for what else was there, a picture that was uploaded with the post. It was a photograph of a newspaper clipping."

Sundeep only paused for a breath before he continued, but in that instant Mitch felt like he had been kicked in the belly with a pointed-toe cowboy boot. He *knew* what was on that newspaper clipping. From the shocked look on the marshal's face, he suspected the same thing.

"The clipping was the announcement in the *Black Bear Forge Gazette* of your wedding on Saturday, the one that has pictures of you and Rileigh, Jillian, and David. I figured the clipping was there as an invitation, or more like a challenge — 'catch me if you can' *at this wedding*."

Sundeep took out his phone then and showed Mitch and the federal marshal the screenshot he had taken of the chatroom.

Mitch managed not to visibly respond, or at least he thought he did, but he felt like the world was spinning around and around too fast, and he couldn't manage to run fast enough to catch it and hop on.

150

"That's what I meant when I said I thought I might know why this guy didn't have any clothes on."

"You think maybe somebody killed this guy because they thought he was the guy who posted on that site," the marshal said. It wasn't a question. "Killed him and took his clothes off, looking for the tattoo."

Sundeep shrugged. "That would certainly explain why he's lying here in his birthday suit."

The marshal looked at Mitch. "So somebody pegged this guy for El Viento."

"Who *is* El Viento?" Sundeep asked.

Mitch's world was still spinning. "A man with a tattoo, apparently," he said, shaking his head.

"*That* certainly narrows it down." Sundeep pointed to the tattoo on his own left forearm, an ornate design in blue and red ink. "And this is just the one you can see."

"I'm not touching *that* line," Mitch countered.

"Nowhere interesting — a Navy insignia on my chest."

No one spoke for a moment.

"Well, besides the bird on his shoulder, this guy doesn't have any other tattoos you can see," Marshal Dylan pointed out. "At least not with the *naked* eye."

Mitch had never met a lawman who didn't indulge in black humor.

"I plan to let Gus be the one to confirm that," Mitch said.

Chapter Twenty

Gus Hazelton made his way past Deputy Rawlings, whom Mitch had stationed at the door to the restrooms to keep the curious out of the area until the ambulance crew could be summoned to take the body away.

"What have we got here?" Gus asked, then nodded hello to Sundeep and the marshal.

"Dead body," Mitch answered, as if it weren't obvious.

"A buck-naked dead body," Gus said, "in case you didn't notice that part." He crossed to the body and then walked slowly around it, his eyes taking in everything.

"Noticed, noted … and I might even have an explanation."

"Hmmm, I'm interested to hear that part."

Gus was in info-gathering mode now, though, and Mitch kept his mouth shut. Mitch had sometimes fantasized about crawling inside Gus's head, just for an hour or two, to watch his mind at work. Your basic fly-on-a-wall fantasy. Mitch was absolutely certain that though he had looked carefully at the body, Gus would inevitably find things he didn't see, notice things he had missed, or had noticed and dismissed, and come up with conclusions that Mitch probably would have gotten to eventually. Or maybe not.

The body was lying face up, and Gus squatted down on one knee beside it. He took out a ballpoint pen from his pocket and used it to straighten out the fingers on the right hand.

"We have a musician among us," Gus said. "Plays the bass or the harp, I'd say."

"The guy plays the harp?" Mitch almost choked.

"The calluses on his fingers."

Mitch hadn't even noticed there were calluses on the man's fingers.

Marshal Dylan knelt and pointed out the tattoo on the man's shoulder — a bird of prey with a rabbit in its talons.

"Besides this tattoo of an eagle, he might have another, more important tattoo on his body somewhere, but Mitch said he'd let you go looking for it."

"That's not an eagle, it's a hawk."

"Looks like an eagle to me," the marshal said. "You sure?"

Mitch shook his head sadly. Yeah, Gus was sure. As the marshal was about to find out.

"The easiest way to tell the difference between an eagle and a hawk is size," Gus said, not looking at the marshal, his words on autopilot as his eyes continued to scan the body and the area around it. "An eagle is considerably larger, with a wingspan that can reach seven feet. An eagle is stronger, too, with a sharper beak and talons. But from just this image, you can see the difference in their structure. Hawks have long and sharp-pointed wings, whereas eagles have wide wings rounded on the ends." Gus tapped the tattoo, then, as he continued. "This is a northern goshawk, not a red-tailed hawk. A northern goshawk has a wide body" — he gestured to the bird's chest — "and its tail feathers don't extend out any wider than its body, see?" The tail feathers were not, indeed, wider than the body. "A red-tailed hawk's body is thinner, and its tail feathers fan out." He gestured, spreading his fingers wide apart. "And a red tail hawk's wings extend straight out from behind the bird's head, whereas a northern goshawk's wings" — he pointed to the spot where the wings were connected to the bird — "are positioned farther down on the torso."

No one else spoke. The marshal let out a breath. "All righty then," he said. "Hawk for the win."

Gus turned to Mitch, oblivious to the affect his expertise had had on his listeners. "So what is your explanation for this man's current state of un-dress?"

Mitch nodded to Sundeep Singh. "Not mine, Sundeep's."

"Hope you're feeling better," Gus said. "You might want to think about getting a lithotripsy — kidney stones suck."

"Tell Gus what you found on the dark web this morning."

Sundeep described the Beyond Here Be Dragons chat room that he found and the post there.

Marshal Dylan answered the question Sundeep had asked before Gus arrived.

"El Viento is a renowned assassin who's wanted all over the world. He's called El Viento, which means the wind, because no one knows what he looks like, where he lives. He comes and goes and leaves no trace."

"Killers always leave a trace," Gus said, more to himself than to anyone else. "You just have to find it."

Sundeep continued his story, pointed out that the post had also included a picture of the wedding announcement that had been published in the *Gazette* of the wedding this

Saturday. He held out his phone with the screenshot. Gus took it, then patted his pockets before pulling out the evidence envelope the Marshal had given him last night. He compared the screenshot of the clipping to the real thing in the envelope. The jagged edge where it was torn out of the newspaper was the same on both.

Gus studied the screenshot and looked up. "One of the guys who responded to the post — his screen name's 'Nighthawk.'" He gestured toward the tattoo on the man's shoulder of a hawk-not-an-eagle.

Mitch hadn't put that together yet.

"Do we have any idea who this guy is?" Gus asked.

Mitch pointed to the clothes scattered around on the floor that the murderer had taken off the naked man on the floor.

"I left them where they were. Didn't touch a thing. Figured you'd want pictures."

"Eight by ten glossies suitable for framing," Gus said, then proceeded to walk around and take pictures.

When he was finished, he went to the clothing and began to go through the pockets. Pulled out a wallet and opened it up.

"I'll still send this guy's prints off for an ID in case this is a fake driver's license, but if it's not, this man is Philip Aubrey Mason, 38 years old, 1282 112th Street, Chicago."

"So Philip Mason, screen name Nighthawk, was here looking for El Viento to collect the million-dollar prize, and one of the other killers thought Nighthawk was El Viento and clipped him," Mitch said.

"I'll buy the second half of that hypothesis — the part about another killer thinking he was El Viento, but the first part, not so much. You remember the finger bones that I sent off for DNA analysis?"

Mitch nodded.

"The man who had lost the finger that was sent to Rileigh was 36-year-old James Spencer Mason, aka Trey Mason, Fats Mason, and Fat Boy. And as I recall, he had a jacket as thick as a large print Bible and sealed juvie records dating back to 1997 when he would have been about nine years old."

"So you think Philip Mason and Fat Boy Mason…"

"Probably related, yeah, since they both live at the same address — 1282 112th Street, Chicago."

Mitch couldn't believe Gus remembered that.

"And you think he was looking for El Viento because El Viento offed his … what? Brother?"

"Cousin, uncle, grandpa … something."

"He was looking for revenge?"

"Yeah, but he wouldn't have stripped the corpse if the multi-million-dollar jackpot weren't a motivating factor, too."

"If we assume the guy missing his fingerprints and his head from the bachelor party was in on the hunt, that's two down," Marshal Dylan said.

"And four left," Gus added.

Mitch gestured toward the doorway.

"So we have four killers wandering around out there pretending to be carpenters or cake makers or photographers or wedding planners … and there's no way to pick them out."

"He's left-handed," Gus said, saw the questioning look on Mitch's face and continued. "Stiletto is in this guy's right eye. You'd definitely use your dominant hand to stab a guy in the eye. Right eye, left hand."

He paused.

"It's illegal to carry a concealed stiletto in California," Gus continued, for no reason other than it came to his mind. "In Texas, you can carry it any way you want — you can also carry an axe, hatchet, dirk, poniard, Bowie knife, or machete."

Mitch didn't know what a dirk or a poniard was but had the good judgment not to ask.

"And look for somebody with blood on his shoe," Gus said. Gesturing toward the almost bloodless crime scene, he continued, "The killer was standing in front of the victim when he killed him. Key word — *standing*. A sharp stick in the eye doesn't gush, but it does bleed some, and that blood *could* have dripped *down*, maybe landed on the top of the killer's shoe."

Chapter Twenty-One

EVERY SO OFTEN, RILEIGH WAS REMINDED WHY GEORGIA Stump was her best friend.

It wasn't just that they'd been friends for so long, and it certainly wasn't that their friendship had had such an auspicious beginning. Georgia had put gum in Rileigh's hair when they were in kindergarten, and Rileigh had punched her in the face for it.

It wasn't merely the shared experiences, though they had pretty much lived in each other's pockets all through school until Rileigh went to the military and Georgia got married and started pumping out babies. But even though their lives separated after high school, there was still that connection between them that was as strong as a piece of catgut and as translucent and delicate as a strand of a spider's web.

It didn't matter how long it had been since Rileigh and Georgia had spoken, whether the six months during which Rileigh was in Afghanistan and then in the hospital from her wounds, or the years when she was a Memphis police officer. When Rileigh was on the battlefield with bullets flying or chasing down bad guys and snapping cuffs on them, and, as she liked to think of it, "depriving them of their freedom in a significant fashion," Georgia had been having one baby after another, changing diapers, holding toddlers' hands while they learned to walk, teaching little kids to ride tricycles, and cleaning jelly off the table.

Through all of that, despite their wildly different lives, the moment they got together, the connections reconnected and they were as close as sisters, closer than most. Tonight was no exception.

Rileigh had been as mad as she'd ever been at Georgia for what Georgia had done to turn her small private wedding ceremony into a three-ring circus. But the thing was, you couldn't stay mad at Georgia Stump. It was impossible, and as Georgia flitted around her and Jillian, unloading the supplies from the trunk of their car into the back of the Methodist Church Fellowship Hall where the bachelorette party was set to begin, her cheeriness warmed Rileigh's heart in a way nothing else could. Not only was Georgia unflappable, she was indomitable; no matter what life threw at her, she wiped the mud off her face and came up smiling. She was having such a gloriously good time arranging this fairy-tale wedding — that any fool could see was what *she* wanted, rather than what *Rileigh* wanted — it was impossible not to have your own spirits lifted by hers.

A thing Rileigh had learned about Georgia in elementary school before their front teeth grew back in was that Georgia Stump was never content just to be happy. She had to make everybody near her happy too, and her bubbly chatter had done that for Rileigh on one occasion after another for their whole lives. Including now, as she was hauling in the box out of the trunk of her car that she said was a surprise.

Rileigh looked at Jillian, and Jillian rolled her eyes.

God only knew what kind of surprise Georgia had come up with. Then she opened up the box, and it was filled to the brim with stupid party favors.

There was a jar of screaming pickles. Little plastic pickles with faces drawn on them and their mouths open, and when you squeezed them, they made a horrible screaming sound.

There were swizzle sticks that had each of the brides-maids' pictures on them. There were medicine bottles containing hangover recovery kits — "fast-acting relief for lifelong memories." There were other medicine bottles containing crazy pills, know-it-all pills, dumbass pills, and...

Georgia pulled out of the box a pair of Groucho glasses and parked them on her nose. Jillian reached into the box and retrieved a pair of sunglasses, punched a button on the side, and lights flashed on the frame around the lenses.

There were also cowboy hats with flashing lights, giant suckers with high school pictures of all the girls on the wrappers, and at the very bottom was what Rileigh loved the most — dozens of small jars of Nutella that said "I love you" on the outside and had little wooden spoons taped to the lids, indicating you were supposed to eat the Nutella out of the jar.

Gus had insisted on footing the bill for the bachelorette party, as he had the bachelor party, paid to have all the food catered so the participants and attendees didn't have to lift a finger, just suit up and show up and have a good time. He'd even gone so far as to get a DJ. When Rileigh asked what they needed a DJ for in a party of only women, he shrugged and said, "Well, I'm assuming you girls are going to dance. You are, aren't you?"

"With each other?"

"You telling me you never danced with another girl?"

The wedding reception would have no DJ. Rileigh wasn't completely certain how the wedding reception differed from the mountain whoop-de-do. Were they the same group of people? They'd have to be — more or less — because there were a finite number of people in Yarmouth County. A Venn diagram, she supposed. The circles of "wedding reception people" and the circle of "whoop-de-do people," and where those two circles intersected were all the same people. It made her head throb to think about it.

Rileigh's mother had somehow found time to send out more than two hundred wedding invitations. Not fancy printed invitations — hand-written invitations on lined notebook paper, each with a personalized note.

My girls picked blue for the bridesmaids' dresses just like your Emma did.

Be sure to bring Granny — we got strong men can carry her wheelchair down the steps.

Please come! I ain't seen you in a month of Sundays!

Those people would be seated on the benches in the amphitheater, and the area on the floor of the amphitheater beyond where the ceremony would be conducted would be taken over by the Audrey and Hank Foote and their band the Foote Notes, who would provide music for the reception and for the dancing afterwards. So there would be dancing and clogging, an open bar, a lot of drinks ... and Rileigh and Mitch would be bowing out early, so she didn't really care what came after that.

The women who had been invited to the bachelorette party included, of course, all ten of the bridesmaids who were members of Rileigh's graduating class and had been pressed into service by Georgia, and fully twice that many other women who had just been invited to have a good time.

Rileigh found herself laughing and enjoying the evening, even though it was not the circumstance she had envisioned. It was glorious to see Georgia having such a good time. She walked up to her best friend, who had just told the story of how her oldest son Liam had pushed a nickel, not a penny or a dime, but a *nickel,* up his little brother Eli's nose, occasioning a trip to the emergency room when Rileigh gave Georgia an unexpected hug.

"What was that for?"

"For all this, what do you think?"

"Are you having fun?" Rileigh hated the anxiety she heard in Georgia's fun. "I mean, really having a good time?"

"Of course I am."

"Really?"

"Really."

Georgia let out a relieved sigh.

"You're certainly enjoying yourself," Rileigh said.

"Of course I am. I've got five kids — *at home.* Chigger's feeding them supper. Chigger is giving them baths. Chigger is reading them stories and putting them to bed, and Chigger is making sure Mayella has enough bananas to keep her mouth shut … and I'm *here.* What's not to like?"

Rileigh knew that she was going to have to rain on this parade, but she waited as long as she possibly could. The women laughed their way through dinner. The open bar was a magnet for her high school friends, and Rileigh knew that she'd best give her explanation of how her friends could help her before everybody got too drunk to understand what she was saying. She clacked her spoon on the side of her glass and hollered, "Ding, ding, ding, hey, can I talk to everybody for a minute?"

The general hubbub of conversation and laughter calmed, and the women all looked her way.

"Boy, do I hate to rain on this parade," Rileigh said. "I have to tell you something, and I need your help, and it's a downer."

"What could be a downer for you two days before your wedding?" asked one of the bridesmaids.

"The fact that somebody is trying to kill me before I get a chance to say, 'I do.'"

That was a conversation stopper.

At that point, Rileigh explained what was going on. She told her friends about the man who'd been stalking her all these months, and that he would be among the guests at the wedding and was probably hanging around through all the preparations for it.

"And since there will be so many strangers doing all manner of things in this enormous celebration of marriage that my best friend so kindly bestowed upon me" — she winked at Georgia to take the sting out of the remark — "the bottom line is that the stalker could be anybody. He could be the guy setting up the chairs. He could be the guy building the grape arbor. He could be the guy serving the drinks. He could be..." She let her words trail off. "He could be anybody, and Mitch and I don't have any way to catch him without your help."

Several of the women knew what was coming because they were the wives or sweethearts of the men who'd been at the bachelor party the night before and had already heard this spiel.

"It's like after 9/11. If you see something, say something. All I can ask is that you guys keep your eyes open. There will be strangers everywhere. Watch them. Mitch and I can't do it by ourselves, even though there's a federal marshal helping us who's looking for this guy, and Gus is on the lookout, and all the deputies, but still…"

"And all the groomsmen," somebody called out.

"Yes, and all the groomsmen. But we need everybody. Please, if you see anything odd, anything at all, tell a deputy, tell me, tell Mitch, tell Gus. Just don't ignore it."

The came the questions.

"Odd like what?"

"Odd how?"

"Odd as in out of place. The only way the stalker could be here is if he's pretending to be somebody who has a right to be here. We don't know who he's pretending to be, and he might screw it up. Like … oh, I don't know … if you see a cook who doesn't look like he knows how to cook. That kind of thing. Just tell somebody."

The mood in the room, of course, had been dampened by Rileigh's announcement, but Georgia's efforts to get everybody back into a party mood were mostly successful. The girls wolfed down the glorious catered dinner and giggled their way through an untold amount of alcohol. The DJ played all their favorite songs from when they were in school. "These Are My People" by Rodney Atkins and "You Shouldn't Kiss Me Like This" by Toby Keith. When Kenny Chesney's "The Good Stuff" came on, several of the girls shrieked in delight. "Wasted" by Carrie Underwood was a pretty good description of the condition most of the girls were headed toward. But Tim McGraw's "Live Like You Were Dying" was a haunting reminder of what Rileigh was facing. The party lasted very late, with only a couple of girls needing the assistance of their designated drivers to make it to their cars. It was long past midnight when Rileigh and Jillian put Georgia into her car and forced her to leave.

"Go home and look in on your sleeping children," Rileigh said.

"I'll do no such thing. I don't want to see their little faces until the morning." Georgia sighed. "I know Chigger didn't make them take a bath." She shook her head. "It's a damn good thing going to bed with dirty feet won't kill a kid. If it did, all of mine would be six feet under."

She grabbed Rileigh in a gloriously tight hug, kissed her on the cheek, and said, "Thanks for letting me do this." Then she hopped into her car and drove away. The catering people had gathered up all their things and were leaving as Rileigh and Jillian walked back through the building, picked up their purses, and headed out the back door to their car parked behind the building. Jillian was in front of Rileigh when she stopped so suddenly that Rileigh bumped into her from behind.

"Jillian? What the—?"

"Look."

Jillian's face drained of color, and her hands covered her mouth. Rileigh had her weapon drawn before she even thought about doing it, pushed Jillian behind her, and swung the barrel of the gun back and forth as she approached their car, where someone was sitting in the driver's seat.

It was obvious the person sitting there wasn't going anywhere, so Rileigh made her way around the car to make sure no one was lurking in the shadows. She checked the back of the building and the trees in the nearby forest, then finally came back with her weapon holstered. Whoever had left the surprise package in her car was long gone.

She pulled her phone out of her pocket, punched favorites, and Mitch answered on the first ring. Rileigh didn't mince words.

"While we were at the party, somebody deposited a corpse in my car. Left a garrote around his neck."

She heard Mitch's grunt and knew that her words had knocked the breath out of him.

"A corpse. Is there anybody—?"

Rileigh cut him off before he could ask. "Everything's fine. I've secured the area. Whoever did it left a long time ago. But you might want to come out and help me get the fellow out of my car so I can go home."

"Do you know who it is?"

"I don't have any friends with a spiky blond mohawk."

"Blond mohawk? One of the carpenters working at Breezy Creek this afternoon had a blond mohawk."

"I don't know who he is, but I do know who left him — our friend who uses dead bodies to deliver messages."

"What's the message?"

"This guy's face is painted yellow, with eyes covered in black paint and a frowny mouth drawn below his nose."

She paused.

"And in black on the front of his white tee shirt is a big circle."

"A circle?"

"I don't think it's meant to be a circle," Rileigh said. "I think it's a zero. Number one isn't the last number in a countdown — zero is."

Chapter Twenty-Two

MITCH LOOKED AT THE BODY PROPPED UP BEHIND THE steering wheel in Rileigh's car. The man appeared to be in his mid-40s. His features were distorted, of course, because his face had been painted smiley face yellow, a frowny face drawn on top of the paint with black paint. His hair appeared to be natural blond, styled in a three-inch mohawk. Definitely memorable. He was wearing a white t-shirt with a black circle painted on the front with the same black paint that had been used to make the features on the face. Rileigh, of course, didn't think it was a circle. Rileigh said it was a zero.

Mitch was so proud of how she was holding it together. She should have been a basket case by now with all that had happened and all that was going to happen. But she was steady and calm, and so he tacked that onto the seemingly endless list of reasons why he loved the woman.

"I mean, I get a doll in a wedding dress with the number one on it and then a dead body with the number zero. That's the end of the countdown, don't you think?"

The first number in the countdown had been the

number six, which had been on the postcard that Rileigh got months ago. The one that had a cemetery on the front and her name written across one of the tombstones in black magic marker with a frowny face on the back and the number six.

Five had been a card inside a box with a finger bone belonging to one Fats Mason, from Chicago — who preceded in death his brother/father/uncle/cousin James Spencer Mason, who had breathed his last this afternoon next to the urinals in the Breezy Creek Recreation Area bathroom.

Number four had been a thumb bone. Three, a piece of tanned skin with a tattoo — flayed from the back of an organized crime bagman named Santiago Suárez — and a key. Two, the jack-in-the-box with a clown sign saying, "Bang, you're dead *this time*." And one, the doll in a wedding dress. Now this life-sized, frowny face doll, had a zero painted on its chest.

Marshal Craig Dylan had been walking around the car looking at the ground, searching for Mitch didn't know what, and he was sure the marshal didn't know what either. Something, anything that would identify who had come and put the body here.

Gus had been examining the body while it still sat in the car before they allowed the EMTs to come and haul it away. He stepped back, stood up, and turned to the others. "Well, it seems to me that the dude-in-the-nude we found at Breezy Creek this afternoon was killed by one of the other killer wannabes who must have believed that he had found El Viento … and was hoping to pass go and collect way more than two hundred dollars. He was sorely disappointed, I am sure, when he stripped the guy and didn't find the tattoo. But this guy has all his clothes on."

"Which means this guy was planted by El Viento,

because only El Viento would know there was no tattoo on this body that'd make him rich." Rileigh shook her head. "It's to send me a message. The countdown's over."

"The headless body that guy dumped last night outside the bachelor party … I'm thinking El Viento killed him, too," the marshal said.

"So why did he cut his head off?" Mitch wondered aloud.

The marshal shrugged.

"I'm running his DNA," Gus said. "I'm sure he's in the system, so it won't be long before we find out who he is, if not what he was doing here."

Mitch put his arm around Rileigh and moved her away from the others, who continued to discuss the body and the evidence and posit scenarios that would explain what was going on.

"You doing all right?"

"Couldn't be better," she said.

"That's a large stinky pile of what you find in the dirt on the south side of a bull going north. So let's try that again. How you doing?"

"I really am fine." She hugged him then, held on tight, and he returned the hug just as tight. He heard her make a sound of some kind, perhaps a little sob, and it broke his heart to think that his bride, the woman he was going to marry on Saturday, was anything but carefree, joyful, full of wonder. He almost ground his teeth, but didn't because he knew Rileigh would hear it and he really didn't want her to know how ragingly furious he felt right now, with an anger in his belly he'd never felt before. Someone was torturing the woman he loved, had been doing it for the last six months, and now was somewhere among all those people wandering around Breezy Creek. And Mitch couldn't do a damned thing about it.

"Unless the EMTs are going to drag that dude out of my car in the next fifteen minutes, I'm ready to go home. Would you take me and Jillian now?"

He leaned down then and kissed her and didn't care that all of the men standing around saw him do it.

When they pulled up at Mama's, Mitch realized it was second nature now to maneuver his car over the hump at the top of the driveway without crashing through the fence. All three of them were surprised to see that house was brightly lit.

"I wonder what's going on?" Rileigh asked, her voice tight. Mitch suspected she was worried that something had happened to/with Aunt Daisy. Rileigh and Mitch had talked at length about what it was like to live in the house with Aunt Daisy and Jillian. Rileigh told him that Jillian was stronger than anybody she'd ever seen, ignored her aunt as if she weren't there, when obviously she wanted nothing more than to leap across the table and strangle the life out of the old bitch.

Rileigh and Jillian hopped out of the car and Mitch followed them inside.

As soon as they opened the front door, Mama squealed. "They're home!" She ran to greet Rileigh with a fierce bear hug. "Guess who's here?"

"Who?"

"The Dalai Lama," Mama said. Rileigh, Mitch and Jillian exchanged a look.

"Goody," was the only response Mitch could muster.

Mama had gone down that rabbit hole in her dementia. But Mitch thought that Mama and the Dalai Lama had broken up weeks ago. Apparently, the romance was back on again.

"Come on, come on, he's sitting in the kitchen. Come meet him."

They aways went along with Mama's fantasies. Rileigh, Jillian, and Mitch followed Mama into the kitchen, prepared to pretend that indeed there was somebody there who looked just like the Dalai Lama. And there he was.

Except, he *really* was.

The *Dalai Lama* was sitting in a chair at the head of the table.

"Who—?" Rileigh began.

"Who—?" Jillian began.

"Oh, stop it both of you. You sound like a flock of owls. It ain't like you ain't never seen the Dalai Lama before." Mama was seated at the table beside him, and Daisy was nowhere to be seen.

The old man seated at the table was dressed in a crimson robe with a swath of gold fabric draped around him. His head was shaved, his body was covered in tattoos. He rose to his feet, put his hands together in a prayerful gesture, and bowed to Mitch.

"My name is Phassakorn Bassui," he said. "And I am *not* the Dalai Lama. I am of the Bhikkhu, a monastic order. The word literally means 'beggar' or 'one who lives by alms.'"

"Oh pooh," Mama said, "he's just being humble. Of course he's the Dalai Lama. You want some coffee, Mitch?"

"Sure, Lily, bring me a cup of coffee," he said, then walked around the table to greet the man who had bowed to him.

"The assertion that I am the Dalai Lama is, I'm sure, awkward for you," the man said. "I am sorry. I did not realize my hostess would ... cling to that belief even after I informed her otherwise."

Rileigh walked up beside Mitch. "Where did Mama find you?"

"And why are you here?" Jillian asked.

The man offered a shy smile. "I was walking along the roadside when she pulled up beside me and invited me to come to her home for dinner."

"And so you just got in the car with her and came here?" Rileigh asked.

"What were you doing walking along the roadside?" Mitch asked.

"I was on my way to the temple in Round Rock."

"There's a Buddhist Temple in Round Rock?" Mitch was surprised.

"Maybe there was once, but not anymore," Rileigh said. "Because Round Rock's not there anymore. It was all washed away in a mudslide."

"So you were *walking* there, just walking — from where?" Mitch asked.

"I was in Knoxville," the man explained.

Mama handed Mitch his cup of coffee. She was absolutely beaming, and he supposed that she had every right to be happy and thrilled. He was sure that none of her imaginary people had ever actually came to life. But then she had imagined before that she was dating Rhett Butler. And Neil Armstrong was in there somewhere. He thought maybe Elvis was, too.

"When I heard about the hurricane, I was at the Nashville Buddhist temple to join other monks in creating a sand mound mandala."

"A sand mandala?"

"A sand mandala is used to help us visualize an enlightened life. Mandalas mean different things to different people, but the one we were creating at the McClellan Museum was serving as a symbol of patience and strength. But it only lasts a moment."

"When you're not making sand" — Mitch caught

himself before he said "castles" — "mandalas, what do you do?"

"I am a teacher of Dharma meditation. We have been constituted by the Buddha to provide those of pure aspiration, who are willing and able to simplify their lives radically, an opportunity and support to base their lives entirely in Buddhist principles. In return, they are made responsible for preserving and promoting the teachings and for ensuring that they are accurately transmitted to new generations."

"So you walked here all the way from Nashville?"

"No, not Nashville. I got a ride as far as Knoxville."

"Oh, well, Knoxville, then. You *walked?*"

Knoxville was less than an hour's drive away, but it wasn't like there were sidewalks along the roads. And it was in the mountains.

Mitch was equal parts fascinated, dubious, and distrustful of the man dressed in crimson with the gold sash.

"I left as soon as I finished the dissolution ceremony—"

"Dissolution ceremony?"

"Yes, after mandalas serve their purpose, they are dissolved in a ceremony that begins with a monk dropping golden flowers into the center. Then he drags one finger through the sand until eight lines are shown. Then a paintbrush is used to mix together the remainder of the sand."

That was either too profound for Mitch to grasp or a total crock of shit. He didn't know which.

"So how did you come to be here? I mean specifically here in my mother's kitchen," Rileigh asked.

"As I said, she saw me on the side of the road and stopped and invited me to dinner. When monks travel alone, Buddha sends people to care for us. We have no money and nowhere to sleep, nothing to eat, but Buddha provides."

He bowed again and nodded to the empty plate on the table in front of him. Mama had obviously heated up the leftovers of pot roast and all the trimmings left from supper.

Mitch connected then with the rest of what the monk had said. "So you carry nothing with you to eat and have nowhere to sleep. Is that right?"

"That is correct," the monk said. "I am protected."

"Protected?"

The man held out an arm, so filled with interlocking tattoos, it put the term "full sleeve of tattoos" to shame. "These are sacred, called *sak yant*, and the images are drawn from Buddhist manuscripts in Khmer, Thai, and Sanskrit. My whole body is covered, for protection and good fortune."

"I'm sure that Lily invited you to stay the night here with her, right?" Mitch said.

"Well, of course he's going to stay here with us. I've invited him to the wedding, and he has agreed to come. Where else would he stay?"

Mitch turned so that he faced the monk with his back to Mama. He hoped the monk could read his face and the undertones of what he was saying.

"I know somewhere you can spend the night. It's *private*. No one there to disturb you, at the Great Smoky Mountains National Park. It's warm and dry."

"That is sufficient. I need nothing else."

Mama stood then. "Whoa, wait a minute, Mitch."

"There'll be plenty to eat and plenty to do — and lots of new people to meet at Breezy Creek, and I'd be glad to give you a ride there *tonight.*"

"The Dalai Lama is staying here with me," Mama said. "I invited him."

"Oh, but Mrs. Bishop," the monk said, "I would very much like to go with the officer here to the place he indicated. I would be very comfortable there. And I would not put your family out."

"Oh, you're not putting us out. You're welcome. We've got a guest bedroom."

"I would enjoy meeting many new people there."

"Well, it's just me and the girls here…"

"I would prefer to stay at the site offered to me by the officer." The monk said the words kindly, smiling, but he was firm, and Mama backed down.

"I am ready to go with you whenever you would like," the monk said to Mitch and sat back down in his chair at the table and smiled.

Mitch leaned toward Rileigh. "He can stay in the admin building at Breezy Creek. I have a key. There are couches, bathrooms … he'll be fine." He leaned closer and said softly, "I'm not leaving you women here with some stranger, whether he looks like a Buddhist monk or not."

"I was thinking exactly the same thing."

Rileigh's brow furrowed.

"Dang … one of Mama's imaginary people finally came to life — why couldn't it have been Rhett Butler?"

Chapter Twenty-Three

EL VIENTO SAT IN THE DARK IN THE SMALL HOTEL ROOM HE had rented. It was close to the Breezy Creek recreation area where he had hung out yesterday, trying to be "useful." But proximity wasn't the reason he'd picked the hotel. The sign out front proclaimed, "Overlook Hotel," and in small print below, in a font that was supposed to look like somebody'd added the words on top: "Not *THAT* Overlook Hotel." The place was old, had been the Overlook Hotel long before Stephen King wrote *The Shining*, and El Viento liked that the owner was sharp enough to use the notoriety of the fictitious hotel to his advantage.

It was not yet dawn, and he savored the darkness. The light hurt his eyes. He'd spent most of the day yesterday attempting to keep his eyes fully open, not squinting in the bright sunlight that seemed to be hundred-watt bulbs two inches from his eyeballs. He needed to get some sunglasses, but didn't want to do it. He burped out a little bit of derision at himself when he realized he didn't want to buy sunglasses because it would be a waste of money. Why buy sunglasses that he was only going to wear a day or two before he died? He had millions in a Swiss bank account, and he was concerned about spending fifty bucks on a pair of Ray-Bans.

It was nice sitting here in the dark, not thinking about anything in particular. Thinking had become difficult in a way he could not explain. It just seemed harder, the way walking through water is harder than walking through air. Everything seemed more difficult now, but he thought he was doing a good job of putting a good face on it. No one he was around appeared to notice anything at all odd about him, except that he was squinting a lot.

He'd not been found out, and it was a miracle that he hadn't, because he had suffered two of what the doctor called petit mal seizures while he was in the company of others. And he was surprised that nobody seemed to notice. At least no one had brought it up. But of course, he was in the company of people who had all manner of other things on their minds besides noticing that one of the people in their midst was standing and staring blankly into space. They were busy — a lot to do — and time was running out.

The doctor said that the frequency of the seizures would increase, as would their longevity. He feared what that could mean. Even now, when he suffered one of them, he had no idea how long it lasted, how long he stood staring before he was interrupted. And so far, he had been able to come back when he was interrupted, too. But it was like wandering around with his head full of static, static so loud he could barely hear the voice of whoever was speaking to him. And he'd had to concentrate with all his mental strength hear their voice, to come out of the seizure and appear normal. It wouldn't be long before he would be unable to come back from the static, he knew, that he would be stuck there, unable to do anything. Until — what? Until he died? Was that how he was supposed to die, how others with tentacles growing in their heads died? Did they wander around inside their own heads full of static and white noise, unable to find their way out? Like being in a room with a light shining so horribly bright that they could only open their eyes a sliver and look at the world through a forest of eyelashes? Is that how he would go? Is that how Ole Arch would kill him. Trap him in an over-bright nothingness full of static and white noise?

Well, sorry 'bout that, Archibald. You lose. That was *not* how Reuben Lablonski would end. That's not how he would die. El Viento had a far, far better and more appropriate end plan for himself. El Viento would not die, lost inside his head with his brain being eaten up with cancer. No! El Viento would go out in a blaze of glory and take a whole bunch of other people with him.

Pulling out his laptop, he logged into the dark web chat room and looked to see what others had posted there. Then he began to type.

El Viento: "A little note for the tidy ones among you who like to keep the contacts in their phones up to date. You can mark BloodHarpy off your Christmas card lists. He is no longer among us. For a couple of days now, BloodHarpy has been assuming room temperature. He was such an idiot. Did he really think I wouldn't spot him? Well, apparently, he did. Fatal error on his part. I saw him instantly and eliminated him just as instantly. And he served a good purpose. He helped me accomplish an end. He was far more useful dead than he had ever been alive."

Another post popped up beside his.

BangURDead: "You think you're the only one who's

made a kill? Well, you'd be wrong about that. From the looks of a tattooed hawk on his shoulder, the man I eliminated today was Nighthawk."

El Viento: "And you saw the tattoo on his shoulder because you were looking for a different tattoo on his body and didn't find it. Ha, ha, ha. You killed Nighthawk because you thought Nighthawk was me. You're really dumber than you look, and given how dumb you look, that's an accomplishment of some consequence."

He started to close his laptop but stopped. He wasn't finished gloating yet.

El Viento: "In case you're keeping track, your little group of five dwarves has now been reduced to two. Iron-Jackal thought he was smarter than me, too. He never even knew I had him pegged. Didn't know until I slipped that garrote around his neck and began to twist. I knew what IronJackal looked like, you see. I met him once. He didn't remember me, but I remembered him. And I have met others in our little group, though I'm sure you can't quite place my face."

El Viento logged out of the chat room as his vision began to blur. He suddenly felt dizzy. This was new, the dizziness. He rubbed his temples as his head began to throb in rhythm with his heartbeat. He started to stand, thought better of it, and crawled from the chair to the bed, where he lay down and concentrated on taking long, slow breaths until the dizziness passed.

Dizziness. No one had noticed him staring blankly at nothing — at least not yet. And that was a thing you could explain away without arousing suspicion. But how could he hide dizziness? Nobody would buy that he was who he was pretending to be if he fell flat on his face.

He ground his teeth, dug deep inside himself for the

iron will of determination that had seen him through a career snuffing out the lives of others. He'd make it. He would. Just had to make it through today. Tomorrow it would be all over.

All over. He would be dead, and so would a whole lot of other people.

Chapter Twenty-Four

"What's this doing here?" Jillian asked, picking up a small can off the kitchen countertop.

Rileigh and Jillian had come downstairs together Friday morning, just mumbling greetings, not yet human beings. First-cup-in-the-morning granted humanity to those who craved coffee, and they hadn't yet had theirs. Mama was out feeding the chickens, and Aunt Daisy was … somewhere. Who gave a shit.

Jillian turned and held out the can toward Rileigh. For a moment, she didn't know what it was. And then she figured it out. As if in a dream, she took the can from Jillian and read the label. "Chainsaw oil."

"What's a can of chainsaw oil doing—?"

"Two words: Aunt. Daisy."

The can of chainsaw oil had the desired effect on Rileigh, the effect she knew her Aunt Daisy intended it to have. Against her will, Rileigh was transported back to the day she'd come home after chasing down leads in the Tina Montgomery murder case and innocently accepted a glass of drugged lemonade from Daisy. The drug had rendered

Rileigh unable to defend herself, and her Aunt Daisy, believing she was Jillian, had dragged her out to the garage, planning to cut off her head with a chainsaw.

"Why would—?"

"Psychological torture."

In one of their many catching-up-on-life conversations since Jillian got home, Rileigh had briefly told her what had happened that day, how she'd tried to fight off the attack — and Aunt Daisy smashed her hand with a sledgehammer.

Rileigh unconsciously flexed the fingers on her right hand. It had taken months to heal, one of the most painful injuries Rileigh had ever suffered in her life. The bones had been shattered. It was months before she had full use of her hand, and it still ached now and then, would for the rest of her life.

Jillian saw the gesture and put it together.

"She's reminding you. She wants to dredge up those awful memories."

"That'd be my read on it." She ground her teeth. "You know, I used to believe she was a psychopath, pure and simple, but now—"

"Oh no, that's too easy. Aunt Daisy is not just crazy. She's evil, pure evil in an ugly old woman's suit. She delights in other people's misery."

And Aunt Daisy would use any weakness Rileigh showed as a crowbar to pry open her chest and eat her still-beating heart.

"I'm not going to play her diabolical game," Rileigh said. Then she paused dramatically. "Wow, did you see *that?*"

Jillian looked around, confused. "What?"

"Aw, you missed it. My 'give-a-shit' just hopped out of my skull and went flying out the window."

Jillian grinned. "Screw Aunt Daisy."

"And the horse she road in on." Rileigh smiled. "You fix the coffee." She held up the can in her hand. "So it doesn't taste like this. I'll go put this back in the garage where it belongs."

Aunt Daisy spent the day puttering around in the garden — when she wasn't setting out emotional land-mines for Rileigh. In her bedroom later that afternoon, Rileigh was picking out the clothes to pack for her honey-moon, when she suddenly heard calliope music. She froze in place. It was drifting up from downstairs, she thought, though the music was so faint, it was hard to determine the direction.

It was a calliope, all right, though. She was sure of it. A calliope just like the one on the riverboat, the Smoky Mountain Queen, where Rileigh had been trapped in a little kids' gerbil tunnel playground. Smashed into that tight space, with the raging case of claustrophobia she'd suffered after a serial killer tried to bury her alive, Rileigh had lost it. She went totally postal, flailed around in hyste-ria. It was truly ugly, and the memory of it now chilled her to the bone.

Which, of course, was the point. Standing absolutely still with the top part of her new bikini bathing suit — tag still dangling — she cocked her head and listened to Aunt Daisy's effort to spoil her happiness. Why? Aunt Daisy needed no reason — pure meanness would explain it all. There was no sense confronting her aunt about it. The old woman would just play the "I'm too crazy to remember all the terrible things I do" card, a defense Mama would buy. In her eyes, though … you could look in Aunt Daisy's eyes, see the merriment in them, the delight in watching someone suffer.

Rileigh wouldn't give her the satisfaction of knowing

she was rattled. But she was. The last thing in the world Rileigh wanted to be thinking about today was having her hand crushed or being stuffed into a kids' gerbil tunnel. She had enough on her mind, thank you very much, wondering about the killer who had been sending her pieces of people and threats, and oh, by the way, she was *getting married* on Saturday. If she lived that long. She realized that sometime while she was standing there, the calliope music had stopped and wondered if it had ever been there to begin with. Maybe she imagined it.

Nah. It'd been real.

Jillian had not spoken a single syllable to Aunt Daisy that initial confrontation when Mama had brought her home, and poor dithered Mama hadn't even noticed. But if looks could kill, Aunt Daisy would have been dead the instant Jillian saw her. The loathing, the disgust, the raging anger in Jillian's look would have soured new milk. But Jillian was keeping her feelings in check because she loved her mother, and Mama was as happy as anybody had ever seen her. She was about to marry off not one but two of her daughters on the same day. Since she had no idea there were any other issues that anybody else was thinking about, she assumed that everybody was as thrilled and carefree as she was. Oh, how Rileigh wished she were.

After she'd selected what she'd take with her — hadn't packed it yet so the clothes wouldn't wrinkle — Rileigh noticed that her handcuffs were missing from the spot on the top of her dresser where she had put them. She went looking for them but hadn't even made it downstairs before her mother called to her from the kitchen.

"Rileigh, honey … it ain't funny."

Rileigh veered toward the kitchen at the bottom of the stairs and found her mother standing with hands on hips, looking at the refrigerator door ... which was handcuffed to the handle of the cabinet next to it.

"I can't get neither one of 'em open with them handcuffs on 'em. Ain't you got better things to do than play jokes on your poor old Mama?"

Rileigh pulled her keys from her pocket.

"You mean you didn't bust out laughing as soon as you saw these?" she said as she unhooked first one cuff and then the other. "My bad."

She kept the smile on her face, refusing to allow her mind to wander to a basement filling with smoke and her ankle handcuffed to a pipe.

Thank God Mason Stump never did what he was told.

Had Aunt Daisy taken notes on every damn case Rileigh'd worked in the last year? How did she know—?

She stopped herself. Nope, she was not gonna rent out space in her mind to a vicious old hag. Not happenin'.

Her resolve lasted through the day, until she, Jillian, and Mama were on their way to the rehearsal dinner and she found on the porch swing an axe smeared with catsup to approximate blood — intended to send Rileigh's mind reeling back to Shagbark Manor where she'd been chased in the dark by an axe-wielding lunatic.

But that lunatic wasn't any crazier than Rileigh's Aunt Daisy. And at least Carly Farrington had had a reason. There was no reason for Aunt Daisy's insanity. It made Rileigh sometimes question whether the incidence of gypsies switching babies in cribs was an old wife's tale or reality. Daisy had been raised in a happy, healthy home with her sisters, beautiful girls named for flowers, and all of them had grown to become lovely women with happy families of their own — all except Daisy, who had grown to be a nasty, angry, bitter woman who believed that her baby sister, Lily, had stolen from Daisy the only man she'd ever loved, J.R. Bishop.

Rileigh shook her head. It would be hard to determine who was the more evil human being of the two — J.R. Bishop, a pedophile who'd molested Jillian and Georgia, or Daisy Gillespie, who was having an affair with him and sold his daughter to a sex slave ring to keep her from going to the police.

They were both going to burn in hell, Rileigh thought. Oh, how she would love to be a fly on that wall and watch it happen.

Chapter Twenty-Five

REHEARSAL DINNERS WERE THE RESPONSIBILITY OF THE groom's family, but Gus Hazelton beat everybody to the check — as he had for the bachelor and bachelorette parties. A lottery winner who'd invested his winnings expertly, he was absolutely delighted to be able to provide for his friends what they could never have afforded for themselves, and he pulled out all the stops — a prime rib dinner catered by the Texas Roadhouse steak house in Gatlinburg.

Marshal Craig Dylan had been invited, and he attended ... just for protection, to be one more gun, she was sure. Since he knew nobody, he sat a little apart from the others, enjoying their merriment from afar.

The rehearsal dinner was held at the Knights of Columbus hall, and once the bar was open, the fun began, with one person after another rising to their feet to toast the bride and groom, or to tell raucous stories about them. It was the responsibility of the best man and the maid of honor to *roast* the couple, like comedians did politicians in an election year.

The first best man to rise to the occasion was Gus Hazelton, Mitch's best man, who told a much-exaggerated story about the day he, Mitch, and Rileigh had gone squirrel hunting and the tough, pistol-packing, you're-in-a-heap-of-trouble-boy, kick-ass sheriff had been too squeamish to skin what they'd shot.

The other best man, David's brother, Rich, had described the day he had stolen David's clothes when he'd gone skinny-dipping, and he'd barely made it out of the water before a group of girls came to swim.

"Dave hid behind a rock, covering up strategic portions of his anatomy with creek mud, and then made a break for the woods." He turned to David. "And when you did?"

"I took two steps … the girls saw me and started squealing … and then all the mud fell off."

Georgia described the day Rileigh had challenged her to a game of chicken when they found the carcass of a dead cow in a field, swollen and *ripe*.

"She dared me to touch it. I crept as close as I could, ten feet from it, but I couldn't stand the reek, and ran away before it made me throw up." Then she gave Rileigh the floor. "Tell them what you did, Rileigh."

Rileigh rolled her eyes. "I won!" She said triumphantly. "That's all you need to know."

"Oh, no, no, no. Not so fast. Tell them *how* you won?"

"I didn't give myself time to smell it, I *ran* up to it as fast as I could…" She paused.

"And…?"

"And I touched it!"

"Actually, she more than just *touched* it. She was running … and she tripped over a tree root … stumbled … and fell *into* it, and—"

A groan rose up from the crowd that thankfully drowned out the last part.

Jillian's maid of honor, Aaliyah Al-Masri, *Dr.* Al-Masri, said she hadn't been a witness to the event she was about to describe, but Jillian had told her in "excruciating detail" about the time that Jillian had brought home a mangy old dog she found on the side of the road. And before Mama could shoo the creature out of the house it got ... sick.

"I believe you Southerners would delicately describe it as 'south-end-of-a-dog-going-north sick.'"

She said Jillian had just stood there screaming while Mama chased the dog through the house, with the creature "making deposits" on the floor, the carpet, the bedspread, the furniture...

"How did this degenerate into tales of dead animals and dog shit?" somebody called out, and as the crowd's laughter rumbled, Rileigh saw the door at the back of the room open and a stranger step inside.

Rileigh's heart froze in her throat. He was a big man, strong, rugged-looking, and with an air of danger about him that was unmistakable. Mitch looked up and spotted him and rose to his feet. Rileigh felt for the pistol at her waist. She never went anywhere without it these days, but she didn't draw her weapon because Mitch didn't draw his. Instead, he walked with purpose toward the man standing just inside the door.

Stopping in front of him, he demanded, "You wanna tell me what in the hell *you're* doing here?"

The man looked at Mitch, then grabbed him — in a tight bear hug.

"What the hell do you think I'm doing here, bro? You think I'm going to let you get *married* without me?"

Mitch stammered, "You're supposed to be on a mission in—"

Then the man put his finger to his lips.

"You're not allowed to say where I'm supposed to be.

189

Just know that I'm not there, and they'll be fine without me."

Mitch turned around to the group, his face wreathed in a delighted smile.

"Everybody, I'd like you to meet my brother, Hank."

There was an instant cheer from the group of people. Mitch's brother Hank was a Navy SEAL who had told Mitch that he was on a mission and couldn't possibly attend the wedding, but apparently, he'd gotten out of it.

Rileigh rose from her seat and hurried to Mitch's side. "I'm so glad to meet you, Hank."

"You're Rileigh?" the young man asked, then went on before she could answer. "And you're actually going to marry this bum?"

She slipped her arm around Mitch's waist. "Yep, I am. I know it's crazy, but I am."

"Oh, *sweetheart*…" Hank said, dragging her arm away from Mitch and fitting it around his own waist, putting his arm around her shoulders, then walking her back to the table and speaking softly and fervently.

"Listen, sweetheart, we need to talk. When I finish telling you what I know about my brother, you not only won't be marrying him tomorrow, you might decide to drive really fast down a bumpy road and shove him out an open car door."

Rileigh was dazzled by Mitch's brother. She'd heard about him often enough but had never met him. As a Navy SEAL, he didn't get a lot of downtime, and Mitch had not seen him in almost two years. As soon as she saw the two together, the family resemblance was obvious and striking. Hank had a square jaw, as did Mitch, and a dimple in his chin, as did Mitch. But where Mitch's good looks came to the crossroads and veered toward rugged, Hank's took the other fork in the road toward dashingly handsome. Hank was handsome like a movie star, had the face of a male model, looked like he had just stepped off the set of some action-adventure flick.

When Rileigh had a moment to do so, she whispered in Mitch's ear, "Holy shit, Batman, you said he was good looking. You didn't say he was *that* good looking."

"Tom Cruise and Matt Damon rolled into one, with a side order of Brad Pitt and … oh, I don't know, Cary Grant on the side," he said. "I know."

Before she could respond, he added, "Just remember, I saw you first."

"Have you noticed how the bridesmaids are looking at him?" Rileigh said. "Like hungry wolves at a side of beef."

"It won't impress Hank," Mitch said. "He's used to it. Girls have been falling all over themselves to get his attention his whole life."

"And what does he do?"

"I'm not completely sure what he has done since he joined the Navy. Hell, he might have a girl in every port. Who knows? All I know is that when we were growing up, Hank cut a wide path around all the girls who were throwing themselves at him. I asked him why he didn't date any of them. And he threw the question right back in my face. Why don't you?"

Rileigh had always assumed that girls had been throwing themselves at Mitch when he was a young man, and he had just inadvertently confirmed her suspicions. "I guess both of us were wary of women — after our mother allowed our aunt and uncle to abuse us for years."

"You didn't seem suspicious to me when I first met you."

"Are you telling me you didn't notice that I was suspicious of you?"

"Well, yeah, okay, I noticed. But I thought it was just that you didn't trust me as a police officer."

"There was that."

"And *more* than that?"

He nodded.

"I got over it fast." He cocked his head toward Hank, deep in a discussion about firearms — pistols, rifles, bazookas, grenade launchers — with Gus. "Before I went to the police academy and he joined the Navy, his shtick was to flirt outrageously with every woman he saw — a bee lighting briefly on every flower, making them all fall for him, which they were going to do whether he paid any attention to them or not. But at the end of the day, picking none of them."

Rileigh smiled. "You've seen my bridesmaids. Do you think he's going to manage to keep all ten of them at arm's length?"

"A couple of them are married."

"Fine … *eight* drop-dead gorgeous single women … and your brother. I kind of wish we weren't leaving so fast after the wedding. It would be fun to watch him fend them off."

"Are you telling me that you want to hang around?"

"Hell no, I don't want to hang around," she said. "I'm about to have you all to myself for a glorious week on the beach. I want to leave *yesterday*. A team of Clydesdales and the Budweiser beer wagon couldn't drag me away from that."

Gus instantly bowed out as the best man, since Mitch would have picked his brother if he'd had any idea his brother could attend. Mitch said the decision was Rileigh's — "it's the bride's wedding. I just have to stand there, say 'I do,' and try not to spill pieces of the cake on her dress."

Hank turned to Rileigh and dropped to one knee in front of her.

"If you're planning to ask for her hand in marriage, you can put a sock in it," Mitch said. "She's already spoken for."

"Rileigh Bishop," Hank said, taking her hand and looking up earnestly into her face, "may I have the honor of standing beside, and holding upright, my worthless, useless, extremely ugly and totally morally bankrupt older brother so he doesn't face-plant into the petunias before he has a chance to marry you?"

They all laughed.

"You may indeed," Rileigh said.

Sundeep, who'd been tasked with escorting *both* of the fatherless brides into the ceremony, quickly did a handoff to Gus.

"Two brides is more than any man could be expected to keep track of," he said. "You wouldn't be willing to take one of them off my hands, would you?"

"I'll take the one who knows how to skin a squirrel," Gus said.

Rileigh grinned at him and nodded, then she turned and caught Aaliyah's attention, motioned her over and introduced her to Hank.

"Georgia Stump is my maid of honor. She'll will be walking in with David's brother, Rich. Aaliyah is Jillian's maid of honor. You'll be walking in with her on your arm. Aaliyah can tell you where to stand and what to do."

Hank offered a thousand-watt smile. "I'm a really slow learner," he said. "I'll need tons of coaching. You'll probably have to spend *hours* showing me the ropes. We should probably start right now."

Aaliyah smiled pleasantly. "My bullshit detector gets a lot of practice, and right now it's going ding, ding, ding."

Rileigh suspected it wasn't often Hank Mitchell got shot down by a pretty woman.

"I'm sure you'll figure it out as we go along," Aaliyah added. "See you tomorrow."

Then she walked away.

Hank's eyes followed her.

"Knock, knock. Earth to Hank," Mitch said, waving his hand in front of his brother's eyes. "You're punching way above your weight class with her. She's a psychiatrist, and she can spot a pickup line from a thousand yards out."

"A psychiatrist," Hank said. "Beautiful *and* smart. Aaliyah. You know that means highborn, exalted, sublime in Arabic." He looked at Mitch. "Hold my drink." Shoving his beer into Mitch's hands, Hank took off through the crowd after Aaliyah.

Rileigh smiled, watching him go.

"Your brother's got his work cut out for him," she said. "Have you noticed the sparks flying between Aaliyah and Gus?"

Mitch's eyes opened wide. "I thought I was imagining it — wishful thinking. You noticed something, too?"

What she'd noticed was that as soon as *Dr.* Aaliyah Al-Masri was introduced to *Dr.* Gus Hazelton, the two had been inseparable. Through all the standing-around time necessary to arrange all the pieces-parts of a huge wedding, they'd hung out together, laughing and talking. They were a perfect match, of course — both brilliant and nerdy and funny. Rileigh'd thought: *wouldn't it be wonderful if…*

"Gus had best turn on the charm … there's a new sheriff in town."

She felt safe here, now, at this moment. All around her were friends and family, as well as the entire sheriff's department of Yarmouth County, a U.S. marshal, and a

Navy SEAL. But she knew this was the last time she'd feel safe until they caught — *killed* — the son of a bitch who was stalking her.

Gus got a call near the end of the evening, and he stepped outside to take it. When he came back in, he gathered Mitch, Rileigh, and Marshal Dylan, and said the call had been the autopsy results on the dead body that had been placed in Rileigh's car at the bachelorette party the night before.

"His name is Magnus Odland, Swedish passport, he's—"

"Wanted on just about every continent in the world," Marshal Dylan finished for him. "Men who frequent that website your friend Sundeep found — they're all mercenaries or assassins, hired killers. Interpol is looking for our Swedish friend, but MI6 in England will be particularly saddened by his demise. They believe Odland assassinated an MP, Member of Parliament, about five years ago."

"Probably wasn't sporting a mohawk at the time," Gus observed.

"It was ugly," Dylan continued. "The guy broke into his house in Guildford, that's a little town in Surrey, just outside London, and murdered him in his bed."

"That's grim."

"Oh, it gets grimmer. He was murdered in his bed with his wife sleeping soundly beside him. She actually woke up because she felt something wet on the sheets, and since it was raining outside, she thought the roof was leaking. She flipped on the bedside lamp and saw that her husband's throat had been slit ear to ear."

"And the guy who did that, El Viento, killed him and stuffed him in my car last night," Rileigh said. "Don't have to ask how El Viento spotted him. A mohawk … and the guy was trying to blend in?"

"Three dead bodies — two killed by El Viento, and one by somebody looking for El Viento," Gus said.

"And we're no closer now to catching El Viento than we were when we started," Rileigh said.

"No," Mitch said. "But we have a lot of lines in the water."

Rileigh and Mitch were able to grab a few minutes alone together while the event was winding down. All Rileigh wanted was to feel Mitch's strong arms around her, to bury her face in his chest and stay there, a frozen moment in time, a scene in one of those snow globes before some little kid shakes it up to watch the blizzard.

"Are you okay?" he asked.

"No. Are you?"

"No."

"Glad we got that settled."

"This time tomorrow, we will be Mr. and Mrs. Mitchell Webster." Rileigh put as much enthusiasm and certitude in the words as she could muster. She knew what he was thinking: "We will, if you live long enough to say, 'I do.'" But he didn't say that, of course, just hugged her tighter.

"And all the ugly will be over for good," he said.

"Do you believe that?"

He pulled her out of his embrace so he could look down into her face.

"Yes, I believe that."

"Really?"

"Really."

She grinned and held up her little finger. "Pinky swear?"

He hooked his little finger around hers.

"Pinky swear."

They stood together, looking into each other's eyes, each drawing strength and comfort from the other and giving strength and comfort in return. For a minute, for five minutes, an hour or a lifetime.

She saw tears form in his eyes that he didn't shed.

"I love you so much," he whispered huskily.

"I love you, too … and we will win, you know."

He nodded, swallowed hard.

"I know … we *will* win."

Chapter Twenty-Six

IT WAS VERY LATE WHEN JILLIAN, RILEIGH, AND MAMA returned to Mama's house after the rehearsal dinner. The dinner had gone blessedly without incident. Well, unless you counted the unexpected arrival of Mitch's brother Hank, who followed Jillian's psychiatrist around like a puppy for the rest of the night.

And then there was Mama introducing the Tibetan monk she'd picked up on the side of the road as the Dalai Lama.

She'd suddenly leapt to her feet and raised her glass, and said, "I want to make a toast to the holiest man I know — the *Dalai Lama*."

Phassakorn Bassui had not wanted to go to the dinner at all, but Mama had absolutely insisted, and it wasn't like he had anything else to eat or anywhere else to go. Mitch had made him comfortable in the admin building at Breezy Creek, for which the monk was extremely grateful.

When Mama raised the toast, everyone in the room looked around until they spotted the old bald man covered in tattoos, sitting quietly in the back of the room in a red robe with a gold sash.

Just sitting there — staring out into space, oblivious to everything going on around him. The monk must have been meditating, though he had not assumed a cross-legged position on the floor, his hands in his lap, palms upwards. He was just sitting stock still, staring ahead vacantly. The raucous crowd quieted, an awkward silence, looking at the old man and wondering what to do.

The silence didn't last, though. Mama hurried to the rescue. Rileigh recalled her old granny telling her often, "Fools rush in where angels fear to tread." And that'd be Mama, all right.

Putting her hand on the monk's shoulder, Mama shook him, hard.

"I done told everybody who you are and offered a toast to you," she said cheerily.

Though startled and momentarily confused, the old man handled himself well. He rose slowly to his feet and bowed solemnly, then said, "While I am *not* His Holiness the Dalai Lama, I am of the Bhikkhu, a monastic order, a teacher of Dharma meditation, and one of our most important principles is hospitality. I want to thank all of you for extending it to me in such lavish proportions."

That drew a thunderous wave of applause.

Beyond that, everyone had had a wonderful time, with the sudden appearance of Mitch's Navy SEAL brother as the icing on the 'cake. The three women were exhausted when they pulled up behind the house in Mama's car. Aunt Daisy, of course, had been left behind, snug in her ankle bracelet tracker in case she suddenly started feeling froggy and decided to jump. She had no role to perform in the wedding, so there was no reason for her to go to the wedding rehearsal. At least that's the logic that Rileigh had used to convince Mama that they were not snubbing her poor older sister by not inviting her. Aunt Daisy had moved herself into Jillian's studio. It was a spare bedroom on the top floor that had been converted into an art studio when Jillian came home, and she had spent hours upon hours there painting, splashing colors on canvases, and then taking the canvases out into the backyard and burning them.

It was easy enough to slip the bed back into the room and move all of Jillian's art supplies over into a corner. After all, it was only going to be for three days.

There was no light on in Aunt Daisy's in the bedroom/studio, which had a window on the back of the house they could see when they drove up, meaning Aunt Daisy had gone to sleep. Rileigh was profoundly grateful for that. It was physically painful to be anywhere near that old woman, and she could not imagine how Jillian felt about it.

They went into the house and Mama announced, "The tired's hit me 'bout half an hour ago and I'm 'bout to fall asleep on my feet." She hugged the girls goodnight, then padded down the hallway to her room, which was on the first floor. Jillian said she would make coffee for in the morning. Rileigh was lousy at making coffee, particularly in the machine that all you had to do in the morning was punch a button.

"Okay, good night, see you in the morning," Rileigh said, and trudged up to the top of the stairs. The tired's had hit Rileigh, too, and she couldn't wait to take a hot shower and hit the sack.

As she started down the hall to her room, she noticed that Jillian's bedroom door was open. That seemed odd. She had walked downstairs with Jillian hours before and could have sworn she had left it closed, which meant someone had opened it after they left.

Rileigh suddenly felt uneasy — no, more than uneasy, anxious. She felt a weight descending on her, and as she approached the open door of her sister's bedroom, her heart began to pound and her mouth went dry.

After all, tonight was "the night before the wedding." Everyone had made a point of ignoring that bit of history. Well, maybe Mama wasn't ignoring it. Maybe she didn't remember, but Rileigh and Jilian certainly did and went to great lengths not to go anywhere near the subject. On the night before Jillian's wedding almost thirty years ago … the whole world had come apart.

A force as powerful as magnetic north drew Rileigh to the open bedroom door. As she crossed the threshold, she tried desperately not to flash back to that night all those years ago when a six-year-old Rileigh Bishop had come into her big sister's bedroom carrying her school picture and a note written in a little kid's scrawl, "Please don't forget me." But like a body drowned last summer that'd worked free of the shit on the bottom of the lake and was now making its slow, ghastly ascent into the sunshine, she was powerless to stop it.

She remembered then the last thing she had done when the world was still normal, before what she found in Jillian's room had turned it upside down and pulled everything wrong side out. She had looked at her school picture in her hand, examined the face — dark hair, hazel eyes, and missing teeth in front. Rileigh remembered searching the face for the image of her sister, Jillian, because Rileigh wanted more than anything else in life to look like her sister. Well, except for her sister not moving out — she wanted that more than she'd ever wanted anything, but she knew she wasn't going to get what she wanted. She wasn't going to look like her sister, and her sister was going to leave.

Rileigh struggled, fought against the memories that rushed at her like the ugly black mudslides had roared down the mountainsides at the people in east Tennessee. But those people couldn't stop the flowing mud ... and she couldn't stop the flowing images.

RILEIGH TURNS the knob slowly so it won't creak and steps into the room that's dark except for a spill of moonlight through the big window on the wall on the other side of the bed. Her eyes are accustomed to the darkness, so she can see well in the full moonlight. What she sees is that Jillian isn't in her bed, but it's not made up, so Jillian must have gone to bed and then got up later and went —where? Downstairs to get something to eat maybe? Sometimes Jillian got up in the middle of the night to get a sweet roll or make herself cinnamon toast.

Rileigh stares at the unmade bed where Jillian isn't sleeping, and there's something wrong. Even in the dim moonlight, she can see that the bed is unmade and there's some dark something smeared on the sheets and on the pillowcase. She edges around the bed, trying to get a closer look, and sees a tiny drip of something dark on one of the little bead things on the front of Jillian's wedding dress, which is lying in a heap on the floor beside the bed. Rileigh reaches out a finger and touches the black whatever it is that spilled on the sheets on the bed. She looks at the wet on her fingertip, and up close it doesn't look black. It looks red.

Suddenly Rileigh is afraid, so afraid she can't get her breath, because she thinks she knows what has spilled on Jillian's bed. In two steps, she reaches the lamp with a lacy shade that Mama gave to Jillian, the one Jillian put smiling faces on and Mama got mad. Light floods the room, and Rileigh freezes in place as stiff as a statue, looking at a small blotch of red on her fingertip so she won't have to look at the blood-stained sheets beyond it. The sheets are hanging off the bed onto the floor, and there's a huge stain of blood — how could there be that much blood? It's more blood than anybody has in themselves, and it is splattered everywhere on the bed. She tries not to think the thought, but she can't stop herself. She tries not to know what she knows, but you can't unsee a thing after you've seen it, and you can't un-know the truth about something once you know it. There's blood on the sheets on Jillian's bed, and it's Jillian's blood. So where's Jillian?

Rileigh wants to look for her, to cry out her name in a shrieking voice that'll wake up Mama and Daddy and Aunt Daisy, but she can't make her mouth form words or her voice form a sound. She's frozen there in her bare feet. The note and the picture she planned to hide in the bottom of Jillian's suitcase slip out of her hand to the floor. She feels them but can't hold on because her fingers don't work anymore, and that's when she sees it and wishes then that it was her eyes that didn't work so she wouldn't have to look. It's right there in the center of the pillowcase, the white one next to the one covered in blood. It's like a cherry on top of vanilla ice cream, a red thing you couldn't miss on the white sheet. Rileigh can see it well, and it seems like the thing is getting bigger and bigger until it's bigger than the pillow it's lying on. It's blue and purple and red and bloody. It's the single most horrible thing Rileigh has ever seen in her life.

She doesn't want to know what it is, but she can see it — it's right there lying on the white pillowcase. Obviously, placed carefully there, on display on a white background so you can't miss it. Rileigh stares at it, uncomprehending, trying not to see, not to know it's lying on the white pillowcase in the bloody sheets in her sister Jillian's bed, trying not to know it's a tongue, a human tongue.

RILEIGH SHOOK HER HEAD VIOLENTLY, literally trying to fling the images of that horrible night out of her mind. She stepped to the light switch on the wall and flipped it. That night, the little girl had gone all the way to the lamp beside the bed to turn on the light, but Rileigh stood now just inside the doorway, her hands still on the light switch, her eyes taking in the scene and not comprehending.

For a few moments, she believed she somehow melded the flashback to reality, that she was somehow seeing what she saw all those years ago.

But this was not what she saw all those years ago. It was the same but different. There was blood all over the sheets on Jillian's bed, all right. Not as much blood as there had been the night she saw her sister's bed when she was six years old, but maybe that's because it looked like more blood to a six-year-old. The blood was splattered all over the bed, and her eyes moved unwillingly to the pillow beside the one that was splattered with blood, and lying on it was a tongue, *a human tongue.*

Years and years after that horrible night when Rileigh'd been six, Aunt Daisy had finally owned what she'd done, described how she'd killed a chicken for the blood and cut out its gizzard because a chicken gizzard looked like a human tongue.

But what Rileigh saw now was not a chicken gizzard that looked like a human tongue. Taking shaky steps to the bed, she reached her trembling hand out and picked it up.

The thing in her hand was cold, like maybe it'd been in a refrigerator, but it was a human tongue all right.

She dropped it back onto the pillow and began to edge back out of the room. She had to get to Jillian before she came in here. She had to stop her from seeing this horror that had been perpetrated yet again by the monster who'd done it the first time — their mother's sister, Aunt Daisy. She couldn't let Jillian see this. Not again. Not on the night before her wedding. Rileigh had backed a couple of steps away, and she turned to run downstairs ... and stumbled into Jillian, who was standing right behind her. Jillian, who had looked past her into the room and seen the nightmare. Jillian, who yet again had been tortured by Aunt Daisy.

Jillian sucked in a gasp and shook her head — as Rileigh had done — willing her mind to reject the reality.

Then Jillian turned toward Rileigh. Their eyes met and locked, and both of them said the same words at the same time.

"Aunt Daisy."

Chapter Twenty-Seven

RILEIGH AND JILLIAN TURNED AS IF THEY WERE ONE PERSON and raced down the hallway to the room that had been Jillian's studio until Aunt Daisy showed up yesterday. Even as she grabbed the doorknob, turned it, and flung the door open, Rileigh was remembering what she had done when she saw her sister's bloody bedroom all those years ago.

RILEIGH RUNS out of the bedroom, down the hall, down the stairs, out the back door, into the night. She runs blindly into the woods. Runs and runs and runs until she can't run anymore because of the stitch in her side and then she crawls into a windfall to get out of the cold.

Huddling in a ball in the dark, Rileigh is shaking so hard that surely the bad guy will see the limbs of the tree moving. The guy who killed Jillian will find her here. He'll kill her too and cut out her tongue, or maybe he'll cut out her tongue first. Then he wouldn't have to kill her because without a tongue she couldn't tell what she'd seen.

She is so afraid, more terrified than she has ever been. And she stays there, cold, shaking and terrified for hours.

Eventually they find her. It's her Aunt Daisy who spots her huddled in among the dead tree limbs. Rileigh thinks that there are too many emotions on her Aunt Daisy's features to tell what she's feeling. Relief, anger, surprise, and other emotions Rileigh doesn't recognize. And then Rileigh is sitting in the kitchen wrapped up in a quilt, with Mama trying to get her to drink a cup of hot chocolate and her aunt washing the dirt off her face and hands with a cold cloth. Why not warm? Why hadn't she bothered to wait until the water on the tap got warm? She's scrubbing hard, too, rough. No gentleness. The image of her aunt's face isn't caring and concerned. There are all kind of other emotions on her face, but it doesn't seem like they're the right ones. Rileigh notices and catalogs all that to be hauled out later and examined.

WHATEVER EMOTIONS RILEIGH had seen or not seen that night, almost thirty years ago, they absolutely will not be the emotions on her aunt's face tonight when she and Jillian find her.

Jillian flicked on the light, and both women look at the bed where Aunt Daisy should be sleeping. It was empty.

"Where the hell did she go?" Rileigh said. "She's wearing a damned ankle bracelet, she's 78 years old, and it's dark, and she doesn't have a car. Where the hell *could* she go?"

Jillian didn't respond, and Rileigh looked full into her eyes then.

"...the finest man I've ever met..." Jillian whispered, her face ghostly pale, a thousand-yard stare in her eyes.

Jillian Bishop had left the building and Rileigh knew where she'd gone.

~

As soon as Jillian knocks, lights come on inside the closed business, and within seconds the door opens, and standing before her is a man in blue coveralls like mechanics wear. There's a name stitched on the pocket. Just Max. That's all. Not Maxwell … the man Aunt Daisy had sworn was "the finest man I've ever met." Just Max. He smiles at her.

"Daisy done called me and told me you'd be coming," he says. "She told me all about you. About all your troubles. Asked if I could help, and I told her of course I would. I'd do just about anything for Daisy Gillespie, her being such a good friend and all. Come on in."

And he steps back and opens the door so Jillian can enter.

The eyes of experience. Oh, if Jillian had been able to read men then the way she could now, she would have turned tail and bolted. No, she wouldn't have run. She would have pulled a knife and cut him, cut him good, because he was a man who needed cutting. But she'd been eighteen years old then, had never lived anywhere but Black Bear Forge, Tennessee. She knew nothing. Trusted absolutely. And after all, it was her Aunt Daisy who sent her there, Aunt Daisy who used to help her cut out paper dolls when she was a little girl. If Aunt Daisy said he was the finest human being she'd ever met, that was good enough for Jillian.

So she takes a step across that threshold, and the man with the word Max stitched on his chest pushes the door closed behind her. And at that moment, Jillian Bishop's life as she has always known it ends. What lies ahead of her at the hands of this fine man her aunt has sent her to is a living hell on earth. But Jillian hadn't known that then, of course. She smiles, just a little nervous. After all, she's here alone in this building with a man she's just met. But she can trust him. Of course she can. He is, after all, the finest man Aunt Daisy has ever … yeah, yeah, yeah. He asks for her car keys so he can have somebody move her car off the street, around back out of sight. And after she gives them to him, the fine man·named Max leads her down the darkened aisles of auto parts. Spark plugs and mufflers and *tailpipes, a big building, all the way through to the very back. He opens a door there, hangs her keys on a nail outside it, and gestures for her to go in. She steps into the room, an office, but there's a bed there, too, a half bed with musky sheets, like maybe Max has been sleeping there. That strikes her as odd, and she turns around to ask about it, but she doesn't get to ask to the question. Max slaps her across the face, an open-handed slap, the kind that causes maximum pain with minimum damage. Jillian is so unprepared for the blow that it staggers her, and she falls to the floor, looking up at him, her hand to her cheek, tears streaming down her face, blood dripping from her lip.*

And then she watches in horror as he starts unfastening his belt.

"What's going on here? My Aunt Daisy said—"

"Your Aunt Daisy paid me to take you. Not twenty minutes ago. Said you'd be worth it, so you better live up to my expectations."

He pulls off his belt and starts unzipping his pants.

She screams, leaps to her feet, and runs for the door, but he's faster and stronger. He grabs her by the hair and yanks her backwards, throwing her onto the bed that smells of unwashed bodies. And another stink, one she soon learns to recognize.

JILLIAN *NEVER* THOUGHT about that night, the night before her wedding almost thirty years ago. But as she stood with Rileigh, looking at the empty bed where Aunt Daisy should be sleeping, she broke her own iron-clad rule. A rule she'd only broken a handful of times in her entire life. A rule she had made for herself to keep her sanity. That rule was she never, *ever*, ever allowed herself to remember what men did to her. Whatever it was that happened, when it was over, it was gone from her mind. There were enough horrible things in her everyday world to spend even an ounce of emotional energy on reliving the pain of the past.

But she remembered now.

· · ·

He rapes her. Of course. She isn't a virgin, obviously. Her own father has seen to that. But this is … different, violent, scary. Max takes her roughly. Angrily. And she cries and screams and tries to get away, and when she does, he slaps her around, splits her lip, bloodies her nose to get her to shut up. Before morning, he rapes her three times, satisfies himself apparently, because as the sun shines through the cracks around the window shade, he gets up and puts his pants back on. Then he pulls the envelope out of Jillian's purse, the one Aunt Daisy put there — the two thousand dollars her aunt had given her to "start a new life."

"You belong to me, sweetie pie," he says. "Don't you ever forget that, or I will beat the living hell out of you. Do you understand me? Are we clear?"

All Jillian can do is nod, mutely.

Max goes out the door, checks the nail by the door. Her car keys are gone and Max locks the door behind him. Jillian leaps up out of the bed, out of the stink, runs into the bathroom and vomits, heaves and heaves until there are black spots in front of her eyes. She tries to clean herself up, tries to clean him off of her.

That was another of Jillian's lifetime rules. No, more just an understanding from a lifetime of living life the way it was. And that understanding was that you couldn't ever get the stink of a man off you. It was futile to try. You just learned to accept that stink as a part of life as you had to live it.

"Jillian … are you all right?"

The voice seemed to come from far, far away. Then the world adjusted, snapped back into place, and Jillian was standing in the open doorway of her studio, looking at the empty bed where her Aunt Daisy should have been.

"No, I'm not all right. Neither are you." She took a

breath. "She's too old to run off. She's here in the house somewhere."

Without speaking, Jillian and Rileigh hurried down the hallway to look for her.

Chapter Twenty-Eight

AUNT DAISY WAS NOWHERE TO BE FOUND IN THE UPSTAIRS of the house. Not in the bedrooms or the bathroom or the linen closet or the clothes closet. Rileigh and Jillian reached the end of the hall at the top of the stairs and their eyes met.

"I know where she went," Jillian said, her voice as cold and as hard as a piece of a glacier buried deep under the Arctic Ocean.

They didn't run then. They walked down the stairs, then down the hallway to Mama's room. This time, it was Jillian who reached out to open the door and pushed it inward. Rileigh flicked on the light switch. There were Mama and Aunt Daisy, both of them in the big double bed in Mama's bedroom.

Aunt Daisy was pretending to be asleep, but Mama's eyes were wide open, and she put her finger to her lips.

"Shh, you're gonna wake her up," she said.

"You bet your ass we're gonna wake her up," Jillian said.

Crossing the room to the bed, she went around to the other side, grabbed Aunt Daisy by the nightgown, and hauled her up to a sitting position.

"We saw your little *gift*," Jillian spit the words into her face. Aunt Daisy did a remarkable job of acting both sleepy and surprised, maybe even a little shock thrown in.

"What in the world were you doing?" Mama asked.

Rileigh crossed to stand beside Jillian looking down at Aunt Daisy. Jillian still had not let go of her nightgown. Rileigh could see that Jillian was so angry that she couldn't even spit words out now.

"What's going on?" Mama asked.

Rileigh bit back her response, grabbed hold of the words, and kept them behind her teeth. Mama turned in the bed and put her arms around her sister. "What were you girls doing? What's wrong? What's the matter with you?"

Daisy leaned back into Mama's embrace, and Rileigh saw the tiniest hint of a smirk on the old woman's lips.

Jillian saw it, too, and it infuriated her. She yanked on Aunt Daisy's nightgown, dragged her out of Mama's embrace and hauled her to her feet. "You're going to clean it up this time."

Aunt Daisy had yet to say anything, but now she began to protest.

"Clean what up? What's the matter with you? Why'd you wake me up in the middle of the night?" She turned back to Mama. "Lily, what's wrong with these girls?"

Mama was bewildered and surprised, had no idea what was happening. Rileigh was not surprised when her mother burst into tears. Mama had been emotionally fragile recently — good stress was still stress, and she'd been under a lot of it in the run-up to her daughters' wedding.

And Rileigh suspected it might go even deeper than that. It was possible that Mama was beginning to put two and two together about her sister. That wasn't a simple thing to do with a mind riddled with the ravages of dementia, but connections were being made. And those connections had to be terrifying.

Mama dissolved into sobbing.

"Why are you doing this?" she cried sobbing. "Why have you been so mean to Daisy ever since I brought her home? Why?"

Jillian and Rileigh's eyes met.

Rileigh leaned close to Aunt Daisy and whispered in her ear. Mama's hearing aids were on the charging station beside the bed so she wouldn't be able to hear.

What she whispered was, "Either you come clean up this mess, or we will tell Mama everything."

Aunt Daisy merely looked at her smugly.

"The only reason we've kept quiet about what you did was we didn't want to upset Mama. Well, she's upset now. Telling her the truth will make it a helluva lot worse..." She actually growled the next words. "But after what you just did, I'm down with that. Question is — are *you*?"

Her aunt said nothing.

"Either you come right now and clean up the mess you made, or as God is my witness, I will tell Mama everything, every nasty, gritty detail — all of it. Then we will haul your ass back to the Carrington House ... but you won't be there long before I have Mitch get you transferred to Nashville." The state's hospital for the criminally insane was there. It was a nightmare horror that looked like a prison, with bars on the windows and howling crazy people inside. "The only way you'll ever leave there is in a casket."

Aunt Daisy realized Rileigh meant to do exactly what

she threatened. Turning back toward Mama, she sat down on the edge of the bed and took Mama's hand in hers.

"I got to confess, Lily. I done a real bad thing, then I come and got in bed with you so I wouldn't get caught. These girls is upset because I left a mess in Jillian's bedroom, and they want me to come clean it up."

"What kind of mess? Whatever it is, it can wait until in the morning." She looked from one of her daughters to the other. "Why would you do a thing like this, come waking your aunt in the middle of the night? You ought to be ashamed of yourselves."

"Now, Lily, don't blame them," Aunt Daisy said soothingly. "You got to grant them some grace. Both them girls is going to get married tomorrow. Their emotions are all over the place. They didn't mean no harm coming in here to get me to clean it up. Everything's okay now. You need to go on to sleep and let me do what they want."

"Well if there's a mess to clean up, I'll help too," Mama said.

All three women spoke as one. "No."

Aunt Daisy reloaded first. "You wait right here. Would you keep the bed warm? Do that for me, please. You remember when we were little girls and you used to come and get in bed with me in the middle of the night when you had a nightmare?"

Mama was calming down, not crying so hard but still confused and upset. "Sure I 'member I done that."

"That's why I came and got in your bed tonight … because I'd made that mess, and I felt bad about it and I was a little kid hiding from the Boogie Man."

Mama looked up at Jillian and Rileigh. "*What* mess?" Rileigh and Jillian said nothing. "Well, whatever it is, you girls can clean it up all by yourselves. You'd ought to be ashamed of yourselves, coming down here and waking up your Aunt Daisy like this."

"It's all right, Lily," Daisy said. "It's fine. I'll feel better if I clean it up, I won't feel guilty no more, and I'll be able to sleep by myself. If I don't, I'll have to stay in bed with you all night."

"I don't mind. When we was little, I used to like to sleep with you."

"You remember that story I used to tell you when you were a little girl and you were scared and you got in bed with me in the middle of the night? You remember that story?"

Lily shook her head dully, but she had stopped crying and now was merely sniveling. "You told me lots of stories. Which one are you talking about?"

"It was that one about the chicken who had baked a loaf of bread, and when she'd asked all the other farm animals to help her gather up the ingredients and make the bread, they refused but as soon as the bread was done they wanted some. You remember that?"

Mama sniffed. "I remember."

"The moral of that story is you got to do your part. You can't expect all the good things in life just to come to you. You got to be willing carry your own share of the load."

Mama didn't reply, but she wasn't crying anymore.

"I'm gonna clean up what I messed up and you're gonna wait here for me and I'll come back down and sleep in the bed with you. How about that?"

Mama looked at Rileigh and Jillian. The face of each was frozen in a rictus of rage.

"There's more going on here than you're telling me," Lily said. "I know there is."

Daisy got stern then, exerting big-sister-to-little-sister authority.

"Yes, there is, and I'll tell you about it sometime. Not right now, though. You need to go on to sleep." Daisy shoved Mama gently back down on her pillows, got up from the edge of the bed, and pulled the covers up around Mama's neck. "Now you stay right here and wait for me. I'm gonna calm these nervous brides down. I'll be right back."

Chapter Twenty-Nine

AUNT DAISY TURNED AND WALKED AHEAD OF JILLIAN AND Rileigh out the door. Rileigh closed the door behind her, and as soon as she did, Jillian grabbed Aunt Daisy's night-gown by the shoulder and hauled her down the hallway and up the stairs and into Jillian's bedroom, where she threw the old woman onto the floor at the foot of the bed.

"You bitch, you hateful bitch," Jillian spat. Rileigh was suddenly afraid of what Jillian might do to Aunt Daisy, so she stepped between them.

"You're going to clean this mess up," she said, "every speck of it, so it looks like it never was here. You know how to do that. You've already done it once."

Aunt Daisy glared at her defiantly. Rileigh grabbed her by the upper arm and lifted her to a standing position. "Get busy."

Turning her back on Aunt Daisy, she pushed Jillian gently but firmly back toward the door, out of Aunt Daisy's way.

"Come on, she's going to clean it up, and we're going to make sure she doesn't forget anything."

Rileigh saw now what she had not been aware of before. And that was that there was very little blood on the sheets of Jillian's bed. In fact, it might not even have been blood. It could have been tomato juice. Or perhaps ketchup. It was only spilled in the one spot, with a splatter or two on the pillowcase.

There was certainly not as much blood as there had been on that night all those years ago. Of course, there might not have been as much blood then as she remembered. In the eyes of a small child, a cup could have looked like a gallon.

As soon as she was sure that Jillian had gotten control of herself, Rileigh turned and crossed the room to the other side of the bed and picked up the human tongue.

"You want to tell me where in the hell you got this?" She snarled at Aunt Daisy.

"That chicken gizzard? I got it out of a chicken. Where do you think?"

"This isn't a chicken gizzard. You used a chicken gizzard last time. This is a real tongue. A real human tongue. Whose is it, and where did you get it?"

Aunt Daisy looked from one of her nieces to the other. "I don't have any idea what you're talking about. That there's a chicken gizzard. Cut it right out of the chicken myself. Always did think chicken gizzards looked like human tongues. Don't you?"

Jillian unexpectedly lunged at Aunt Daisy, who, to her credit, did not cringe, just stood her ground. But Rileigh caught Jillian before she could put her hands on the old lady. She shoved Aunt Daisy aside and pulled Jillian back to the doorway. "We're going to stand right here and watch. She's going to clean it all up."

"You bitch," Jillian snarled. "You whore."

"Well, I suppose it takes one to know one."

Jillian lunged again. And Rileigh was ready this time. Got between her and Aunt Daisy.

"Look, Jillian, I'd like to kill her, too. I'd like nothing more than to put my hands around that old bitch's throat and choke the life out of her. But—" Rileigh cut her eyes toward the door. "Mama." Just the one word. "Mama's waiting downstairs for her big sister to come get back in bed with her. That's more important than revenge."

Jillian looked at Aunt Daisy. "One day. Mark my words. One day, I will knock that smirk off your face. Not a threat, a solemn sacred promise — I will bury my fist in your ugly face and feel your teeth and your nose break."

Aunt Daisy didn't respond, but she didn't get to work, either.

Rileigh looked at her watch. "I'll give you half an hour to clean this mess up."

"And if I don't?"

"Then I'll haul you back to the Carrington House and dump your ass there. And tell Mama I don't have any idea where you went. Then I'll see to it that they confiscate that cell phone you're not supposed to have. And I'll block your number out of Mama's phone. Good luck trying to get your baby sister to come to your rescue again."

Aunt Daisy made some kind of grunting noise. She trudged off to the bathroom to get a washcloth and a towel to clean up the mess. While she was gone, Rileigh examined the tongue that had been laying on display on the white pillowcase. It was cold. Not room temperature. Cold. It had been in a refrigerator somewhere. Maybe it hadn't been cut recently out of a human body. Maybe it had been cut out a few days ago, and somebody had to put it in the refrigerator to make sure it didn't start to stink.

"I need to call Mitch," Rileigh told Jillian. She pulled

her phone out of her pocket and stepped out into the hall where she could keep an eye on Aunt Daisy and her sister.

Mitch answered on the first ring. "Please tell me you called just to tell me you love me so much that…" He paused, searching for words. "That you feel as light as a soap bubble and you're afraid you're about to float away."

"I do love you so much I feel as light as a soap bubble and I'm afraid I'm about to float away."

"But…?"

"But that's not what I called to tell you."

"I was afraid of that."

She filled Mitch in on how Aunt Daisy had spent her evening turning Jillian's room into a recurring nightmare while everyone was at the rehearsal dinner. She described how her aunt had recreated the scene from almost thirty years ago on the night before Jillian's wedding when six-year-old Rileigh walked into the room and found blood everywhere and a human tongue nestled purposefully on a pristine white pillowcase. Rileigh heard him grind his teeth. And he only did that when he was absolutely furious.

"Well, I'm as mad as you are," she said.

"Oh, I don't think so. I don't think so at all." He let out a breath. "What did you do?"

"I tried to keep Jillian from seeing it, but she got past me. And then the two of us went looking for Aunt Daisy."

"How'd you keep from killing her? Or if you didn't keep from killing her, tell me how I can help you hide the body."

"She wasn't in her room. She had better sense than that. She'd gone down and gotten in Mama's bed. She was pretending to be asleep."

"That had to be ugly."

"You don't want to know."

"So now Mama knows what Daisy did all those years ago."

"No, we managed to keep it from her. I threatened Aunt Daisy. Told her I'd tell Mama everything. And that you would see to it that she was transferred to the prison for the criminally insane in Nashville. And the only way she'd ever leave there was in a coffin."

"That's an absolutely glorious idea. Why didn't we think of it sooner?"

"You'd have my vote," Rileigh said. "But now she's cleaning up the mess. And by morning, when we get up, I'm sure — I *hope* — Mama will have forgotten all about it."

"Dodged a bullet."

"There's one little detail I left out."

"And that is?"

"The human tongue on the pillowcase. Remember how Daisy told us that she cut out a chicken gizzard because she'd always thought it looked like a human tongue?"

"I remember."

"Well, she didn't bother to kill a chicken this time. The red splattered everywhere was just for effect. She may have used tomato juice or ketchup. But the tongue looked real all right." Rileigh took a breath. "Because it *was* real."

"What was real?"

"It's a real human tongue, Mitch."

"Real?"

"It was cold when I touched it. It's still cold. Meaning it had been in a refrigerator."

Mitch seemed to be stumbling a little, trying to follow the train of Riley's thought.

"Oh," he said. "So it wasn't fresh. It was cut out of somebody's mouth some time ago."

"That was my thought. And it would explain why the body that was dumped outside the bachelor party on Wednesday was missing a head."

"The killer didn't want us to see that what it was really missing was its tongue," Mitch finished for her.

"Seems reasonable to me."

"Wait. Wait a minute. If Daisy got that tongue from someone…"

"Where else could Aunt Daisy have come by a real human tongue? She must have gotten it from the killer."

"Which means…"

"Aunt Daisy knows who the killer is."

Chapter Thirty

It was Saturday morning, October 12, 2024, just after sunrise.

Reuben Lablonski was awake, but he stayed in bed with his eyes closed.

When he opened his eyes, he saw nothing. He was staring at the ceiling, but there was nothing there to see, no ceiling. Inside his head was just static and white noise, and he was lost in there, unable to find a way out, unable to distinguish up from down, floating around in white, glittery nothingness.

He had slept, sound and deep, and then he awoke. But there was no difference between sleeping and wakefulness. He heard a sound then, something that had found its way through the tiny sparks of light that held him captive. And that's what they were, the glitter and the static were particles of light, not tiny as they should be, though. The particles were the size of marbles, and he could touch them. He reached out both hands, scooped up handfuls of marble-sized light and let them dribble down in a cascade between his fingers.

Then there were more marbles, then more and more. He couldn't reach out his hand to grab them because they were all around him, pressing in on him, smothering him. He was buried in an avalanche of them, swallowed up by them, swirling around and around like water racing toward a drain.

The sound came again, and he tried to focus on it. When the sound came a third time, he recognized it as his phone ringing, and the white noise and the glittering chunks of light rolled away from him, like he had risen up out of a coffin filled with marbles. Then he was sitting up on the side of his bed, looking around at his hotel room. And he was present then, he was there, he was *aware*. He reached for the phone and put it to his ear.

"Hello."

There was no answer. The line was dead. Had he imagined the phone ringing? But imagined it with what? He no longer had a mind that could imagine. His head was full of marbles of brilliant light.

He looked to see if the phone had rung, and if it had, what was the number. That's when he noticed his hands, realized how scratched and scuffed they were. So were his knees, rubbed raw like when he was a little kid and he'd fallen down on the sidewalk. And the scratches hurt. That was absurd, but it was true. Each scratch screamed in pain like an inch-deep knife wound.

Ole Arch. That was it, had to be. Ole Arch. Thanks a bunch, pal.

Holding the phone in his hand made him aware of the stinging, and he examined the marks, wondering if anybody would notice that his hands were scratched. If so, he'd come up with some excuse, some explanation. The scratches couldn't be helped. He's had a job to do last night and he'd been scratched doing it. Scratched, but not *seen*. He was certain that no one had seen him.

He'd spent a little time in his criminal career as a cat burglar, dressed all in black. He could scale buildings and creep into someone's house, steal millions of dollars' worth of jewelry, in and out, and no one had ever saw him or knew he was there. It was like that last night.

There were times in his life when he thought perhaps he *was* invisible, genuinely invisible, because people always seemed to look right through him. And that was definitely a plus, given his line of work, and it had helped out last night too. There were people around at the recreation area. It wasn't like there was a guard posted, because there was nothing to guard, but there were people there, doing jobs, even after all the principals had gone through the wedding ceremony to see how it would be played out today, and then they'd all adjourned to the Knights of Columbus hall for the rehearsal dinner.

And once the crowd had been behind closed doors, he had crept as silently as a black cat. Entered on silent feet, did the work that he had to do, was gone without leaving a trace.

Blew through like the wind.

The work that he had to do was difficult, tedious, and had to be perfect. It wasn't necessarily dangerous, though. He was working with a very stable explosive. It couldn't be detonated by a gunshot or by dropping it, even setting it on fire. It needed a specific kind of spark from a detonator. He had, as usual, done every task masterfully, and when he was finally finished, he had stood at the top of the hill, looking down on the rows of satin-covered benches, and tried to imagine what it all would look like after El Viento had blown through here with the force of a category five hurricane, the wind a mile-wide twister, wreaking havoc and destruction.

And death.

Oh, my yes. Death. Death on a grand scale.

He put his phone aside, got to his feet, went to the hotel room desk, opened up his laptop, and dived deep into the dark web. Entering the chatroom called Beyond Here Be Dragons, he read the postings there, grinning.

BangURDead: "I've got your number now! I get the 'catch ME if you can' reference. I understand how come you always manage to get away."

El Viento: "How do you figure that is?"

BangURDead: "Oh, I don't want to spoil the surprise. It'll be our little secret, just between you and me."

El Viento: "Fool! You know nothing."

BangURDead: "Oh, but I do. Now, I understand how you've been able to hide from everybody for all these years. You've been hiding right out there in plain sight."

Born2BEvil: "In plain sight? Where might that be?"

BangURDead: "You think I'd tell *you?*"

El Viento: "Idiots! Both of you."

El Viento knew the moron was chasing a rabbit down the wrong hole. He'd stood ten feet from Born2BEvil this afternoon and the cretin had never noticed.

El Viento: "You don't have any idea what you're talking about. But I, on the other hand, have you figured out. Your impersonation isn't half bad, I'll give you that. But I see through the disguise. And I'm going to enjoy sliding a blade into your navel today. I can't wait to see the look of surprise on your face."

Of course, that was a bluff. He had no intention of wasting his time ripping BangURDead's guts out. Oh, he'd kill the man, all right. He'd kill them all. He just wouldn't use a knife.

BangURDead: "Good luck with that. You're the one who's not going to live to see another sunrise. By this time tomorrow, I'll be collecting the money out of your Swiss bank accounts, and you will be as dead as a post."

By this time tomorrow, we'll *both* be as dead as posts! But El Viento didn't say that. He merely typed, "Good luck with that."

Chapter Thirty-One

It was Saturday morning, October 12, 2024, just after sunrise.

Mitchell Webster was awake, but he stayed in bed with his eyes closed.

Was the night really darkest just before the dawn?

It had often seemed like that in Mitch's life that the hesitation between night and day was the time when all bad things were possible, when the Boogey Man would come roaring out of the closet and bring all his nasty friends. It was the hour when everyone he loved was in imminent danger of drunk drivers, brain aneurisms, and stray bullets and death seemed as near as the darkness, as cold as the moonlight, and as certain as the coming dawn.

Today was it. Today was the day when the rubber would meet the road — on every highway that mattered in his life. Today, Rileigh Bishop would become his wife.

If she lived that long.

Mitch slammed the door on that thought and all the others like it that waited in the dark recesses of his mind, ready to attack him, chew up his resolve and paralyze him with fear.

Fear was a luxury he couldn't afford. Not now. Not today.

To calm his nerves that had been worn down to the loose ends of a frayed rope, he ticked off in his head all the precautions he had taken, the protection he had erected to shield his bride from harm.

It had begun with the "if you see something, say something" admonition he'd given to his friends at the bachelor party and Rileigh had given to hers at the bachelorette party.

He'd checked out maybe a dozen different "sightings," and while none of them had turned up a live killer, one of them had come close, and led to the discovery of the body of the videographer, a victim of one of the other killers in the Catch Me If You Can posse.

Then he'd required every person — man, woman, and child over the age of twelve — who was on the Breezy Creek Recreation Area property preparing for the wedding extravaganza to sign in — to put their name, address, phone number and the reason for their presence on a sign-up sheet. He'd collected dozens of names — so many he had nowhere near the resources it would require to clear them all. And right about that time, he'd gotten a call from Collier Atkinson, the sheriff of Weatherford County. He'd met Collier when he and Rileigh had been trying to save the life of FBI agent Lamar Devereaux. Atkinson had only been on the job for a few months at that time, appointed until there could be a special election to replace the sheriff who had died. Mitch had taken an instant liking to the man because he was all business. One look at him told Mitch he was former military — erect posture, haircut high and tight, and you could have cut a piece of steak with a crease in the pants of his uniform.

Atkinson had called to congratulate Mitch on his upcoming wedding, and Mitch found himself unloading on his counterpart from the neighboring county. He told Collier what was going on with the wedding ... the killer who'd been stalking Rileigh ... the other killers stalking the stalker ... the dark web, all the precautions he was taking — everything.

By the time he had completed his litany of woe, he was embarrassed for unburdening himself to Atkinson, but to his surprise, Atkinson had offered to help.

"How about I wrestle up a deputy or two, maybe talk Sheriff Huxley in Buchanan County and Barker in Whitley County into doing the same. We could take that sign-up list you compiled and check out the names. You sure as shit don't have the manpower — or the time — to do it right now."

Mitch had gratefully accepted the offer.

Then Mitch had recruited a small army of "wedding guest" security guards — half a dozen local men who would be on the lookout for any strange occurrence, all of them packing, men who would be armed and had experience using a weapon.

He had set out a perimeter around the recreation area, guards patrolling the woods to prevent a sniper from setting up there. Then he'd placed his own snipers, three of them, strategically in the trees — one with a clear sightline to the back side of the amphitheater stage and another one on each side. They would be examining the crowd through the scopes on their rifles, could have their crosshairs on any threat in seconds.

He'd found out last night what Aunt Daisy had done to

Rileigh and Jillian, and that the old biddy obviously knew who the killer was. While there was no hope she would divulge that information, it was possible she might make contact with him today. So he'd called Craig Dylan to enlist his help.

"Hate to bother you, Craig, but I'm wondering if you could do me a favor," he'd said when he reached him. "I'm looking for a babysitter."

Then Mitch told him the story.

"You're saying Rileigh's Aunt Daisy knows what El Viento looks like?"

"I don't know how else Daisy could have gotten a human tongue if he hadn't given it to her."

"So how are you going to get her to identify him?"

"You *can't*. Nobody can get Aunt Daisy to do anything she doesn't want to do. She looked Rileigh dead in the eye and said that what Rileigh had in her hand was a chicken gizzard, not a human tongue."

"So you can't get her to?"

"No. But maybe he'll contact her today. Whoever he is, he'll be at the wedding today, he'll be in that crowd. If you could just keep an eye on Aunt Daisy and see if anybody approaches her…"

"I'll be on that old lady like white on rice," Marshal Dylan said.

As Mitch lay now in the growing dawn light, he realized he was going over and over the precautions he'd taken, fingering them one after the other like a rosary. He had done everything he could do. And now…

Now, all he could do was *trust*.

He had to trust Rileigh. She was their final line of defense. He absolutely adored the woman … but did he *trust* her? Did he believe that if the guano came into contact with the air conditioning, she could handle it?

Then he answered his own question. Rileigh Bishop was one of the finest police officers he had ever worked with. She was smart and quick, with the reflexes of a cat.

If it came down to it, Rileigh would stop El Viento.

Chapter Thirty-Two

It was Saturday morning, October 12, 2024, just after sunrise.

Rileigh Bishop was awake, but she stayed in bed with her eyes closed.

When she opened her eyes, in that gauzy place between sleeping and waking, she was a little girl again. Six years old, waking up on her big sister's wedding day … only her big sister wasn't going to get married. Her big sister was dead. Rileigh'd seen the blood and the human tongue … but nobody believed her.

Rileigh blinked, and she was back in her own bedroom, a young woman on her own wedding day. She didn't move, just lay there in the receding shadows with only the beginnings of light creeping in from outside. Oh, the sun had risen out there on the flat, but it hadn't cleared Tucker Mountain yet. And when it did, it would shine out over Rileigh's *wedding day*.

Like most little girls, Rileigh had dreamed of the day when she would walk down the aisle in a beautiful white dress with a handsome man standing at the altar waiting for her, but unlike most other little girls, she had put those fantasies aside. Rileigh never allowed herself to indulge in that kind of imagining, because Jillian's wedding day had so traumatized the little girl that she didn't realize until years later that she had grown to dislike all things associated with weddings. The Here Comes The Bride melody she and Jillian would hear as they walked down the aisle — for years, it had made her skin crawl. Wedding dresses were like Halloween costumes — she'd never liked anything frilly and fancy and girly like that. So many things in her life, the decisions she'd made, the places she'd gone, had been a result of the trauma that six-year-old girl experienced when she went into her sister's bedroom to put a note in her suitcase — "Please don't forget me."

And then Aunt Daisy had rubbed their noses in that horror last night, staged the whole thing over again, tried to spoil everything for both Jillian and Rileigh. That woman was wicked and evil. Rileigh would like nothing better than to lock her up somewhere and never see her again. And she would, too. Except Mama. Mama didn't know that her sister had sold Jillian to sex slave traders and destroyed thirty years of Jillian's life. Mama didn't know her precious husband J.R. had been sleeping with Daisy, and had abused his own *daughter* and his other daughter's friends and was engaged in all manner of other pedophilia before he was left hanging from an extension cord in the barn. Rileigh would do just about anything to allow her mother to go to her grave without ever knowing any of that.

They were approaching the finish line now. It wouldn't be too long before Mama's dementia overtook her, and she wouldn't be able to understand the horror of her husband's and her sister's betrayals. Just not yet. And so

Aunt Daisy had gotten away with her nasty prank last night.

After she and Jillian had slipped Aunt Daisy back into bed beside Mama, they had walked slowly back upstairs, then Jillian had made an odd request. She turned the tables on Rileigh.

"So how about I sleep in your room tonight with you?" Jillian said.

Rileigh threw her arms around her big sister. "Of course you can."

"It's payback for all the nights you came and got in bed with me when you were scared."

"Are *you* scared?" Rileigh asked Jillian.

"Yeah. Terrified."

"Of what?"

"Of tomorrow and all the tomorrows stacked up on top of each other out there in front of it. Of trying to live a normal life when I'm not normal. Of trying to make David happy."

Before Rileigh could say anything, Jillian had put her fingers over her lips. "Let's not talk about this now. Let's just go to bed. After all, we're both getting married in the morning."

At some point during the night, Jillian had returned to her own bedroom, and now Rileigh lay in bed as morning light began to warm her room and considered the incredible reality: today she would marry the man she loved more than she'd ever thought she could love anyone. She smiled then in the lightning dark. She hadn't wanted to love him. She had done everything in her power to keep from falling for him. All those months working on first one murder case and then another she had felt herself being drawn toward him as inexorably as metal filings to a magnet. And she had fought it, oh my goodness had she fought it, had dug her heels into the dirt and tried her dead level best not to care about Mitch Webster.

It had been a useless effort. She had fallen head over heels in love with the sheriff, and he with her, and now the two of them were about to become one, as the ceremony would say. They were embarking today on the first day of their lives together. They would build a home and a family, have kids, grow old together. Someday she would sit in a rocking chair on a porch in the mountains somewhere and reach out her old hand, gnarled with arthritis, skin wrinkled, spotted, and freckled, and take the gnarled hand of the man in the rocker beside her. Beginning today, she and Mitch Webster would live the rest of their lives together.

Today they would get married.

Or Rileigh would get killed.

On her wedding day.

Rileigh had become a master at pushing aside the thoughts of the monster who had been sending her pieces of bodies for the last six months. Had managed not to think about the impending doom of the countdown. Had kept her eyes focused on whatever case she was working on, on Mama, on Mitch, on something besides the bastard who, for reasons she could not fathom, had decided to kill her. At least she knew his name now, or the name he went by. El Viento, the wind. What was it Marshal Dylan had said about him? He blew through people's lives as silently and invisibly as the wind. You couldn't see him. You only knew he'd been there after he passed through by the trail of bodies he left behind.

That guy was still out there. She had been determined, and had talked Mitch into being equally determined, to stop the guy here and now, the one time they knew where he would be. But now it was her wedding day, and the killer was still out there, as were probably two other assassins bent on killing the killer. Rileigh shook her head to clear it. This was her *wedding day*. She needed to concentrate on that, on the fact that she was marrying Mitch and they were starting a life together. But as hard as she resisted, the sinister figure of the killer still stood between her and the sunlight of happiness, casting a pale shadow of fear and anxiety over Rileigh's whole world.

El Viento.

She clenched her jaw, found that her hands had been curled into fists at her side. Well, she and Mitch still had a card or two in their hands left to play, thank you very much. Cards *nobody* knew about. This wasn't over. They would not go blithely into the activities of this day carefree. They would appear to be ignoring the threat of the monster out there, but they were *ready*, and Rileigh trusted that their final line of defense would stop him. She *had to* put her faith in the skill of two fine police officers — she and Mitch.

After all, she and Mitch had tracked down killers and stopped them from killing again — over and over during the months they'd worked together. They'd stopped Aunt Daisy after she killed Tina Montgomery. They'd stopped Angus and Sarah Park, who'd used fire as a murder weapon. They'd put an end to Brandon Hollister, the copycat serial killer, and Charlie Hayden's murder spree on the Queen of the Smokies. They'd also caught the little-kid kidnapper, who'd snatched Mason Stump from Walmart, and the ex-sheriff, Mum, who'd murdered J.R. Bishop almost three decades ago. Stopping the minister's son who used witchcraft to cover his crimes and the "gang war" between the Hatfields and the McCoys were additional feathers in their caps, as well as saving the life of an FBI agent and stopping a murderous "ghost" at Shagbark Manor. They'd even saved Jillian from the murderer who *wasn't* the daughter she'd given up twenty years ago. In all those cases, they had made it through and caught the bad guy.

This was the money shot. This was the gold ring, and they'd catch this bastard, too.

For almost three decades, Rileigh had lived without Jillian in her life, and then in the miracle of miracles, Jillian had escaped her captors and come home, and today Rileigh would stand beside her sister and the two of them would marry the men they loved. Rileigh would not let *anybody* get in the way of that. El Viento thought he was smarter than everyone else, had eluded capture for years, had killed God only knows how many people and gotten away with it. But he had met his match in Rileigh and Mitch. He wasn't going to get away this time. They were ready for him. Today, they would kill the notorious assassin El Viento, and then they would live happily ever after.

So let it be written, so let it be done.

Chapter Thirty-Three

THE TEN BRIDESMAIDS BEGAN SHOWING UP AT THE BREEZY Creek Recreation Area's Visitors Center late Saturday morning. They all carried bushel baskets or buckets or washtubs or cardboard boxes full of fall leaves, each leaf coated in wax that had been painstakingly applied from wax paper onto the surface of the leaf with a warm iron.

Rileigh was there to greet them and to thank them for helping out — with a bright smile on her face that convinced them all she was *thrilled* by the huge wedding Georgia had planned for her.

Each girl deposited her collection of leaves on the tables that would be used later to seat the crowd at the whoop-de-do but were now placed end-to-end, forming a big surface they could gather around to transform the leaves into centerpieces, garlands, bouquets, and end caps for each of the rows of satin-covered benches set up for the wedding guests. At any other wedding, all those beautiful decorations would have been made from flowers.

Phoebe Phillips from Phillips Florist Shop in Black Bear Forge had volunteered to come out and help the girls arrange the beautiful leaves into displays like floral displays. She brought ribbon, but not the pale blue and white and pink that usually adorned wedding decorations. She had brought bright green, yellow, red, and gold ribbons, and the girls set to work making centerpieces with big ribbons tied in bows around handfuls of brightly colored leaves.

The girls also set to work decorating the grape arbor that Ian McGinnis and his crew had taken all day to build yesterday. It was gorgeous. The brides and grooms and the minister would stand beneath it during the ceremony, and it would be covered in fall foliage as if it were the forest floor after a strong breeze.

Rileigh remembered grade school science class where she learned why leaves changed color — an explanation that'd surprised and charmed her. All leaves started out green in the summer, of course, because of the presence of a group of green pigments known as chlorophyll. When these green pigments were abundant in the leaf cells during the growing season, they masked the color of any other pigments that might also be present in the leaf. Chlorophyll in the leaves was the tree's main means of producing nutrients during the summer, but autumn brought the destruction of chlorophyll, and the demise of green pigments allowed other previously *masked* colors to come forward. Rileigh had loved that explanation. She had always assumed that the autumn colors appeared and covered up the green leaves of the forest, but to discover that the green in the leaves was actually covering up the fall colors was a glorious revelation. She'd look out in the summertime at the beautiful mountains and consider that the green in every leaf on every tree was hiding some wonderfully brilliant color that would show up as soon as there was frost on the pumpkin.

The colors of the leaves the girls provided was determined by where in the mountains they lived and what trees happened to grow in the woods near them.

Ashley Brooks brought in huge tulip poplar leaves as big as dinner plates, bright yellow ones.

Brittany Durant brought in blue ash leaves, a stem with tiny leaves extending out from it in different shades of yellows and reds and golds.

Rileigh remembered Alexis McCauley from third grade when she had just gotten in the two top adult teeth and everyone had teased her that she looked like a rabbit. She certainly didn't look like a rabbit now, and Alexis lived on Dogwood Ridge which — *duh!* — was covered in beautiful, yellow-leafed dogwood trees.

Rachel Ewing brought birch leaves in shades of pale yellow and elm leaves that were both yellow and gold.

Hickory leaves were among Rileigh's favorites, and Victoria Whitworth dumped out a bushel basket of them, painstakingly covered in wax, of course, that were green with yellow stripes running through them.

Nicole Garrison lived in Sweet Gum Hollow, and the sweet gum leaves she brought were red and gold and yellow in combination. The shape of sweet gum leaves had always reminded Rileigh of a stick figure — a very fat stick figure — with a head at the top, two arms, and two legs extending below. The ones Nicole brought in were both red and yellow in a swirling mixture, each leaf unique.

One of the things Rileigh loved best about autumn leaves was that they were as unique as snowflakes. No two were exactly alike. Cottonwood leaves were bright yellow and heart shaped. Poplar leaves looked like golden teardrops. Ash leaves were a violet color of red. Sweet gum leaves were red, too — the bright red of a fancy sports car or a candied apple. Sugar maple trees, the delicate design of their leaves forming little points like stars, were both yellow and red in combination — different in every leaf.

Stephanie Wakefield had gathered a basket full of prickly holly leaves — deep, dark green year-round and interspersed with red berries — from the holly trees in the woods beside her house. She had the scratches on her hands and arms to prove it.

The girls arrived dressed in sweatshirts and jeans and Crocs. They would be transformed into ten chiffon-clad fairy princesses for the wedding this afternoon, but it would take them all day to get there. Each would go through a caterpillar into a butterfly metamorphosis *individually*. Two hairdressers were on hand to "do hair." Shelby Hicks, David Hicks's cousin, was one of the markup artists for stars appearing at Dollywood, and she had volunteered to "do makeup" for each girl. That process would begin with spraying base makeup on each girl's face, rendering her skin absolutely flawless. Then would come the application of powder, blush, eyeshadow, eyeliner, and mascara — after the false eyelashes were glued in place, at least for those inclined to wear false eyelashes.

Rileigh wandered down the length of tables, gathering her favorite leaves — several of the dinner-plate sized tulip poplar leaves, some red maple leaves, yellow beech tree leaves, and orange hickory leaves that were the shape of four-leaf clovers, except there were five leaves. The girls were making bouquets for all of the bridesmaids as well as using the leaves for decorations, but Rileigh was selecting leaves individually for her own bouquet. The brides' bouquets would, of course, be the biggest and most beautiful of all. Hers would be huge. She would make it herself with big, colorful leaves, and streamers of colored ribbons. It would be unique — and special.

———————————

Chapter Thirty-Four

Almost-five-year-old Mason Stump was pissed on. That's what Daddy called being mad — pissed on.

No, not on — *off.* Daddy called being mad "pissed *off*," and Mason was pissed off. He was grumpy and he was tired and he didn't want to wear the stupid suit that was too hot and the tie that made him feel like he was choking.

Daddy had been in charge of getting all the kids ready for Aunt Rileigh's wedding because Mommy was *in* the wedding. And it had been such a mess at the house trying to find Eli's shoes and Liam's socks and Connor's underwear. Mommy always managed somehow to find everybody's clothes when they were all getting ready to go somewhere at the same time, but Daddy didn't even know that the Spiderman underwear was Eli's, not Connor's. Connor wore Batman underwear! Mason's little sister Mayella had been parked at Mamaw's house because Daddy had told Mommy that he couldn't haul enough bananas with him to keep her quiet during the wedding and he didn't plan to try.

Mason was the only one of his siblings who had to

dress in a stupid suit and a tie because he was the ring bearer. It had sounded like fun in the beginning, being the ring bearer. He was supposed to walk very slowly holding this pillow out in front of him with the wedding rings on it, down the aisle in front of Chloe, but not get too far in front of her. And Mommy said he couldn't talk to anybody that he saw sitting in the audience. He couldn't wave at anybody. He couldn't do anything but walk very slowly down the aisle and then up to the steps and hand the pillow to Dr. Hazelton. Then he was supposed to walk very slowly to the seats that were saved for him and Chloe on the front row. And he was supposed to sit there until the wedding was over.

That'd sounded like fun. But Mason found out as soon as they started practicing what he was supposed to do that they weren't going to let him carry the *real* wedding rings at all.

"Are you kidding me? Put *Mason* in charge of the wedding rings?"

That's what he'd heard his mother say, and then she had rolled her eyes. He found out then that they were going to put pretend wedding rings on the white cushion that he would be carrying in front of him, but the real wedding rings would be in the pockets of the guys standing beside Sheriff Mitch and Uncle David.

So why did he need to go to all the trouble of wearing the stupid, uncomfortable suit if he wasn't going to carry real rings? And he had to walk really slow in front of Chloe Morgan, who was throwing things on the floor, tiny red leaves or something. Chloe Morgan was the little girl who had been kidnapped the same time he was last summer, when he'd believed that the little girl with the blonde hair in Walmart had some puppies in a box, and he'd wanted to see the puppies, so he'd followed her out — and bang! He got locked in that camper. He pitched a green fit, screamed and hollered and yelled and banged, but nobody heard him. And then he wound up spending the night in a dog kennel. If it hadn't been for Aunt Rileigh, he might still be stuck in that kennel. But in the end, he had disobeyed Aunt Rileigh. She'd told him to help Chloe get out of the basement because the house was on fire and then she said he was to run into the woods to get away from the fire and wait until people saw the smoke and came.

But that was *stupid*. If he just stood around, that house would burn down right on top of Aunt Rileigh! And he wasn't going to let that happen. So he grabbed Chloe's hand and dragged her out to the road. It was a long way. Maybe longer than he'd ever walked. Certainly longer than he'd ever walked by himself. And then he just stood in the middle of the highway. He knew nobody would run over a little kid standing in the road. Whoever came along would stop. And he was right. That nice farmer man came along and stopped and Mason told him what was going on.

Of course, he hadn't been spanked for running away in Walmart because Mommy and Daddy were so glad to see him after he'd been kidnapped that not only did he *not* get spanked, but he pretty much did anything to do for about a month after that and nobody corrected him. That was a long time ago, though, and now life was back to normal.

Mason had fallen asleep in the car on the way into town — until Liam stuck his tongue in his ear to wake him up. Mason had tried to punch Liam in the nose, but he missed, and then Daddy told them to stop fighting. It was Daddy's fault that Mason was sleepy. While Mommy was at the big rehearsal dinner thing last night, Daddy let Mason watch *Jurassic Park* with his older brothers, Liam, Eli, and Conner. But Daddy had made them promise, cross-your-heart-and-hope-to-die, pinky-swear promise that they wouldn't tell Mommy he had let them watch that movie because she didn't think it was appropriate for small children.

Mason had *loved* it. It was the best movie he had ever seen — *ever*. Better than all those kiddie movies like *Toy Story* and *Monsters, Inc.* and *Despicable Me*. There were all these dinosaurs and they were kept in a pen on this island until the dumb guy let them out. But boy was he sorry! He got eaten by a whole bunch of little dinosaurs taking little bitty bites of him all at the same time — which was almost worse than the big dinosaurs eating whole people in one bite. Mason thought *Jurassic Park* was so good he would have watched it ten more times. But it had lasted really late — so late Daddy had barely gotten him and his brothers put to bed before Mommy got home.

Mason was still awake, heard Mommy tell Daddy that she knew he hadn't given the boys baths before he put them to bed. Mommy always knew those kinds of things even when she wasn't home and nobody told her. Mommies were just like that, he guessed. He'd listened to Mommy and Daddy talk, something about not dying if you went to bed with dirty feet. He didn't understand that part and then he fell asleep. But in the middle of the night, Mason woke up. There were big monsters with sharp white teeth chasing him in the dark. He was *scared* and he started crying and ran and got in bed with Mommy and Daddy. He couldn't stay asleep after that because every time he nodded off, the monsters came after him again. Mason thought maybe Mommy figured out what the deal was, because Conner had bad dreams last night, too. Liam and Eli probably did, too, but they were too old to sleep with Mommy and Daddy.

What it all came down to was that now it was late in the afternoon, and Mason didn't feel like doing a wedding.

Mason felt like taking a nap, but Daddy put him in a suit that he didn't like and put that tie on him and told him that he was gonna have to walk down the aisle in front of the bride even though the rings he had on that white pillow were just pretend. He didn't see any reason why he had to do it, and so he did what was his … what was it Daddy called it? His *default* behavior when he didn't get what he wanted. He threw a tantrum, a big one. He said he *wasn't* walking down the aisle, wasn't going to carry that stupid pillow with its pretend rings, and then he fell down on the ground, crying really loud and banging his feet and fists in the dirt.

Mommy never did anything whenever Mason or any of the kids threw a tantrum. It wasn't like she punished them or anything like that. Sometimes throwing a tantrum got you what you wanted, and sometimes it didn't, but Mommy never got mad about it.

But Daddy did, though. He grabbed Mason by the arm and shook him and whispered in his ear, sounding really mean, "You straighten up, young man."

You knew you were in big trouble when they called you "young man."

"Or when we get home, I'm gonna bust your little butt."

That had put the fear of God in him. But he was still sniffling and snuffling, still mad, and then it came to him. He could run away and hide!

Sure! It was the perfect solution. With all the people in the wedding, and the wedding guests showing up, and the whoop-de-do getting started, it'd be easy to slip away. And he knew exactly where he could hide that nobody'd find him.

Mason Stump smiled, happy for the first time that day.

Chapter Thirty-Five

THE LOGISTICS OF GETTING THE RIGHT BRIDESMAIDS hooked up to the right groomsmen to walk down the aisle together before the two brides came in was a tactical maneuver reminiscent of Rommel in North Africa during World War II.

Gratefully, the building lent itself to organizing the event. Located on the hill above the amphitheater, it was U-shaped, with a northern wing, and a southern wing connected by a central hallway. Brides and bridesmaids were assigned to the north side, grooms and groomsmen in the south. If they lined up in the proper order, each bridesmaid from the northern wing would meet her assigned groomsmen from the southern wing in the central hall connecting the two. The bridesmaid would hook her arm through the arm of the matching groomsmen and down the aisle they would go.

It was in that central hallway that Georgia sprang her final surprise.

"Close your eyes, don't look," she'd told Rileigh, Jillian,

and Mama, leading them reluctantly into the hallway where all the bridesmaids had gathered waiting.

She let go of Rileigh's arm and stepped back. *"Surprise!"*

The three opened their eyes to see a statue on a three-foot pedestal. No, not a statue, not something made of stone. It was a beautiful bride, stunning, standing before them. It was a moment before Rileigh understood. Mama was the first to react.

"Is that *my*…?" she gasped.

"It is indeed," Georgia said, beaming. "Your wedding dress!"

All the bridesmaids cheered and applauded.

Georgia scolded Rileigh and Jillian, still mystified by their lack of imagination.

"I can't believe you didn't want to wear it. I sure as hell would have!" Except, of course, the dress would have been far too small to fit around Georgia's I've-had-five-babies shape. But it was the fairy-princess wedding gown from Georgia's childhood fantasies … all the way down to the fifteen-foot train. "So I sneaked it out of your house, got a mannequin from Susan's dress store, and put it up here. It's just so *beautiful* — the most gorgeous wedding decoration of them all. And now Mama gets to see her wedding dress on her daughters' wedding day … even if neither one of them's wearing it."

Mama hugged Georgia, tears in her eyes. Rileigh had to admit the beautiful bride standing right outside the room where she and Jillian would dress added just the right final touch.

Rileigh had worked much of the afternoon on her huge bridal bouquet of leaves, and it rested on a table beside the door with Jillian's and Mama's bouquets, easy for them to snatch up as they left the room. They would be the last of the line of women to file into the central hallway for their walk down the aisle between the rows of satin-covered benches where the audience would be sitting, and on down onto the stage area of the amphitheater below where the ceremony would take place.

Rileigh stood by the window, watching the guests get out of their cars in the parking lot and file down the steps to find a seat on the benches, each adorned with a ribboned spray of autumn leaves attached to both ends. They had dispensed with the bride side, groom side for this occasion and called it festival seating all around. The curtains on the window opened just enough so that she could look out at the guests as they arrived.

Unfortunately, she wasn't just enjoying seeing familiar faces coming to her wedding. Black Bear Forge was, after all, a community as close-knit as steel wool, a place where your neighbors showed up for the significant events in your life: weddings, funerals, and graduations, and everyone looked for your face at their significant events as well. And as she looked into the faces of friends and family getting out of their cars and coming toward the amphitheater, she was saddened by the fact that she wasn't just enjoying the guests at her wedding; she was eyeing everyone for something out of the ordinary, anything that seemed strange, anything that someone could report to her as had been reported to Mitch.

If you see something, say something.

While Rileigh watched, Wally Hansford and his wife crossed the parking lot with Stephanie Papadopoulos. Wally was the head of the Good Guys Investigation Agency, The Good GIs, in Gatlinburg, where Rileigh had worked part-time when she first came back home to Yarmouth County from Memphis. Stephanie Papadopoulos was Wally's receptionist, a reasonably attractive young woman with big eyes, a bright smile, and the highest-pitched voice Rileigh had ever heard. It was a squeaky squeal, fingernails on the blackboard of Rileigh's soul, reminding her of nothing so much as the squealing cry that Georgia's youngest child, Mayella, a squeal used to hold her family hostage and to get whatever she wanted, and of course what she wanted was a banana to be stuck in her mouth to shut her up.

Rileigh spotted Big John Clancy, who owned the Red Eye Gravy Diner; he'd come with two waitresses from the diner, Beth Ann Huntington and Reba Simmons.

Evelyn and Clive Foster got out of car and started across the parking lot. Rileigh hadn't seen them since the spring festival at the elementary school when Chloe Morgan had been kidnapped. Rileigh saw Smitty Arnold, who was a proprietor of the Rusty Nail Tavern in Gatlinburg, which she had frequented often when she'd been working for the Good GIs, tracking down bail jumpers and those dodging summonses. She saw Elijah Row, the riverboat captain of the Smoky Mountain Queen, and Belle Watson, the boat's pilot. Behind them was Whit Nash and his family. Whit was the funeral director in Gatlinburg who'd helped pull off the elaborate ruse that Rileigh and Mitch had put together to convince the Arabs who were looking for Jillian and her daughter that they were already dead.

There was Mildred Sandusky, who ran the *Gazette*, where Rileigh had gone to look up back issues when she was working on arson cases last year for the Good Guys.

And prancing officiously toward the building was Yarmouth County Mayor J.P. Rutherford and his little bird-like wife, Phylis. J.P. was going to be blown out of the water on November fifth. Sundeep Singh, who had decided to run for office because J.P. behaved so abominably on so many occasions, would win the election in a landslide.

Then she saw Chigger Stump, herding his four boys across the parking lot, the two oldest fighting about something. But the youngest, Mason, was smiling, adorable in a black suit, white shirt and blue satin tie, looking like a miniature magician, ready to pull a rabbit out of a hat, or disappear in a puff of smoke.

As Mason crossed the parking lot with his father and brothers, he was smiling, planning how he would disappear — poof, like some kind of magician. He'd be there one second and gone the next. He just had to find the right moment.

The ride from home to the wedding had been what Mommy would call *tense*. After Mason fell asleep and Liam woke him up, and he'd tried to punch Liam ... all the kids were yelling and fighting and then Daddy said they had to shut up and say absolutely nothing, and anyone who spoke would get a spanking.

So the car had been silent.

And the quiet was good, because it gave Mason time to think about what he was about to do, which was run away so he didn't have to be the ring bearer carrying a pillow with rings that weren't real.

Daddy had allowed his brothers to start talking again when they got out of the car in the parking lot, and Liam and Eli had immediately gotten into a fight because Eli said Liam was wearing his socks, and Daddy said to hush; it didn't matter whose socks they were so long as they had socks on.

Daddy herded all four boys ahead of him as he went

down the steps to find a seat on the benches. They finally found a spot about halfway down, on the aisle so Mommy could see them. She was supposed to come get Mason when it was time for him to line up.

Then Liam's shoes came untied, and Daddy was busy tying it back. Eli and Connor started arguing about who got to sit on the aisle...

And nobody was looking at Mason. This was his chance.

Mason dropped to his knees on the ground in front of the bench, and in one quick motion slid under the bench and pulled the satin down behind him. Now he was in a cave that stretched from one end of the bench to the other. It was like a tent with fabric on all sides, not dark because the fabric was white, so light shone through it. It was dim though, cool, and sorta creepy — in a good way, not a *Jurassic Park* kind of scary — and he could crawl down the length of the bench and then go to the next bench and then the next bench. This would be way more fun than having to walk down the aisle in front of Chloe, who'd be throwing tiny leaves on the floor while he carried a pillow that didn't even have the real rings on it.

He crouched very still in the dim cavern created by the satin covers over the benches, but only for a moment. Then he took off crawling as fast as he could toward the end of the bench. If Daddy missed him and started looking around, he would look under the satin cover and see him under the bench. But if Mason could get out from under that bench and under the next one in line, Daddy wouldn't see him if he lifted up the satin.

Crawling along on the grass on his hands and knees, he was getting stains all over his suit pants. And grass stains all over his hands too. But he didn't care. He had to get out from under this bench and under the next one in line.

When he finally got to the end, he lifted up the satin and peeked out. There was a space of about a foot between one bench and the next. So he had to reach out and lift up the satin on the second bench and then slide from one to the other and let both the ends of the satin drop into place without any grownup noticing. He suffered only a moment of indecision — should he go back before he got caught? But he was not a kid given to second guessing his own behavior. He acted on instinct, dropped to his belly and commando crawled across the small open space between the benches, from the first to the second bench. And let the fabric drop back down behind him.

Mason froze then, waiting for some random grown-up who'd seen him crawling in that little bit of open space to call out to him. But there was no sound, no cry of a mad adult.

Then he collapsed on his belly in the dirt, panting, grinning. Oh, he was *sooooo* going to get his butt busted for this!

Chapter Thirty-Six

MITCH PACED.

Back and forth. Back and forth.

Making a circuit from one window to another window and back, until his brother Hank held up his hand as he passed.

"You keep pacing, and I'm gonna hand you a sign."

"Sign?"

"A picket sign. You know, like maybe the sheriff's union is on strike."

"The sheriff's department doesn't have a union."

"That was a joke."

Mitch gave his younger brother a wan smile.

But damn, he was glad to see Hank.

"You're a man about to get married in..." Hank looked at his watch. "Half an hour. So you're nervous. I get it."

"I told you, I'm *not* nervous."

"Bullshit."

"I'm gonna wash your mouth out with a bar of soap if you keep cursing, little brother."

"*Little* brother?"

Hank had been seated on a stool and he hopped down off of it and stood next to Mitch. He had two inches and probably thirty pounds on Mitch.

"Okay, okay," Mitch said, "how about younger brother, does that work?"

"Look, it's real hard to screw up a wedding," Hank reassured him. "Just don't fall down walking in. If you do, don't worry about it. My job's to grab your collar and haul you back to your feet, dust you off and keep you going. You don't even have to remember your lines. All you have to do is repeat what the minister says, and those guys usually use little words and short sentences. He'll ask you one question, and you just have to say two words — little bitty words — 'I do.' How hard is that?"

"You got the ring?"

Hank licked the end of his finger and made an imaginary mark in the air.

"That's number two hundred twelve. The answer is the same as it was the other two hundred eleven times you've asked me — yes, I've got the ring."

"Show me."

Hank reached into his pants pocket, felt around. He got a horrified look on his face and stuck his other hand in his other pocket. Then he started patting the pockets in his suit jacket.

Mitch was afraid he was going to throw up.

Then Hank burst out laughing. He held out his hand and the delicate gold band Mitch'd gotten for Rileigh rested in Hank's palm. When they'd first started talking about wedding rings, Rileigh had been adamant — she didn't want a big rock on her finger.

When she'd pointed out, quite reasonably, that a ring with a diamond on it might catch in her holster when she was drawing her weapon, he'd grabbed her in his arms, whirled her around, and said she was his kind of woman.

They had decided on fingerprint wedding bands. Simple gold bands — Rileigh's would have Mitch's fingerprint on it, and Mitch's ring would have Rileigh's print.

"I'm good with this thing," Hank said, slipping the gold band back into his pocket. "Just a little advice. You can fake it if you have to. Nobody in the audience can see the ring, so if Rileigh can't lay hands on yours, just pretend there's a ring and go find it after."

"Why would Rileigh not find it?"

"That maid of honor of hers…"

"Georgia."

"Whoo-ee, she's a house a'fire."

"You have no idea." Then Mitch stopped. "You know I'm surprised you even noticed Georgia, what with gawking at Aaliyah Al-Masri ever since you met her last night."

What he didn't say was that Hank had also ignored the flirtations of all the other bridesmaids, who — as Rileigh had predicted — were throwing themselves at him.

To Mitch's utter astonishment, Hank had no handy comeback. In fact, he looked a little glum.

"I'd afraid I'm going to have to put her down in the 'one that got away' column," he said.

"How you figure that?"

"Your buddy, Gus, is leaving me in the dust. You didn't tell me he was a doctor."

"I told you he was the coroner. That makes it kind of obvious."

"Do you know that man can recite the whole Periodic Table of the Elements from memory?"

Mitch wasn't completely certain he remembered what

the Periodic Table was. But whatever it was, he wasn't surprised Gus could recite it.

"What'd he say?"

"I don't remember how it came up, but suddenly he's describing how the man who invented it — in *1869!* — Dmitri Mendeleev had started collecting the properties of elements like he was playing a game. Then Gus started *naming* them — hydrogen, lithium, sodium, magnesium, potassium — and I'm standing there with my mouth hanging open."

Mitch could see how that'd be a hard act to follow.

"What'd you say."

"Nothing. I didn't think Aaliyah'd be impressed that I could recite the Super Bowl winners for the past five years."

Mitch was grinning at his brother's discomfort, but the smile drained off his face when he saw who had stepped into the room behind him.

"Collier!"

Collier Atkinson was the sheriff of neighboring Weatherford County. He and several of his deputies had taken over checking out the IDs of the people from Mitch's signup sheet.

Collier was all business.

"I wanted to tell you personally — there was an imposter on your signup sheet. When I catch him, I'll likely be charging him with murder."

Mitch's heart was in his throat.

"I went out to check on one of the names — Cole Chandler, because he lives in Weatherford County. Thought about it as I was driving out there that it wouldn't be strange in Yarmouth County that nobody knew him."

One of the dozens of away-from-here's at Breezy Creek last week.

"Cole Chandler is a park ranger. I found his cruiser in front of his house but nobody was home. Did some checking and found his brother, who told me that Cole had left a couple of days ago to spend ten days wilderness camping. So if he was off duty camping, why was he in uniform at Breezy Creek?"

Mitch remembered the ranger, a big guy, just hanging around being helpful. Breezy Creek was, after all, in the Great Smoky Mountains National Park.

"I went back to his house again, started looking around. I found his car still parked in his garage … and his dead body was stuffed in the trunk. Which means—"

Mitch finished the sentence for him. "That the guy who's been walking around here in the ranger's uniform with the name tag Cole Chandler is probably the man who killed him."

"That'd be my call."

Mitch had not noticed the ranger today — didn't mean he hadn't been there, just that Mitch hadn't seen him.

Mitch turned to Hank.

"I need you to go tell Rileigh what Collier just told us. Tell her to be on the lookout for him."

"I'll hang around here if you don't mind," Collier said. "I'd like to catch the bastard."

"Not nearly as bad as I do," Mitch said.

Chapter Thirty-Seven

THE ROOM WHERE MAMA, JILLIAN, AND RILEIGH WERE dressing was the largest of the rooms in the north hallway of the visitor center. It served as a meeting room — used by local clubs, sometimes the school board, and by banks for their annual meeting of their boards of directors.

They'd left the big oak table in the room as a place to set makeup, blow dryers, slips, dresses, and all the accoutrements and paraphernalia two brides and a matron of honor needed to get ready, but they'd moved the chairs that had sat around the table out into the room across the hall.

Mama had started out in the morning clear and lucid, but as the day progressed, the thousand-yard stare came into her eyes, so Rileigh kept her "present" by giving her tasks to perform, such as moving the chairs. She had pressed Marshal Dylan into service to help out, since all the usual suspects — Mitch, David, Gus, Sundeep — and Hank! — were sequestered on the other side of the building getting dressed. Mama had also gotten him to fetch out of the trunk of her car a box that was sitting on the far end of the table. She wouldn't tell Rileigh and Jillian what was in it, but she'd apparently filled the marshal in, leaning close, chattering gaily in his ear about it for a full five minutes. The conversation reminded Rileigh of conversations she'd watched Mama have with imaginary people, and she was glad this guy was real. Mama'd taken a particular shine to the federal marshal, since she'd actually been a fan of the black-and-white western, Gunsmoke. He was dressed in a golf shirt and khakis today — one of half a dozen looks-like-a-wedding-guest security officers scattered among the crowd, and Mama teased him about not looking a thing like James Arness, the actor who'd played the lead.

"You need a hat, a great big ten-gallon hat."

"The last time I wore a hat was when I was walking a beat back in the day, and it was more like a three-cup hat, a quart hat at the outside."

"And look at them arms, all decorated up but skinny as pipe cleaners."

"Hey, I got guns," the marshal protested, flexing his bicep muscles. Mama studied his "guns," inspected them … and was not impressed.

"If them's guns, they's cap pistols. And Matt Dillon was tall! When that man got on a horse, he had to hold his feet up so's his boot heels wouldn't scrape the ground."

The marshal gave her an it-is-what-it-is shrug before hurrying back to where he'd parked Aunt Daisy beside one of Collier Atkinson's Weatherford County deputies.

Someone had had the presence of mind to line the walls of their dressing room with mirrors so the brides could have a 360-degree view of themselves. Rileigh hated it. Who in their right mind wants to see themselves 360 degrees around, even a bride on her wedding day? That was a little much.

Rileigh realized she was being judgmental, and nit-picky, finding fault, negative — all the things she did when she was nervous. And she was definitely nervous.

Mama was getting dressed along with Rileigh and Jillian. The maids of honor — Georgia and Aaliyah Al-Masri — were dressing with the other bridesmaids. Georgia would pop out of their dressing room when it was time to start the ceremony to go fetch the ring bearer, Mason Stump, who was sitting with his father and brothers in the audience.

The hairdresser, whose name was Fabian, made of Rileigh's hair a riot of chestnut curls, with a few small gold and yellow leaves strategically placed to look like they'd been blown into her hair by the wind. Then he had care-fully fit her veil on her head, affixed the crown of daisies and green leaves to her hair with a couple of hairpins, and straightened the veil down to her shoulders. Fabian draped Jillian's long blonde hair over one shoulder, entwined in a tiny vine with red and gold leaves. He set the veil, with its inset bluebells, on her head, and poofed the sheer netting out around her waist. Mama's hair style was dignified and chic — a simple bun, captured at the nape of her neck in the sheer fabric of a veil, inlaid with tiny white pearls.

When Fabian was finally satisfied with his handiwork, he left. The makeup artist finally left, too, after she finished making everyone look absolutely flawless.

Now, the three of them were alone in the room. Mama looked at herself in the mirror. She was dressed in a blue chiffon dress, as were all the bridesmaids and everybody else in the wedding, except Jillian and Rileigh and the groomsmen. Even the little flower girl, Chloe Morgan, was wearing a blue chiffon dress. Chiffon was the fabric they had to work with, and Bestowing Sewing had done a masterful job of outfitting the entire wedding with the bolts of fabric given to them by Cynthia Waters. Mama's chiffon dress was floor-length. The bridesmaids' and the maids of honor's dresses were knee-length. Mama had been the beneficiary of her best friend, Mildred's, expertise at cross-stitch, and the whole front of her dress was adorned with tiny pearls. Mildred had spent untold hours affixing them — plastic, of course, but sparkling and beautiful — to the filmy fabric.

Since Mama's dress was floor-length, it was too long for her unless she had her shoes on. Not spike heels by any measure, but shoes with heels. Now she was walking around barefoot in the room, holding her dress up off the floor to keep it from dragging. She had slid in and out of lucidity as the day progressed, but she seemed to be a hundred percent "with it" now.

"Have you girls forgot all about tradition?" Mama dropped the non sequitur into the room with a thump.

Rileigh had a bit of mascara in her eye and was blinking as fast as she could, trying with all her might not to tear up in that eye, because the tears running down her face would wash off at least a streak of that makeup that had been so patiently and professionally applied. She was leaned over the mirror, dabbing at the little black speck, not daring to turn her head to look at Mama when she spoke.

"I think we pretty much ticked all the boxes on tradition," Rileigh said.

"Have you? What about something old, something new, something borrowed, and something blue?" Mama asked.

Georgia had talked incessantly about that in the beginning, but gratefully she was so busy with other details that she'd let it slide, and Rileigh had been far too preoccupied with trying to stay alive to be concerned over making sure she was wearing blue underwear.

"You don't have to worry about it, I've got it all taken care of," Mama said and went to the box at the far end of the table.

"Them wedding dresses is good for the something new, and I have something old for both of you."

Mama held up what Rileigh instantly recognized as one of her grandmother's crocheted flowers.

At one time, when she was a little girl, there had been Grandma's crocheted things on every possible surface in the house because Grandma loved to make them, and they were beautiful. When Grandma died, Mama had gathered them all up and packed them away, and Rileigh hadn't seen them since.

"Here's one for you." Mama handed to Jillian a delicate crocheted rose. It was pale now and faded, but probably had once been a beautiful bright red. The petals were so delicate, the stitches were so small, that it looked like a single piece of fabric, rather than individual stitches that Grandma had put in half a century ago.

Then Mama handed Rileigh a crocheted flower. It was pale yellow, a lily, and so real that Rileigh could have sworn it was a silk flower rather than a crocheted.

"I figured you could put these flowers in your bouquets — just add them to the leaves."

"Thank you, Mama," Jillian said and took her mother's shoulders and leaned in and kissed the top of her head. Mama was barefoot, and Jillian had her shoes on already, and it looked like she was kissing a little girl.

"I think you need to rethink leaving what Grandma made in that box in the attic," Jillian said. "You need to put them out again so we can all enjoy them."

"Maybe I will when you girls are gone," Mama said.

She said the words lightly, but Rileigh and Jillian exchanged a glance. Though Mama was thrilled beyond measure that her daughters were getting married, it was having the same effect on her that Jillian's getting married had had on Rileigh all those years ago. Rileigh'd realized that when her sister got married, she would move out. She wouldn't live there anymore, wouldn't be down the hall for Rileigh to run to in the middle of the night, crawl in bed beside when the boogeyman was peeking out of her closet.

Mama was feeling some of that as well.

The four of them — Jillian, David, Mitch, and Rileigh — had talked about the fact that Mama couldn't live by herself. She'd either burn the house down trying to cook something or forget to cook at all. But Rileigh and Jillian had come up with a solution. Mama's best friend Mildred was going to stay with Mama while the girls were away on their honeymoons … but what Mama didn't know was that Mildred had agreed to move in permanently. They'd spring that on Mama when they got back home.

While Rileigh carefully added the pale-yellow lily to the huge bridal bouquet she had made for herself out of leaves, and Jillian added the rose to her own bouquet, Mama reached up and unfastened the pendant necklace she wore almost every day. It was a little gold heart with a hinge that opened it. In one side was a picture of Rileigh, and in the other was a picture of Jillian when they were little girls.

"This here's *my* necklace," she said, "and can't neither one of you *have* it. But you can borrow it for the ceremony. There's only the one necklace, though, and I've been thinking and thinking what else I could let you borrow that'd be as pretty as this necklace, but I couldn't think of nothing. So I finally just decided one of you gets to borrow the necklace, and the other…"

She reached into the box and pulled something out.

"This here b'longs to me," she said solemnly, holding out her hand. In the palm lay an ordinary rubber band. "You can't have this here rubber band — it's *mine*. But I will let one of you borrow it."

Rileigh burst out laughing, grabbing Mama in a hug.

"Now, don't you be making fun of my rubber band bracelet," Mama said huffily. "You're gonna fool around 'til you hurt my feelings, cause I'm right proud of it."

"So which one of us—?" Jillian began.

"I ain't 'bout to do the picking. We'll let chance decide."

Rileigh assumed Mama meant to flip a coin, maybe draw straws or pick a number between one and ten. When Mama reached into the box and pulled out a fresh, still-in-the-box deck of cards, Rileigh couldn't stop herself from laughing again.

"You need to get hold of yourself, child. You don't wanna go walking down the aisle giggling. Folks'll think you ain't draggin' a full string of fish."

At that moment, the door to the room opened, and the photographer stuck his head around the corner.

"I figured you'd want me to get pictures of this last-minute stuff."

"Absolutely," Rileigh said, delighted. "If I can't produce pictures of this, Mitch is never going to believe it happened."

The photographer came in, closed the door behind him, then took the camera that hung around his neck and started snapping. Rileigh turned her attention back to the deck of cards in Mama's hand as she shuffled them with the expertise of a croupier at a blackjack table in Las Vegas. Even with her stiff arthritic fingers, the one skill Mama never lost was shuffling cards. Finally, she spread the cards in a fan and held them out to Rileigh and Jillian.

The photographer came up close, popped the 100-500 mm zoom lens off the nose of the camera and put an 85mm portrait lens in its place.

"Pick a card, any card," Mama said, as all-business as a professional card shark.

Rileigh reached out and pulled a card from the fanned-out deck. Jillian did the same. Then both of them flipped the cards over at the same time. Jillian had drawn a queen. Rileigh had drawn the seven of hearts.

"You won, Jillian!" Mama cried. "You get to pick."

"I want the rubber band bracelet!" Jillian said.

"Aw, I wanted that," Rileigh said.

Mama shook her head. "I always did say if Jillian had a dead horse, you'd want half."

Jillian fit the rubber band around her wrist and Mama helped Rileigh with the necklace.

Hurrying back to the box, Mama pulled out two some-things she had made special for her daughters — blue garters. Not just the pale blue of the chiffon dresses. These were made of bright, royal blue lace. Mama knelt down as Jillian lifted her dress up, and she fit the garter on Jillian's leg while the photographer snapped away, and then she did the same with Rileigh.

Mama stood up and intoned solemnly, "Something old, something new, something borrowed, and something blue." Then she reached back into the box. "And a penny in your shoe.'"

Mama handed a shiny copper penny to Jillian and another to Rileigh. "Now we're set to go," she said, beaming.

"Except one of you is not going anywhere."

Rileigh whirled around to find the photographer no longer holding a camera. He was holding a gun.

Chapter Thirty-Eight

"WHY?"

Rileigh knew why. This was El Viento, the killer who'd been torturing her with ugly surprises for months, finally here to claim the prize. And her gun was on the other side of the room.

She'd asked the question as a diversion, to buy time. She knew the assassin was smart enough to stay so far away from her that she couldn't jump him. He'd already backed up to the far wall by the door he'd entered.

"This doesn't have to end in a bloodbath," he said. "No reason to kill you if I don't have to. I could let you go —just show me the tattoo."

"Tattoo?" Rileigh asked confused. "What tattoo? Wait a minute. You think *I'm* El Viento?"

"I'm the only one who has figured it out. How can El Viento move in the circles he does, get in and out of the places he goes, and nobody ever notices him? Nobody finds him because it's not a him at all. It's a her. All that combat experience everybody thinks you have. I'd wager you were never in the military. When you claimed to be on deployment, you were just at *work*. Doing your job. Fulfilling contracts."

"You can't honestly think *I'm* El Viento," she said.

Rileigh didn't have to fake the incredulity in her voice. She'd assumed the only threat to her was El Viento himself and had cherished the hope that one of the assassins would find El Viento and kill him before he could strike. She'd never dreamed that one of the assassins would come to the ridiculous conclusion that rather than the intended victim of El Viento, she was the assassin.

"You tried to rub our noses in it, but I'm the only one who figured it out — 'catch ME if you can' — right under a picture of YOU!"

Rileigh thought of the screenshot Sundeep had taken of the post on the dark web. Indeed, the words "catch me if you can" were under a picture of Rileigh — and Mitch, Jillian, and David.

"I wasn't the only person in that picture." As she spoke, she was inching her way toward her gun, knowing it was too far away, that she'd never make it. "There were four of us."

The man wasn't listening.

"Now, we can do this one of two ways," the man said. "One, I can shoot you and your mother and your sister. And then I can" — he looked her up and down — "*enjoy* myself taking your clothes off to find the tattoo. Way number two is you strip and show me the tattoo, and I won't have to kill any of you."

Bullshit. Once he pulled that gun and blew his cover as the photographer, he was committed. He couldn't leave any live witnesses behind to identify him.

"So which one are you?" Rileigh asked, again stalling, buying time. He could open fire at any second on her, Mama and Jillian. Every second she could keep him

271

talking was another second of life. " Not IronJackal, right? Born2BEvil? I know you're not BloodHarpy or Knighthawk because both of them already bought the farm."

"You killed IronJackal?" he said. "I wondered where he went. Stupid mohawk … what was he thinking?"

"*I* didn't kill anybody. El Viento did. I don't know who El Viento is, but I know who he *isn't*. He isn't *me*."

"Riiiight. I made you an offer — to spare your lives. You don't cooperate, and your mother and sister are going to die needlessly. Is that what you want? Give me that number — now."

Rileigh reached up and began to slowly unbutton the tiny buttons on the front of her dress. She stared straight into his eyes, didn't look away, grabbed his gaze and held it as tight as she could.

Because in her peripheral vision, she could see the door behind him begin to open. Rileigh didn't blink and certainly didn't flick her eyes toward the movement. Neither did Jillian.

But Mama…

The photographer caught the change in Mama's expression and his attention faltered.

The photographer began to turn toward the door, swinging the barrel of the gun around to point it that direction. As soon as his focus shifted, Rileigh grabbed the only thing within her reach — the camera lens he had left on the table in front of her, a zoom lens about the size of a shoe. She hurled it at his head as she launched herself at Mama, knocking her down and covering her body with her own to shield her.

The camera lens caught the photographer in the left temple, snapped his head to the side, and he staggered back. The man in the doorway moved fast, caught him before he had time to regain his balance, grabbed a handful of the photographer's hair yanked his head back and sliced across his neck with a hunting knife. The wound was so deep it went all the way through to his spine, almost decapitating him. Blood gushed out of the man's throat, soaking the front of his shirt and pants and splashing down on the floor. Then the photographer's body folded up and collapsed beside where Rileigh lay atop Mama.

What followed was several moments of stunned silence before Mama said in a small voice, "That nice young man wanted to kill us. I don't think it was me done something to piss him off that bad. Was it you girls?"

Realizing she was crushing her mother to the floor, Rileigh rolled off and staggered to her feet. Jillian reached down a hand to help Mama up off the floor. Jillian had stood frozen, hadn't so much as blinked since the photographer pulled the gun and demanded Rileigh take off her clothes.

Clothes.

Wedding dress.

Rileigh looked down. Her gorgeous emerald-green satin dress was covered with blood. The pale green chiffon overlay was soaked, and her legs and shoes were splattered. And there was a growing puddle of blood oozing out from the body.

Mama looked as white as a sheet. She had both her hands over her mouth and her eyes were huge. Jillian's face was unreadable, as it often was. And Rileigh suspected that at those times when there was no expression at all on her face, it was because Jillian Bishop had left the building, Jillian disassociating from herself when bad things happened. That's how she'd survived for all those years enslaved in the Middle East. She left the building and was not a party to, nor allowed herself to be aware of or react to, whatever happened to her body. But Rileigh was fully present. She had not disassociated. And Mama was fully present, though she might just pass out on the spot.

Rileigh turned toward the man in the gray uniform and green jacket of a park ranger, who took another couple of steps into the room, bent down, and retrieved the pistol with a silencer the photographer had dropped on the floor.

She opened her mouth to thank him for saving their lives, but she closed it again without speaking when she saw that he wasn't just holding the photographer's gun. He was pointing it at her.

Chapter Thirty-Nine

OUT OF THE FRYING PAN, INTO THE FIRE.

Rileigh shook her head slowly, trying to deny the reality. The photographer was about to kill her because he thought she was El Viento. And now this not-a-park-ranger was about to kill her because he *was* El Viento.

She played dumb.

"What's all this about? Why are you pointing that gun at me?"

"This is the end of the line. The train stops here, baby. Everybody off."

Rileigh gestured toward Mama and Jillian, knew it was a lost cause, but she had to try.

"You came for me. Well, here I am. Let them go."

"Now you know better than that. In this line of work, there is a single cardinal rule. Never leave any witnesses."

"That's how you rise to the top of the profession — you blow through people's lives, killing everybody."

"That's what people say about assassins, isn't it. El Viento — *the wind*. Maybe the most feared assassin of all time. I've been waiting a very long time for this moment, and I plan to enjoy it." He smirked. "The look in your eyes — fear. You feel fear just like everybody else, don't you?"

"Of course I do."

"Are you afraid now? Tell me. Say it. Are you afraid?"

"Of course I'm afraid. Is that what this is about? You get off on scaring people?"

"Oh, it's easy to scare most people. But not you. You're as cold blooded as a shark. I've been looking forward to eliminating you." He paused, gestured toward her with the barrel of the gun. "But don't let me interrupt. Go on."

"Go on what?"

"Unbuttoning that dress."

"Why?"

"Go on," he said, leering. "Do it. Finish what you started."

Rileigh did as she was instructed, slowly.

"You're a remarkable woman, Miss Rileigh Bishop. Absolutely remarkable. A formidable adversary. It's no fun to match wits with a pushover. You have definitely given me, given all of us, a run for our money. "

All of us?

There was a blur of movement then. The door flew open and then everything seemed to slow down — and to speed up, both at the same time. Every moment lasted an eternity, and the whole event started and ended between one heartbeat and the next. The man in the Smoky Mountains National Park Ranger uniform began to turn, swinging the pistol away from Rileigh and toward whoever was coming in the door. But he wasn't fast enough. The person coming through the door flew into the room like a bullet. He was dressed in a uniform, too, and he knocked the park ranger's gun aside with one blow, then grabbed the ranger's chin in one hand, put his other hand on the back of the ranger's head, and twisted sharply. *Snap!* Rileigh actually heard his neck break before he collapsed to the floor like a puppet with the strings snipped. The man standing above him was not wearing a park ranger uniform, or a sheriff's department uniform. He wore the pure white dress uniform of a naval officer, and the Navy SEAL wasn't even breathing hard.

"Hank!" His name was the only word Rileigh seemed able to form. He stepped to her quickly, reached out to take her into his arms, but she held out her hand and stepped back.

"No, don't … your uniform."

Some part of Rileigh's mind stepped outside her body and commented on her behavior. *You almost got killed, not once but twice in the last five minutes, and you're worried about getting a spot on his uniform?*

That was absolutely crazy and completely normal — both at the same time.

"Mitch sent me to tell you this guy isn't a park ranger," he said, nodding to body lying at his feet. "But looks like you figured that out already." Hank looked around for the source of the blood all over Rileigh's dress and noted the man lying in a puddle of blood with his throat slit. "You've been busy."

All the air seemed to whoosh out of Rileigh then, and she stepped back and leaned against the big oak table in the middle of the room. Too fast. The events of the last few minutes had just happened too fast. She had to concentrate to focus on what Hank was saying.

"…sheriff in a neighboring County, first name's Collier … something—"

"Collier Atkinson from Weatherford County."

"Yeah, that's it."

"What about him?"

"He went out to verify this ranger's ID and found his dead body in the trunk of his car."

The magnitude of what had just happened began to penetrate Rileigh's shock and fear.

"So this is … *him*," Rileigh said, staring down at the body at her feet. "This is … is…" She shifted her gaze to Hank's eyes, marveled at how they looked just like Mitch's. Except not. They were an entirely different color and shape, but still … it felt like staring into Mitch's eyes. Maybe it was what she could see beyond the eyes, *through* the eyes — the characters of the two men were the same. "He told me he'd been waiting a long time to kill me."

"So who is this guy?" Hank asked, nodding his chin toward the photographer laying in a huge pool of blood on the floor.

"One of the assassins. I'm not sure which one."

Jillian spoke then for the first time. "The fake ranger killed him," she said.

Rileigh had forgotten that her mother and sister had just lived through the same few minutes of terror that she had, and neither one of them was freaking out. That was impressive.

"It sounded to me like the photographer thought *you* were El Viento," Jillian said. To Hank, she said, "He wanted her to undress and show him the tattoo."

"Why would he think a thing like that?" Hank asked.

Rileigh shook her head. "I don't know." She let out a breath, pulled in another one and let it out in a slow sigh. Then she felt her eyes well with tears. Still looking at Hank, she said, "We got him. *You* got him. El Viento was posing as a park ranger. It's over."

And suddenly relief washed over her in a warm wave that sent the tears that had welled in her eyes over the rim and down onto her cheeks, sliding across the perfect makeup that had been spray painted on earlier.

"It's over, I can … we can … just *get married.*" She looked at Jillian, and her sister's face was split by a broad smile.

Mama was still looking from one dead body to another, and practical woman that she was, she said, "So what're we gonna do with these here dead men? I mean, there's three or four hundred people out there come to celebrate a wedding. I'd sure hate to haul these bodies out in front of 'em. Kinda spoils the mood, you know."

"This room has a lock on the door," Hank said. "I say we lock them in here. You marry my brother, and we'll worry about them later."

"You need to go tell Mitch that it's all right now, that everything's fine, you need to go tell him that … we're good." She giggled, then reached up and wiped tears off of her face. "Looks like he's actually going to have to marry me after all."

"But what about … that?" Hank was looking at Rileigh's dress. And then it sunk in for the first time that she couldn't get married in the dress she was wearing, all splattered with blood. What could she do? Just put on the jeans and t-shirt she'd worn here this morning?

"Listen, my brother wants to marry you, and he won't care what you're wearing." He pulled his phone out of his pocket, then shook his head. "What's up with the cell coverage?" He didn't wait for an answer, just said, "I'll go tell him myself, then I'll be back to walk Ali down the aisle."

"*Ali?*"

"Yeah, Aaliyah Al-Masri."

Hank turned on his heel, marched out the door and

279

closed it, leaving Jillian, Rileigh, Mama, and two dead bodies in the room behind him.

"It's ruined." Rileigh looked down at her destroyed dress. But even the dismay over her spoiled wedding dress couldn't dampen the growing joy that lit her from the inside at the realization that it was over. It was finally *over*.

"Oh, don't you worry 'bout that dress," Mama said. "You go wash the blood off your arms and legs." She smiled. "We got this."

Chapter Forty

As Mason lay on his belly on the grass beneath the bench where wedding guests were seated, waiting for Aunt Rileigh's wedding to begin, his heart pounded. He was excited, and also a little scared. This might be one of the worst things he'd ever done, and he'd done a lot of pretty bad things. Oh, it wasn't as bad as running away in Walmart that day had been. That had been unquestionably the worst thing he'd ever done, but by the time he finally got back to Mommy and Daddy, they weren't in the mood to spank him. He was pretty sure he wouldn't get that lucky this time.

What Mason was doing now, bailing out on being the stupid ring bearer in Aunt Rileigh's wedding, and instead hiding beneath the satin-covered benches where the audience was sitting, he was sure that was a crime worthy of being spanked as a punishment. Running away like this would have been, even if he hadn't been part of the wedding. But he was supposed to line up out there with everybody. Mommy was going to come and get him when it was time, and when she got there and Daddy couldn't find him … Mason shook his head. She knew Mommy would be just about as mad at Daddy as she was at Mason. And he didn't know if that would work out better for him in the end than her just being mad at him alone.

He was pretty sure that his absence would throw a monkey wrench into the works, that the little boy who was supposed to be carrying the rings had vanished, but he didn't care. He didn't want to do that. And crawling around in these tunnels was about worth a spanking.

As he lay there thinking, his eyes adjusted more and more to the dark so he could see pretty well, since the satin forming the tent was white and the light shined through. When he thought about getting a spanking for what he was doing, he realized, as he had at a couple of other times in his life, that he was really a whole lot smarter than most people thought he was. He figured out when he was real little how to escape the pain of the spanking, and that had been to pretend it hurt really bad.

That might have been one of the smartest things he'd ever done, which was to act like a spanking hurt really bad, to scream and cry for a long time, and then have those hiccup-y sounds coming out of your throat that you make after you've cried for too long.

That was ridiculous. Spankings didn't hurt. I mean, it hurt a little bit, but it certainly didn't hurt as much as he made it sound like it did, and he wondered why nobody knew that. Why did grown-ups think it hurt? It was their hand landing on your butt. If it didn't hurt their hand, why did they think it would hurt your butt? There were some things Mason just didn't understand. But the bottom line was the pain of the spanking wasn't enough to keep Mason from doing anything he really wanted to do, and he really wanted to do this.

Mason got up on his hands and knees and began to crawl slowly down the tunnel. He could see the backs of people's shoes, some of them, and sometimes one of the grown-ups would push their feet back under the bench, and the feet would stick out into the space where Mason was crawling. A man with big black shoes suddenly did that right in front of Mason. Mason started to ease his way over them, but realized in time that if the grown-up felt somebody touch his leg or his foot or his shoe, he would absolutely reach down and pull the satin up to see what it was, and then he'd catch Mason. And maybe Mason hadn't even been gone long enough that the wedding hadn't started yet. Maybe if they dragged him back now, they could still make him be the ring bearer.

No, they wouldn't make him be the ring bearer. He'd messed up his suit, crawling in the grass too bad for that. But he still didn't want to get caught. He wanted to play under here. And just a few minutes of escape would be a poor trade-off for a spanking. He needed to make the most of this.

And so Mason sat as patiently as he was able to sit beside the shoes of the man who had stuck his feet under the bench until the man finally wiggled again and moved them. The bench above Mason creaked when the man moved, and he was sure that the man was a great big fat man, and it was hard for him to get comfortable on that bench because he took up so much of it. Mason quickly crawled past that spot in case the guy stuck his foot back under there again. And as he did, he noticed that there was something stuck up under the bench at the far end. He didn't know what it was, but it appeared to just be stuck to the wood of the bench like a piece of gum. He would have thought it was a piece of gum, except that's not what color gum was. And besides, it was huge. It was way too big to be gum. And it didn't look like it had been chewed or that somebody had mashed it.

The gum that people stuck under things was always about the same shape because when you stuck your gum under something, your fingers made dents in it, and pretty much the same dents no matter who stuck the gum there. What he was looking at now didn't have finger dents in it, and besides, it was way, way bigger than a piece of gum. It was as big as the pencil box that Liam carried to school. The one that Mason had begged Mommy to get him. It was the best pencil box Mason'd ever seen. But Mommy said he was too young for it. She promised him she'd get him a case just like that when he started to school, but he knew she wouldn't. She wouldn't remember by then. Grownups were always promising to get you something later, and then they never did remember it.

Mason crawled slowly down the length of the bench until he was right under the thing that was stuck there. He noticed then that there were strings or something, kind of like wires, poked into it. He studied it, wondered if he pulled hard enough, could he pull it down off where it was stuck to the bench and play with it? When he reached up his finger and poked at it, his finger sunk into it, and he realized it was clay or something just like clay, a big chunk of clay.

He sat there poking his finger into it for a little while and then wanted to pull it down because it had occurred to him that if it was clay, he could make something out of it. But first he had to get those strings, those wire things out. He pulled on the first one, it was black, and it came right out. They weren't stuck in there very hard at all. It didn't take him any time to get all the wires out. And then he reached up and pried at the chunk of clay stuck there above his head, pulled on it as hard as he could.

He tugged and tugged and suddenly it came off right into his hands. This clay was cold and stiff. The clay that he played with at Sunday school was always cold and stiff too when you first started playing with it. You had to squeeze it and squeeze it and squeeze it and get it warm and then it would become soft and you could make whatever you wanted. This piece of clay wasn't very big.

But wait a minute. If there was clay like this stuck up under this bench, maybe there was some more of it stuck up under the other benches.

If there was, Mason Stump would find it.

Chapter Forty-One

LILY BISHOP'S HEAD WAS SPINNING. IF SHE CLOSED HER eyes, the spin would make her dizzy. She felt like she did when she was a little girl, standing out in the front yard — upwind of the outhouse, of course — playing with her sisters, the other flowers in the Gillespie bouquet.

The girls had a few toys, a couple of hand-carved dolls, other dolls made out of straw. They had a ball that they threw around even after it got a hole in it and went flat. But one of their favorite things to do was just to be silly and get dizzy. They would spin around and around and around, their arms extended, and when Lily closed her eyes, it always had seemed to her that her feet left the ground and she floated up into the air by the power of the spinning.

She felt a little like that now, but of course, she wasn't a little girl anymore. Still, she felt dizzy the way she'd felt then, like she'd just stopped spinning and couldn't walk straight and fell down when she tried. Too much was happening too fast, and Lily didn't understand any of it.

She knew there was someone out there who had been sending really terrible things to Rileigh for a long time. She'd even found one of the boxes before Rileigh got to it and hid it so Rileigh wouldn't have to open it up and find something terrible. But of course, they found the box eventually and hiding it for a while only made it worse. There were terrible things in those boxes the others didn't think she knew. Nobody told her about those things, so all she knew was what she could eavesdrop on. And eavesdropping was not an easy task when you were hard of hearing. But if she just kept her own mouth shut and listened, she could find out a lot. The trouble was, even when she knew what they were talking about, she usually didn't understand what it meant. How could there have been bones in those boxes? Human bones, a finger and a thumb? She must have been mistaken.

Still, she knew that Rileigh had gotten one of those terrible boxes again a couple of days ago, that it had been in with the wedding presents in that pile in the living room. Rileigh had opened it up, and nobody would let Lily see what was in it, but she knew what it was. She heard them talking about it. They said it was a doll in a wedding dress, all broken up with a frowny face where its face should have been, and with a bullet hole through its chest!

And Lily knew, though nobody would tell her, that everyone was afraid that whoever it was who had been doing these terrible things to Rileigh knew that she was getting married. Otherwise, why would he have sent a doll in a wedding dress? And she knew everyone believed he was planning to be here at the wedding to do something terrible to Rileigh. No, not just something terrible. He would be at the wedding to *kill* Rileigh.

Lily had had to force herself to understand the reality

of that. It was so horrible, she could barely think about it, and thinking was not easy for Lily anymore. But even though Lily's mind was not as full of fog as it so often was, the reality of what was actually going on in the world where her mind was clear had to be some kind of hallucination or craziness, because it was nuts. The photographer who was taking wedding pictures had pulled out a gun and was going to kill Rileigh with it, and then the park ranger came in and killed him and got blood all over Rileigh's dress, and then Mitch's brother Hank came in and killed the park ranger. It was crazy. The world was crisp and clear and not foggy, but this couldn't be real. The foggy stuff made more sense than this did.

But everybody else seemed to be seeing the same crazy things.

When Mitch's brother left, Jillian and Rileigh and Mama were left in the room with two dead bodies. How could this possibly be real? She opened her mouth to ask Rileigh but then realized it had to be real, because Rileigh was looking down at her wedding dress in horror, and there was blood all over it, splattered all over it. It was ruined.

This was her wedding day. Her wedding dress was ruined on her wedding day.

And then everything became bright and clear in Mama's mind, because *she could fix this*. She couldn't protect Rileigh from a killer. She couldn't do anything about the dead bodies in the room, but she could fix the problem with Rileigh's wedding dress.

"Don't you worry about that dress, sweetheart. We got this," she said. Rileigh looked at her and the anguished look on her baby daughter's face broke Lily's heart. She'd had a beautiful green dress that she'd picked out herself, and now it was ruined. And she was supposed to walk down the aisle in it any minute now. But in truth, when Lily thought about it, she suspected that it was supposed to be this way all along, that her baby daughter wasn't supposed to go walking down the aisle in that green dress.

While Rileigh was in the bathroom washing the blood off her arms and legs, Lily turned to Jillian.

"Sometimes God just gets you to do things and you don't know why. And I think that's what happened to Georgia."

Jillian looked like she didn't have any idea what her mother was talking about.

"I think God told Georgia to bring my wedding dress out here and put it on that mannequin so it would be here when Rileigh needed it."

Jillian's face lit up like a Christmas tree.

"Mama, I hadn't thought of that!" She flung her arms around her mother.

Lily and Jillian hurried out into the hallway and stripped Lily's wedding dress off the mannequin. The dress was staggeringly beautiful. Lily remembered asking her parents, time and again, where on earth Daddy had gotten the money to buy a dress like that for her to get married in. But no one would say. They always changed the subject when she asked. And it didn't take her long to figure out that he might not have come by that dress legal.

The dress had a high neck with a collar like a priest's collar all the way up under the chin. Then below the collar, spreading out across the shoulders, was pure white lace. The sleeves were poofed at the top with white satin, and then the lace hung tight to the lower arms and stretched out halfway across her palm. The dress had fit Lily snug in the waist tiny and tight and then billowed out below her waist in a sea of white satin and white taffeta with lace on top and little pearls sewn all over it. The dress touched the

289

floor all the way around, and the train stretched out behind it ten feet.

When Rileigh emerged from the bathroom, wearing nothing but her bra and underwear, the blood was cleaned off of her arms and legs.

"You can walk down the aisle in the jeans and tee shirt you were wearing this morning," Jillian said, "or…"

Mama and Jillian held out Mama's dress and Rileigh was too surprised to say anything at all. Mama and Jillian helped her into the wedding gown, which was a garment you definitely had to have help getting into. The zipper stretched all the way from right below the hairline to below the knees.

When they'd got it all zipped up, Rileigh turned around toward them. Lily heard Jillian gasp, "Oh, Rileigh, you're so beautiful."

And then Lily watched Rileigh turn toward the mirror on the wall, and she gasped, too. Certainly her wedding dress had been beautiful. She'd picked it out. It was a perfect color for her eyes. But though Rileigh's dress had been beautiful, Mama's dress was magical. Rileigh looked like a fairy princess with sparkling jewels and sequins on the dress and train catching the light and shining. Lily picked up the veil and fit the crown of it, white crocheted flowers in a circle on the top of Rileigh's head. The handful of colored leaves that the hairdresser had put into her hair added just the tiny little bit of color to make it all perfect.

"The colored leaves in my hair will match my shoes," Rileigh said. The only shoes she had to wear were the green ones that had been the same color as her dress.

"I don't think anybody's going to notice," Jillian said.

"Oh, Mama," Rileigh said, and her eyes filled with tears.

"Don't cry, for Pete's sake. You're going to ruin the makeup that woman went to all the trouble to spray on your face so you'd be perfect as a doll. You get it wet and it's going to run. It's not like a tattoo or nothing."

As soon as Mama said the word, an image formed in her mind. The image was foggy because it had been foggy when she saw the image. It was just a little piece of memory, but it was surrounded by fog because she'd been in the fog when she saw it.

"It ain't a tattoo that won't wash off," she said again to nobody.

Jillian and Rileigh were hurrying around putting on final touches, smoothing their hair. Rileigh carefully picked up her bouquet and held it regally in front of her.

The spot where the bridesmaids linked up with the matching groomsmen in the hallway was now marked by a naked mannequin. They would walk slowly down the center steps to the altar and the arbor that Ian McGinnis had made out of wood and carved leaves where Rileigh and Mitch and Jillian and David would stand. It would almost be like they were out in the woods.

Mama could hear the music and the sound of footsteps in the hallway and soft giggling as the bridesmaids walked down, pacing themselves as they'd practiced in the rehearsal.

She heard Georgia's voice above the others — "... gonna snatch that boy bald-headed when I catch him."

"There was vines and pretty flowers and such in that tattoo," Mama said. Rileigh looked at her, her face questioning.

"What tattoo, Mama? What are you talking about?"

"Why, that tattoo on his arm, it had vines and flowers, but you know, if you looked close, there was numbers in it."

"Numbers?"

"Sure, they was like them pictures you look at and see one thing, then you look again and see something else entirely. The vines in that tattoo formed numbers. One of them was a two and there was a six. There were two eights together. Those were two flowers. It was real pretty. I was gonna say something to him about it, but he run off."

"I'm sure it was, Mama. Really pretty," Jillian said, and Mama could tell that Jillian was humoring her, just saying whatever she had to say to get Mama to move along.

Rileigh came forward and helped her sister gently shove Mama toward the door because in just a minute or two, it would be Mama's turn to walk down the aisle. She would walk ahead of her daughters, as they had done in the rehearsal, and she'd stand down front as the matron of honor for both of them. Georgia would already be there, the maid of honor for Rileigh, and that nice Arab doctor who was seeing Jillian and helping her get over all the bad things she lived through was Jillian's maid of honor. Her name was Aaliyah, and she didn't like bacon. She was probably down front on Hank's arm already, too.

"It's about your turn, Mama," Jillian said. Jillian would march in behind Mama, and Rileigh would come in last behind Jillian.

The three of them stepped out into the hallway in turn, each pausing to pick up the bouquet they'd left on the table beside the door. She watched Rileigh punch the little button in the doorknob so it would lock behind them. Then Rileigh carefully picked up her big bouquet in both hands, and Gus leaned past her and closed the door firmly.

Mama was to walk by herself, but Jillian would walk on the arm of Sundeep Singh, and Gus Hazelton was waiting to escort Rileigh. He took one look at Rileigh in the wedding dress and gasped, "You are one fine lookin' squirrel hunter, girl!"

Jillian whispered into Mama's ear, "Okay, Mama, it's your turn."

Mama turned and smiled at Rileigh. "Them numbers in them flowers sure was pretty," she said, and then she started down the aisle.

Chapter Forty-Two

RILEIGH BISHOP WAS A MESS. AN ABSOLUTE MESS.

Her emotions were all over the map. Thoughts were spinning around in her head so fast, she was afraid the friction was going to catch her hair on fire.

She had believed that she would be walking down the aisle with the crosshairs of some sniper right on her, between her eyes. And then the photographer who had taken so many shots of them...

Was it crazy to wonder if they'd still get the pictures now that he was dead? Yes, it was crazy to wonder that, but she did.

Images from all that had happened in the last fifteen minutes — enough fear, murder and mayhem to last a lifetime for the average person — flitted randomly through her mind's eye.

The photographer was one of the assassins after El Viento and had decided that *Rileigh* was El Viento. How crazy was that?

But it must have made some kind of sense to him. He figured that was how the assassin had managed not to get caught for all those years because he was a she, an unlikely combination that might have aided an assassin.

She wondered which one he was. Was he BangUR-Dead or Born2BEvil?

She let the thought go, spinning away through the carousel of lights in her head. She tried to calm her breathing, tried to center herself.

She looked down at her dress.

It was beautiful. Mama's dress. The dress Rileigh'd picked out for herself was now lying in a heap on the bathroom floor. It'd been ruined, splattered with blood, when the park ranger killed the photographer.

The park ranger. El Viento.

He'd gotten so close, so very close, if it hadn't been for Hank. And she hadn't even gotten to thank him properly. Everything was moving too fast. The bodies in the room hadn't even gotten cold when the music started. What if somebody stumbled into this room and found two dead bodies?

She couldn't think about that. That was for later. Now it was time for her to center herself, concentrate on the only thing that mattered now. She was a bride, and this was her wedding day. She was about to march down the aisle and stand beside the man she loved and pledge to spend her whole life with him.

She looked down at the gown she was wearing. It was perfect. She was a princess, wearing her mother's wedding dress on her own wedding day. It didn't get a whole lot better than that.

The relief that had washed over her at the realization that it was over now, it was finally over, welled up in her heart again and brought tears to her eyes. She was so grateful to all the people who had helped make this happen, to all the people who are waiting out there now to celebrate with her that she was going to marry the man of her dreams.

She watched her mother walking slowly down the aisle ahead and thought about what she had said as she was walking out the door, about the vines and the numbers. What was that all about? Something about a tattoo.

A tattoo with numbers.

She felt a cold chill, like ice water was sliding down her neck, inside, on her skeleton, dripping from one pale white vertebra to another.

Drip, drip, drip.

A tattoo with numbers.

Had Mama seen the tattoo El Viento had bragged about in his post on the web? The tattoo that contained the numbers of a Swiss bank account containing millions of dollars? The bait he had used to get all other assassins to converge on Rileigh's wedding to kill him while he was trying to kill her?

The music changed. Rileigh looked at Jillian. Jillian looked at her, and they both smiled. Then Jillian stepped out and began walking slowly down the aisle. In the bridal walk cadence, Rileigh would step out too in just a few moments. She was supposed to count to ten before she stepped so there would be the proper spacing between them.

One.

Two.

When did Mama see the numbers mixed in with vines on the park ranger's tattooed arms?

Four.

Five.

He'd been hanging around for the past three days. Mama must have struck up a conversation with him at some point, noticed his tattoos.

Six.

Seven.

But he had been wearing a park ranger's uniform, and the uniform had long sleeves. He was wearing a jacket over the uniform, and it had long sleeves, too. How could she have seen a tattoo on his arm when he was wearing long sleeves?

Eight.

Nine.

Did he roll up his sleeves for some reason? Men did that all the time — rolled up their sleeves. Maybe the ranger had done that and Mama had been there and seen his arms. How likely was that? Why hadn't they checked the body of the park ranger for the tattoo, just to be sure? She hadn't thought of it and now—

Ten.

Rileigh shook the thoughts out of her head and began to move. She felt the presence of the crowd around her. Everyone she loved in the world was gathered for her special moment, all turned her way, looking at her and Jillian as they walked majestically down the aisle.

Then Mama stepped to her spot.

Jillian moved out of Rileigh's way so she'd have a straight line of sight to Mitch.

When she looked at him standing erect in his dress uniform, her heart caught in her throat and she couldn't get her breath. She was stunned by the flood of emotion and the realization that she was about to pledge her entire life to this man. If it had not been for the decorum of the occasion, she would have reached down and grabbed her skirts, lifted them up so she could run, and raced down the aisle into his arms.

When Mitch saw Rileigh, she watched his eyes widen, and the smile on her own face was so wide, if the ends of it had met in the back of her head, the whole top of her head would have fallen off.

She could tell he was stunned at how she looked in the wedding gown that had been her mother's and was grateful to be wearing it rather than the one she had picked out. This was the dress she *wanted* to be married in.

She got to the bottom of the steps as Jillian took her place under Ian McGinnis's grape arbor across from David.

The music was rising to a crescendo.

It was all about to begin, but the little niggling itch in Rileigh's head would not leave her. Mama was just a few feet away, and Rileigh leaned closer and in a rough whisper, she said, "Mama."

Mama looked at her.

"Mama, the tattoo with numbers ... whose arm was it on?"

Mama's face went completely blank.

"Think, Mama."

"I don't remember," Mama said. "It was ... I think..."

Then her eyes turned. Rileigh' watched as they fell on the front row where the Dalai Lama sat in his red robe and purple sash, his arms, his *tattooed* arms, not covered up with long sleeves but bare for all to see.

Chapter Forty-Three

Mitch hadn't meant to see Rileigh's wedding dress before she walked down the aisle in it. He knew that was inappropriate, and he'd gone to great lengths to ensure that on their wedding day the two of them weren't in the same room together.

But he'd seen her wedding dress anyway. He'd been looking for Hank early this morning in the visitor's center before the women arrived, and he'd poked his head into the female domain, which would make any man tremble in his boots. There were blow dryers, curling irons, makeup, and all manner of frilly things to get Mama and Rileigh and Jillian prepared today.

He'd called out for Hank, and then his eye was drawn to something that was a beautiful shade of jade green — a dress hanging in a plastic bag on the hook on the outside of the door to the bathroom.

And he knew it was Rileigh's wedding dress. It had to be. That shade of green would have brought out the green in eyes Rileigh maintained were hazel but that Mitch knew for lead pipe certain were jade green. It was a dress she would have picked. It was stunning, gorgeous. And he couldn't wait to see her in it. But he also didn't tell her that he'd already seen it.

Hours later, after Mitch dispatched Hank to warn Rileigh about the park ranger, Hank returned to tell him a harrowing tale — how the photographer had tried to kill Rileigh, whose life had been spared by the park ranger, who it turned out was El Viento himself.

"Chill, Bro," Hank said, a millisecond before Mitch leapt to his feet and raced down the hallway to Rileigh. "I handled it."

"Define 'handled it.'"

"Handled it as in there are now *two* dead bodies in that dressing room."

"You *killed* El Viento?"

Hank said nothing, just made a neck-snapping motion with his hands and Mitch suddenly felt weak-kneed.

El Viento was dead.

The relief that washed through Mitch's soul at the realization that the life of the woman he loved was no longer in danger was as sweet a feeling as anything he'd ever felt up to and perhaps including the realization that he loved Rileigh. No, not the realization that he loved her, the realization that he was "in love with her." He'd known it, of course, for months before he ever said it, and he'd said it because she had been within inches of dying, cut to pieces by the fan she was crawling through when he'd dragged her out of it in the basement of Shagbart Manor. He'd held her then, kissing her face, murmuring "I love you, I love you," without even realizing he was doing it.

He knew then that he wanted to marry her. He'd barely been able to hold onto his enthusiasm long enough to propose properly … in a romantic setting, with candles and soft music.

At least that'd been the plan. As it turned out, he'd just blurted out, "Will you marry me?" as she stood before him, soaking wet in a raging storm.

He had lain in bed this morning with the fear eating at his guts that El Viento was still out there somewhere, ready to kill Rileigh. It had taken all his resolve to ignore his fear and do what needed doing.

And now it was over. She was safe, he was safe, they were going to be married, and everything was fine. He was almost floating an inch or two off the floor when he heard the change in the music and turned to look up the aisle leading down between the benches of the amphitheater to catch sight of his beautiful bride in her green dress, except Rileigh wasn't in her green dress. She was, she was a vision in pure white, as beautiful as any fairy princess in any fairy tale. He sucked in a gasp at the sight of her. The veil over her face couldn't hide her radiant smile, and he realized he'd been wrong. Doubly wrong. The beautiful green dress he'd seen was not her wedding dress, and she was more beautiful now than she would have been wearing it.

Rileigh was so staggeringly gorgeous that all he could do was stare at her, gawking, stunned that this vision of loveliness was about to become his wife.

When she reached the bottom of the steps leading up onto the raised platform where Ian McGinnis had built the beautiful grape arbor, she looked into his face and locked eyes with him for a moment, and the electricity that passed between the two of them should have set her veil on fire.

Then she did something odd.

She leaned over and whispered something to her mother, who was standing in her spot as the matron of honor for both of her daughters. Her mother whispered something back. The whispered conversation lasted only a few seconds, but when Rileigh turned her face back to

Mitch, the smile was gone, the joy was gone, the excitement was gone.

It had all been replaced by fear.

Rileigh leaned toward Mitch and whispered, "Mama saw the tattoo with numbers."

Why did Rileigh feel the need to tell him that her mother had seen the park ranger's tattoo?

"It's not the ranger," Rileigh hissed. Mitch felt like a wrecking ball had had him square in the chest.

Not the park ranger?

"Who?"

That was all he could get out, that one little syllable.

"The Dalai Lama."

Mitch's eyes snapped to the man seated on the front row of visitors, wrapped in his scarlet robe and golden sash — a garment where you could have hidden an Ak-47 and no one would notice.

The Dalai Lama. Of course. Mitch had thought all along it was suspect that Mama suddenly runs into a Buddhist monk after she'd been imagining she was dating the Dalai Lama, and half the people in town knew it. It had seemed odd that this guy had just shown up out of nowhere, and now Mitch understood. He looked at the man wrapped in the golden shawl, with his bare arms completely covered in tattoos.

"These tattoos are sacred, called sak yant, and the images are drawn from Buddhist manuscripts in Khmer, Thai, and Sanskrit. My whole body is covered, for protection and good fortune."

Right, protection and good fortune. Not to mention being so intricately designed that you could hide numbers in them and no one would notice. The man was seated quietly, but Mitch knew that was a facade, that any second he would leap up and strike down the vision of white loveliness standing beside him.

Not happening.

As a part of his dress uniform, Mitch was wearing his sidearm, and without a moment's hesitation, he took two steps out into the aisle that separated the visitors from the wedding party, drawing his weapon as fast as Billy the Kid ever drew his, and pointing it directly at the tattooed man sitting on the front row.

"Freeze!" Mitch called out, and the old man did.

So did every other human being in the amphitheater. Maybe four hundred people sucked in a gasp and froze at the sight of the groom stepping away from the bride, drawing a gun, and pointing it at a Buddhist monk.

Mitch crossed the distance between him and the not-the-Dalai-Lama in seconds, grabbed him by the robe at the shoulder, and yanked him to his feet.

"Where's the gun?" he demanded.

"I'm sorry, I don't know what you're talking about," the monk said.

"The hell you don't." Mitch had the gun pointed directly at the monk's chest. "Drop the gun. *Now!*"

MAMA WAS horror-struck when she saw Mitch spin on his heel and pull his pistol out of his holster and march across the wide aisle to where the Dalai Lama was sitting. He pointed the gun right at the Dalai Lama, dragged him to his feet, and demanded that he give up his gun.

What was Mitch thinking?

Why?

And then Mama knew. Well, duh. It was because she'd told Rileigh that she'd seen numbers in that tattoo on the Dalai Lama's arm. And she *had* seen numbers in the tattoo. They had been very intricately woven in with the beautiful greenery and flowers so that you had to really look hard to see them at all. But they were there.

When Mama thought about seeing the numbers and the tattoo, it was hazy and foggy. It had happened at some time when she hadn't had the mental clarity she had right now. She'd cycled in and out of the fog all day, but she was crystal clear now. No fog anywhere. And she searched frantically through the foggy memories trying to remember.

And then she did remember.

Mama gasped.

"No!" she cried out, her voice sounding quaky and squeaky. "No, it's not the Dalai Lama."

Every eye snapped to Mama as she stood in her beautiful pale blue gown in front of the grape arbor. Every eye except one.

"I don't imagine he's armed," came a voice from the other side of the aisle, "but I am."

Mitch let go of the monk's robe and began to turn back toward the bridal party beneath the grape arbor.

"Drop that weapon, or I'll shoot you where you stand."

Mitch stared into the face of the man who was speaking. Mama was already gawking at him.

U.S. Marshal Craig Dylan.

Chapter Forty-Four

CRAIG DYLAN — WHOSE FIRST NAME WAS NOT MATT, whose sidekick was not Chester, and whose girlfriend was not Miss Lily — had taken a position behind the grape arbor and the bridesmaids and groomsmen to guard against an attack from the rear.

As it turned out, he was the attack from the rear.

"You have to the count of one to drop that pistol, or I open fire on the crowd."

His voice was as cold as a stone at the bottom of the ocean, coming from a man who looked so normal, so garden-variety ordinary. It was hard to imagine he was saying something like that, but he was.

And he meant what he said. Rileigh was certain he did. So was Mitch, and his fingers opened and he dropped his pistol to the ground.

"Excellent," Dylan said and held up his left hand, which had a small device in it, a transmitter of some kind. His thumb hovered over the button on top. To everyone's surprise, he shoved his pistol back down into his pocket and held out the device.

"Message to all you fine citizens who came here packing, hoping to help your friend Mitch defend his bride." He raised his voice and shouted, "And all you snipers out in the woods — this is a weapon far more dangerous than any of the pop guns you're carrying. I've placed explosives under all those benches that I can detonate with a signal from this device. If my finger touches this button, everybody dies."

There was a communal gasp from the crowd, who were all standing, as they'd been watching Rileigh come down the aisle. A peep of a scream escaped someone's lips, and several people on the top row of the amphitheater, far from the man holding the detonator device, turned and bolted away.

"Stay right where you are," he called out. "Everyone freeze. I'm warning you."

No one else moved.

"Don't guess your name's really Craig Dylan," Mitch said.

"Nope. He came for me in a hotel room in Nashville. I killed him and took his credentials. It was a good thing for me he wasn't six feet tall and black, but as it turned out, I have been saved yet again by my ordinary face."

He smiled a self-deprecating smile. "I didn't look like that ID picture, but you never noticed the difference, did you?"

He wasn't Craig Dylan, and Rileigh didn't know his real name. It didn't matter. Standing before her, holding death in his hand, was the famed assassin, El Viento.

Suddenly, his brow furrowed and wrinkled, and he appeared to be in pain. She remembered seeing that pained look on his face before. She didn't remember when, just knew she'd thought nothing about it at the time. He grimaced, but his finger hovering above the detonator never wavered, and he kept his hand steady. He grunted as if something hurt, and then gradually his face relaxed.

When he began speaking again, his voice was softer, though, and airless, sounding like someone who was speaking with a finger smashed in a car door.

"I got rid of his body and reported in from his phone, so the marshal's service is none the wiser yet. They'll find out when I blow this place."

There was a gasp from the crowd, followed by a rumble of uneasy murmuring. El Viento didn't even look their way, just called out curtly, "Shut up, dammit. I don't have long, and neither do you. There's no time for stupid babbling."

Rileigh noticed then that Aunt Daisy had stepped forward from where she'd been seated on the front row bench. Mama had parked her there next to Millie, Mama's best friend, who was told to watch over her, and if she tried to go more than five feet from Millie, Millie was to start screaming. Mama and Mildred Hanover had been friends since they were children, and Mildred had never liked Daisy. Nobody in the family did. It was hard to like a psychopath. She understood that Mama was too impaired to understand that Aunt Daisy had conned her way into being allowed to come to the wedding, and nothing would have suited Millie better than to turn her in and have her hauled away in handcuffs back to the Carrington House.

Aunt Daisy's eyes were like black holes in her face, pools of dark water where small, slimy creatures had drowned.

"I used the little gift you left for me," she said to the man holding the small device. No one in the crowd had any idea what she was talking about, but Rileigh did. They'd been right. Aunt Daisy had gotten the tongue she'd put on the white pillowcase in Jillian's bedroom last night from the killer himself, who'd obviously cut it out of the mouth of the headless man whose body he had dumped at the American Legion Hall the night of the bachelor party.

The man with the detonator either ignored Aunt Daisy completely or didn't hear. El Viento merely turned his head slowly, as if doing so caused him excruciating pain, and looked toward Rileigh. She'd frozen when he told the crowd to, so her back was to him, and he spoke to her.

"Turn around."

Rileigh turned slowly around to face him.

"I just want one last look at your face," he said.

Rileigh's mind flashed to the day her firearms instructor at Fort Campbell had explained what the T-Zone was.

"The T-Zone is essentially the center mass of the head. The eyes are roughly halfway between the top of the head and the chin. The nose is obviously in the center. That area on your face forms a T. That's a target for snipers. Not for regular troops. Just snipers."

Then the instructor had explained that every shot a soldier took at the enemy was to be at the biggest body mass. No shooting for arms or limbs or head shots — put a bullet right smack in the chest. Only special ops snipers aimed for the T-Zone.

Her firearms instructor at the police academy had said the same thing, that officers should aim for a body shot. Trained police snipers aimed for the T-Zone, though, to place a bullet literally right on the bridge of someone's nose between their eyes — because that bullet would travel through their skull and hit the medulla oblongata, the brain stem.

"If a suspect is holding a gun to a hostage's temple," her instructor had said, *"the only way to stop him is with a shot to the T-Zone. Any other shot, even if it's fatal, will allow the knee-jerk response that would pull the trigger and kill the hostage. But hit the*

medulla oblongata, and you shatter all responses. Hit that, and the body goes instantly limp. There is no time for the brain to send any signal, even a knee-jerk reactive signal. A T-Zone shot ensures that the assailant can't carry out whatever threat he is using."

Even if Mitch hadn't dropped his gun, he would never have been able to pull off a T-Zone shot. That kind of accuracy was impossible if you were lifting a weapon to fire. That kind of shot required a still, steady hand and grip.

Rileigh finished turning toward the killer and began to beg for her life.

"Please don't," she whispered, lifting up her hands in supplication, extending her bouquet toward him. "I'm begging you, please."

He smirked at her.

"Please!"

Rileigh took a breath and held it.

Bang!

The sound of the gunshot and the bullet ripping through the leaves of Rileigh's bouquet startled everyone.

The bullet struck El Viento right between his eyes, and the assassin collapsed in a heap. The detonator to set off the explosives dropped out of his limp hand without his finger touching the button.

The device clattered to the floor, then slid across the amphitheater stage and came to rest next to a shoe. The shoe belonged to Aunt Daisy. She reached down and snatched it up off the floor. She held a finger over the button and her ugly mouth twisted in a maniacal grin.

Holding her finger just as El Viento had held his, she looked at the two brides standing beside the altar. She made eye contact with each one.

Rileigh.

Jillian.

"You little bitches, little whores," she growled in a voice that hardly sounded human at all. "I've wanted to kill both of you my whole life and now…"

Her voice rose to a high, shrieking wail.

"You're going to … *die!*"

She shoved her finger down on button on the top of the device. Rileigh tensed.

Nothing happened.

Daisy looked startled. Then the surprise morphed into hate-filled rage, and she poked her finger down on the detonator button again and again and again.

That's when Jillian moved. She dropped the bouquet she'd been holding, crossed the space between her and Aunt Daisy in three big strides, and slammed her fist into Daisy's face. The blow made a crunching, sickening sound. It knocked the old woman backwards. She fell into the bench where she'd been sitting, then crashed to the floor, dragging the satin covering on the bench off onto the floor with her.

With no covering on the bench, it was possible to see what was under it. *Who* was under it. Mason Stump.

And what was he holding?

C-4 explosive.

Mason got to his feet and looked around, knowing he'd been caught and was in trouble and wondering why it was so quiet and everyone was staring at him.

Then he saw Rileigh and beamed.

"Look, Aunt Wileigh," he said, holding out the mound of C-4 he'd pulled out from under the benches. "I made a dinosaur."

Chapter Forty-Five

THE WEDDING OF RILEIGH JOSEPH BISHOP TO MITCHELL Andrew Webster was not the small intimate ceremony Rileigh had envisioned.

But as it turned out, it wasn't the fairy-tale wedding Georgia Stump had tried to transform it into either.

For a significant period of time, what it became was *pandemonium.*

To some extent, Rileigh was oblivious to the uproar.

From the moment her pistol jumped in her hand and the man standing in front of her dropped to the floor, Rileigh checked out of reality. Well, to some degree. She was aware of what was going on around her in a distant, observer's kind of way. She saw the man fall, knew she'd done it, that she'd nailed the T-Zone shot, shattered his brain stem and killed him instantly. After that, there was a dreamlike quality to everything.

She'd watched in something of a daze as the phone dropped from his dead fingers, slid across the floor to Aunt Daisy, and she'd picked it up and tried to push the button. She'd watched her sister Jillian smash Aunt Daisy in the face with her fist. That may have been the single best part of her wedding.

Or maybe not. Maybe it was Mason Stump holding up a big lump of C-4 molded into a dinosaur.

The crowd had been holding its communal breath at the unexpected spectacle that played out in front of them, and once they exhaled, it became bedlam.

Some people tried to run out of the amphitheater, still in the clutches of a knee-jerk *get-away* response. Others stood in place with their mouths open, just shocked. A few women squeaked out cries, a couple of children burst into tears, and a few men grumbled — and Mitch's deputies swarmed around him and Rileigh in a protective circle that would have repelled an attack by Attila the Hun and a murderous horde of barbarians.

With everyone talking at once, talking and laughing and crying, Rileigh noticed a scene begin to play out between Mama and Aunt Daisy.

Aunt Daisy was still sitting in the floor, blood gushing out of her mouth and nose where Jillian had slugged her, when Mama approached her.

"Did you see what she done?" Aunt Daisy cried in outrage through her mangled teeth. Rileigh could tell she was working herself up into a self-righteous, I'm-a-victim rant. "She *hit* me, broke my nose!"

"'Pears to me Jillie just done what needed doing," Mama said coldly. "You was gonna punch that button and kill everybody."

Her response surprised Rileigh, and she sidled closer to hear better. If she hadn't, she would have missed what Mama said after that, because she leaned close and spoke to her sister in a gruff half-whisper.

"For my whole life, I been pretending my eyes wasn't seein' what they was seeing, that you wasn't the person everybody else knew you were. Wasn't no hiding the truth today, though. And you know what Mama used to say: 'You can't un-know the truth. Once you know it, you're responsible for doin' something 'bout it.'"

Aunt Daisy sat up straighter, fire in her eyes. "Now, you listen here to me, Lily Bishop."

"No, Daisy, you listen *to me*. You done something terrible to Jillian, and I don't know what it was. All these years, I ain't 'llowed myself to know what, a'feared that if I did, I'd put my fingers around that skinny neck of yours and choke the life out of you. I've decided to go to my grave 'thout ever knowing that one truth, 'cause I discovered another that's more important — that fella who's been tormenting Rileigh, he ain't the only person who died here today. Turns out the 'lily' is the last surviving flower from Mama and Papa's bouquet. I ain't got no living sisters. Daisy Gillespie is dead to me. It shore ain't punishment enough for all you done, but you gonna spend the last years of your life utterly *alone*, a bitter, hate-filled, evil old woman whose whole family has left her to rot."

Mama did something amazing then.

"I ain't never gonna lay eyes on you again, sure's hell ain't gonna show up for your funeral, so *here.*" Then Mama spit on the floor next to Aunt Daisy. "Consider that me spittin' on your grave."

Mama drew herself up tall and walked away with dignity. She stopped in front of Mitch, and Rileigh only caught "...slap her in handcuffs and haul her ass back to the Carrington House..." but that was enough. Rileigh had never been so proud of her mother as she was at that moment.

Then Jillian appeared beside Rileigh, and the next thing she knew, Jillian was hugging her, holding on so fiercely, squeezing so tight that neither of them could breathe, and that was fine with both of them.

Rileigh pulled out of Jillian's grip enough to reach up and wipe away a tear that had slid down Jillian's cheek. She started to straighten the tiara of Jillian veil, and that's when she realized she was still holding the remains of the bouquet of leaves she had made to cover up her Glock that she'd held in her gun hand — with her finger inside the trigger guard — from the moment she picked it up to walk down the aisle.

Georgia appeared out of nowhere.

"I'm s'posed to take your bouquet when you're done with it ... that's what we rehearsed, remember? And looks to me like you're done with it."

Georgia's face grew serious.

"You are one badass babe, Rileigh Bishop! You know that, don't you? Damn I'm glad you're on our side."

Then Georgia took the bouquet and the Glock away, and Jillian and Rileigh stood alone again. People were crying and carrying on all around them, but at that moment, there didn't exist anybody else in the world except Rileigh and her big sister Jillian. On their wedding day, about to marry the men they loved.

"It's been a long road to here," Jillian said. Rileigh found that her throat was suddenly so tight, she could do nothing but nod. Jillian smiled, then Rileigh forced words out of her constricted throat.

"We made it, the two of us. We made it."

At that moment, Rileigh had never felt closer to her sister, and her mind briefly flitted back to that day almost thirty years ago, the night before Jillian's wedding when Rileigh was six years old and went into her sister's bedroom to put a note into her suitcase. Now she held her sister's hands tight and looked into her eyes. "Please don't forget me," she said.

Jillian's smile lit up the world, "I won't."

And then the bubble around them burst and Mitch was there and David was there and somehow the crowd was calmed, and the minister brought back from where he'd been hiding behind the piano, and Rileigh stood with Mitch holding her hand as Jillian stood with David holding hers.

Rileigh looked up into Mitch's face, and the smile on it was so bright she almost had to squint — it was like looking into the sun. Then she heard the words the minister was saying, "Do you, Rileigh Bishop, take this man..." and she listened to the rest of the words, eager to speak. And when he was finally silent and it was her turn, her voice was hoarse with emotion but firm.

"I do."

The End

About The Author

Lauren Street has always loved a mystery. As a kid growing up in bible belt country she devoured every whodunit book she could get her sticky little hands on and secretly investigated all of her (seemingly) normal boring neighbors. Sometimes their pets and farm animals too. All grown up now and living in the UK with her thoroughly unsuspicious (and often unsuspecting) husband, she writes domestic psychological thrillers about families torn apart by secrets and lies. And she sometimes still peers over garden walls to check up on the neighbors.

Also By Lauren Street

The Bishop Smoky Mountain Thrillers

Hide Me Away

Fuel To The Flame

Closer By The Hour

A Gamble Either Way

Calling My Children Home

Too Far Gone

Here You Come Again

A Friend Like You

The Company You Keep

One By One

Come Back To Me

The Only Way Out

Replaced with Nolon King

Replaced

In Her Place

Irreplaceable

The Salazar Redwood Forest Thrillers

The Girl Who Couldn't Stop Dying

The Girl Who Couldn't Get Out

The Girl Who Couldn't Be Found

Standalone Novels

Postpartum